RAVE REVIEWS FOR TIM LEBBON!

"Tim Lebbon moves me, challenges me, and makes me remember how rich our particular strange bent can be."
—Jack Ketchum, bestselling author of *Peaceable Kingdom*

"Lebbon is quite simply the most exciting new name in horror in years." —*SFX Magazine*

FACE

"Intense and affecting, *Face* will seize and hold your attention from the opening paragraph to the end. A writer blessed with extraordinary gifts, Lebbon's chief talents lie in exploring the darker moments of everyday life. . . . A true disciple of the dark, Lebbon's imagery wrings true fear from his audience."

—*Hellnotes*

"Lebbon's novel will reward the careful reader with insights as well as gooseflesh."

—*Publishers Weekly*

"Lebbon draws the reader into this nightmare to experience the horror with his characters. Lebbon taps into our universal fear of the unknown, the unseen."

—CelebrityCafe.com

THE NATURE OF BALANCE

"Beautifully written and mysterious, *The Nature of Balance* will put some readers in the mind of the great Arthur Machen. But with more blood and guts."

—Richard Laymon, bestselling author

"Vibrant, exploding with imagery, Tim Lebbon takes you on a white-knuckle ride of uncompromising horror. This is storytelling at its best."

—Simon Clark, author of *Vampyrrhic*

"As fascinating as his plot is, it's the beauty of his prose that raises his work to a higher level."

—*Gauntlet*

THE CITY OF THE DEAD

The ruins lay in a wide hollow in the desert. There was not one high wall. There was not even a single building. Spread across the floor of the depression in the land, seemingly growing from the ground, lay the remains of several large and dozens of smaller buildings. Sand and grit was skirted around bases and against walls, drifted up and through openings that may have been windows, may have been wounds. Some of the ruins rose above the level of the desert floor, but many more had been revealed below, shown the sunlight for the first time in eons when the terrible sandstorm had opened them up to view. The hollow must have been a mile across.

"Let's go down," Scott said. "I want to see. I want to know where the dead live. Look, over there!" He pointed over to our left, and before the dark stone of the first tumbled building there was something in the sand, something dark, moving.

At first I thought it was a scorpion or small lizard. But as we moved closer I saw the reality. It was a foot, still clad in the remains of a sandal, bones stripped of flesh and dangling with scraps of skin, snapped or broken at the ankle.

Other *Leisure* books by Tim Lebbon:

FACE
THE NATURE OF BALANCE

TIM LEBBON

FEARS UNNAMED

LEISURE BOOKS NEW YORK CITY

For Daniel, my little mate.

LEISURE BOOKS ®

February 2004

Published by

Dorchester Publishing Co., Inc.
200 Madison Avenue
New York, NY 10016

ISBN 0-8439-5200-8

Visit us on the web at www.dorchesterpub.com.

FEARS
UNNAMED

CONTENTS

Remnants

Scott always loved digging down to history. When we were nine years old we would spend time in the local woods, me climbing trees and searching for bird nests and damming the local stream, Scott excavating through the accumulated carpet of leaves and other forest debris in his search for hidden things. Usually he found nothing but mud, muck and crawling things, but on those rare occasions when he went home happy instead of dejected, he would be carrying something of interest. A small skeleton once, easily identifiable were we to ask our parents, though we didn't because we preferred the mystery. He also found a buried box, about the size of a house brick, and we undertook to smash the lock with a rock. Those few seconds were a magical time—the impact of stone on metal reverberating through the woods, the endless possibilities rich and colored by our childish imaginations—and even when the lid flipped open to reveal nothing but rust, we weren't truly disappointed. It was empty of treasure or maps or hidden truths, but the box itself was still there, and that was good enough for us. Scott walked home that day happier than I had ever seen him, the box tucked beneath one arm, his small trowel dirtying his trousers where it protruded from a pocket. He was beaming. "There's always something there," he said. "Everyone reckons that what we see is it. They forget about all the buried stuff."

His progression from school, to university, to a career in archaeology was no surprise to anyone. We kept in touch, even though my work took me on a vastly different route. Scott would disappear from my life for years on end, and then I would receive an e-mail or letter out of the blue, inviting me to join him in Bolivia or Uzbekistan or Taiwan. More often than not I would have to decline, but several times a rush of excitement grabbed me. It was often his young, enthusiastic face I thought of as I sat there in my office at home, dreaming, persuading myself that I should go. The wonder in his eyes. The knowledge that when I saw him again that wonder would still be there.

I was a jealous friend. Jealous when we were nine, and jealous when we were thirty-nine. Scott had always known what he wanted from life, and he pursued it with vigor. I lived my life unfulfilled, and worse, felt that I had no potential *to* fulfill.

So I would talk to my wife and children and, with their blessing, jet off to some far-flung corner of the world to spend two weeks in a tent with my old friend. He never changed, only became fuller. Each time I saw him he seemed more alive and I felt more dead, ground down by life and work, impulsiveness slaughtered by necessity. And each time, Scott seemed to be digging much deeper than even he knew. It was not only lost things he was looking for, but things unknown, and even things that had never been. He was looking past history and into the abyss of unadulterated truth.

He sometimes told me what he had unearthed. I was no longer a child, so I often found it difficult to believe, a leap of imagination that I was not able to make. He would smile and shake his head, and that simple gesture hurt me to the core. He was so used to miracles.

His final calling came in a series of brief, enigmatic e-mails.

I've found a city that no one has dreamed of in centuries, the first said. I smiled at the words on the screen, my heart quickening in unconscious sympathy with the excitement bleeding from them. I imagined Scott's eyes wide and childlike in their amazement.

The following night: *It must be a city of ghosts.* A thrill went through me. Scott could imbue text on a screen with so much emotion and feeling . . . but then I knew that my memories of him were providing that effect. He gave me sterile, blank words, and I fleshed them out with his passion.

Matthew is here.

Matthew was Scott's son. Scott had had a brief, passionate affair when he was twenty, and six years later he learned from his ex-lover that he had a child. She only told him because the boy was dying of leukemia.

This wasn't even funny.

What the hell are you talking about? I wrote back, angry and disturbed at the same time. Scott was a dreamer, a thinker, someone whose imagination led

3

him places not only unheard of, but long forgotten. I had never thought of him as a fool.

Come to me, Peter, Scott mailed back. *Please.* It was the "please" that convinced me I had to go. I was certain that Scott needed my help, though not in the way he believed. Perhaps, somewhere deep inside me where I did not care to look, there was a smugness. Here was the great adventurer—glamorous, passionate, so rich in intellect and enthusiasm—asking for my help. Not outright, but I could read between his digital lines, perceive a desperation that I had never expected to find. A desperation, and perhaps a fear. Until now he had always invited my presence, not requested it.

Matthew is here, he had said.

What could that mean?

I stood from my computer desk after receiving that last message and walked around my home. My wife was at work, my two children at school, and I should have been working through some submissions. But Scott's words had fired my comatose imagination, their mystery setting a fire in the dried out landscape of my mind and struggling to light its shadowed corners. I walked from room to room, bathing in the history of my life as it lay revealed in photographs. Here was Janine and me standing by Victoria Falls, our glasses splashed with spray, wide smiles as magical as upside-down rainbows. And here, the two of us in the hospital with our daughter a bloody bundle at her breast, suckling her way into the world. Another picture sat on the dresser in the hallway showing us on our honeymoon, sheltering beneath a heavy palm tree while a tropical storm thundered its way across the small island. Neither of us could remember who had taken the photo.

There was an old shelf of books in the living room, various first editions I had collected over the years. I liked to think of myself as something of a detective, hauling out my guide to British bookshops every time we found ourselves in a strange town or city, exploring a few here and there, searching old cobwebbed shelves and delving deep into overflowing bargain bins in my search for that elusive rare tome. My collection filled one glass-fronted shelf and was worth over ten thousand pounds.

Worthless. Meaningless. If this was all I had to show for a life . . .

A dried nut, as large as my fist, sat on the fireplace. I had climbed a tree for it in Australia, supposedly braving spiders and snakes to grab a piece of that country for myself. Janine had been watching, camera at the ready in case I slipped and fell. I had been in no danger at all.

I tried to think of the most daring thing I had ever done. I had abseiled over three hundred feet down the side of a cliff. It was raining, the rock was slippery and, in places, loose. I had a safety line attached, and an expert climber stood on top of the cliff slowly feeding me rope. I had raised five hundred pounds for charity. At the time, I had felt on the edge.

Scott once showed me his collection of scars. Shark off the coast of South Africa, snake in Paraguay, a goring from running with the bulls in Spain, a bullet in his hip from a brush with Chinese soldiers in Tibet, the ragged wound in his throat where he had given himself a tracheotomy after being stung by a deadly scorpion, airways closing, life fading away in his poisoned blood, his knife so sharp and sure. He had a tattoo on one shoulder blade, put there by an old woman in Haiti who claimed it would keep him alive when death came knocking. On the other shoulder, a gypsy woman in Ireland had painted a bird, hugely feathered and colorful, the carrier of Scott's soul. The ink had never faded, and sometimes it still looked wet. Scott could not explain that, but it did not concern him. He simply accepted it. He had a wooden mask dating from one of the great Egyptian dynasties, a Roman soldier's spear tip found in Jerusalem and dating from around the time of Christ's crucifixion, and around his neck hung a charm, a diamond inset in white gold, the heart of the diamond impossibly black with the sealed blood of a saint.

I had some photographs and memories, trinkets, meager evidence showing that the most adventurous thing I had done was to go on holiday and book the hotel and flights myself.

"Damn you, Scott," I whispered at the empty house. I closed my eyes and tried to imagine the memories and dreams he must have every single night of his life. When Janine came home I would talk to her, and she would give me her blessing to go and stay with Scott for a week or two.

Perhaps the fact that I wanted to steal a dream sealed the fate of that journey from the start.

Scott was waiting for me at what passed as the airport. I had changed three times since Heathrow, each trans-

fer resulting in me sitting aboard a smaller, more dilapidated aircraft, and I finally flew into an airport
somewhere in Ogaden in an antique that must have
begun service before World War Two. There were
eighteen seats in the cabin, fifteen of which remained
empty. The other two passengers spared me not a
glance. They were enrapt in the frantic conversation
that came through the open doorway from the flight
deck. Not understanding the language, I watched
them for any reaction that should give me cause for
concern. I had the distinct impression that the whole
flight skirted the brink of disaster, and that the intermittent shouts of glee from the pilot or co-pilot marked
another severe problem somehow overcome. As the
propellers spun down and the tang of burning filtered
into the cabin, the two other passengers swapped
strangers' smiles.

"Peter!" Scott shouted as I descended the rickety set
of steps. He ran across the landing strip, kicking up
puffs of dust. "Peter! Christ, mate, it's bloody good to
see you!"

I could only smile. Here he was again, my old friend
who somehow instilled a very private, very deep jealousy in me, and I couldn't help but love him.

"You too," I said. I held out my hand for a shake,
but he dodged it, ducking in for a hug, his arms strong,
his scent that of someone used to a hard life. I hugged
him back, certain that my ribs would crack within seconds.

"How's Janine?" he asked. "The kids? How are
they?"

"Janine sends her love," I said, even though she

hadn't. "Gary's starting comprehensive school this year, and Sandy's taking her exams."

"Shit me. Time, eh? Time, my old mate. Time slips away."

I looked at Scott then, really looked at him, and though his skin was leathered by the sun, his hair graying and thinning rapidly, his jowls drooping lower and lower each time I saw him, he had the manner and bearing of someone much younger. I felt old, even though I tried to keep in shape. Scott had a sense of awe to keep him youthful, and he found wonder every day, in everyday things.

"Yeah," I said. "Nice fuckin' life."

Scott smiled at our old catchphrase, but he did not respond. He was looking at me, appraising me much more openly than I had just assessed him. "You need to see what I've found, Peter," he said.

Someone shouted behind us, one of the other passengers, and a group of people standing at the edge of the runway waved and shouted back. The laughter belonged in the hot dry air, but so did the sudden sense of import between Scott and me, hanging there with the laughter like its solid, immovable counterpoint. Scott's eyes did not shift from mine. I waited for him to say more, but he was silent. He smiled, but there was a sadness there as well, so deep that I wondered if he was aware of its existence.

"What is it?" I asked.

Scott seemed to snap out of a brief trance. He looked around, pointed out the ramshackle shed that served as an airport arrivals and departures lounge, the watchtower where an old man sat with a table-top radio, the collection of huts and shelters that lined the airport perimeter on both sides, people wandering among them like shadows ignoring the sun. The whole place looked run-down, wasting away, and as Scott spoke he was exuberant, a brighter spark in the glow of the day.

"This is no place for wonders," he said quietly. "This country has its paradise, but it's a distance from here. I can't mention it until we're closer." And then he turned and started walking away.

"Scott!" I said. "Why did you ask me to come?"

"You'll see," he said, almost dismissively. He did not even turn to me when he spoke. "This is the cradle of civilization, you know. This place." He waved his arm around and moved on.

I looked around at the plane, the pilots gesticulating at one of the steaming engine compartments, the joyful reunion over by the airport buildings. In the sky dark shapes rode the currents. They were too high to make out properly, and I frowned at the childish memories of vultures in old films, circling, waiting on a fresh death.

My luggage had been unceremoniously dumped on the ground beneath the open luggage compartment. I grabbed the holdall, snapped open the handle on the suitcase and followed Scott toward the potholed car park. The heat had hit me. I was melting.

"Thanks for the help with my luggage!" I called lightly, hoping for an abusive response, hoping for normality.

But Scott only raised his hand and waved back at me without turning around. "I'll tell you when we get nearer," he said. "I can't tell you yet. Not yet. Not here."

The family watched me walk from the runway, but they ignored Scott. Perhaps they knew him. More likely, he looked like he belonged.

Scott had an old World War Two jeep, left over from that conflict and probably not serviced since. It screeched at us as he started it up, a high-pitched whine intermingled with the sound of something hard spinning around inside the engine, ricocheting, trying to find its way out. A cloud of smoke erupted from the vehicle's back end.

"Shit," I said.

"Don't worry," Scott said, "I've cursed it. Wouldn't dare let me down." He grinned madly, smashed the gearstick into first and slammed his foot on the gas.

My first instinct was to look for a seat belt, but if there had ever been one it was long since gone. Instead I grabbed on to my seat with one hand, the rusted window frame with the other, trying to ride out the jolts and bounces. The road was rough as a plowed field, not even bearing the ruts of frequent use.

"Fun, eh?" Scott shouted, laughing as the underside of the jeep crunched against the ground and sent a solid shudder through the whole chassis.

Perhaps we were in a town, but there was not much to see. The most salubrious building we passed was an old church, its tower tall and bell-less, walls rough-rendered and pocked here and there with what could have been bullet holes. Empty windows hid a dark interior, untouched by the strong sun. Contrasting this seemingly unused shell was the church's garden, fenced in with a clean white picket fence. It held a profusion of bright shrubs, lush and thriving even through the dust that had settled on their leaves, gorgeous orchids nestling at the bases of thick green stems; green and purple, blue and red. They could have been artificial, such were the colors. An incredibly old man approached the church as we passed by, carrying a plastic water container on his shoulder, its contents spewing from a rent in its base. He looked our way but did not appear to see us.

"Where are we going?" I shouted.

"The desert!" Scott replied. "Hot as Hell, beautiful as Heaven! Hope you brought your sunblock."

I nodded, though he was paying little attention. I had coated myself on the plane, drawing a single amused glance from one of my fellow passengers. Perhaps the sun was the least I had to worry about, and maybe he knew.

We soon passed out of the small settlement. The shacks and rubbish-strewn streets ended abruptly, as did any sign of cultivation. What few sad fruit trees and root crops I had seen had no place past the town's outer boundary; now, there was only the wilds. The road suddenly seemed to smooth out and calm down, as if pleased to be leaving civilization behind, and before us lay the desert.

I had been aware of its presence for some minutes. It could be seen beyond the town, hunched down, spread as far as the eye could see. Its smell permeated the air; hot and dry, barren and cruel. I could even feel its weight, its distance, its vastness affecting my emotional tides like the sky at night, or the sea on a stormy day. But now for the first time I really *noticed* it. I saw its beauty and danger, its mystery and shapely curves. And I perceived the sharp edges that waited for those unacquainted with its harsh truth.

Now that the road had levelled to merely uncomfortable—and Scott had dropped his speed as if mourning the potholes left behind—I had a chance to talk.

"Scott, you have me confused."

"It'll all become clear," he said. "Or . . . clearer. More obvious." He shook his head, trying to rattle loose whatever he was trying to say. "Just wait and let me show you, Pete."

I nodded, tried to return his smile, but the sun must have stretched my skin. I uncapped the lid of my sunblock and coated my face and arms once more, taking off my cap and rubbing it into my scalp. It grated and scratched. Glancing at the mess on my hand, I saw that a thousand grains of sand had become mixed in, turning the cream into an effective exfoliant.

"Ha!" Scott laughed. "Just like being at the beach. You get used to the sand eventually, just like you get used to being thirsty, sweaty, tired. You can get used to anything, really. Remember going to the beach as a kid? That time when our families went together, you wanted to go canoeing, but I dragged you over to explore the rock pools and caves?"

"You got me into so much trouble."

"I was a kid, what was I supposed to know about tides?" He laughed again, wild, uninhibited, untempered by normal worries like mortgages and jobs and love. I loved him and hated him, and for the thousandth time I wondered how that could be.

"We could have died."

"We should have gone farther into the caves. But you were scared."

I shook my head. "You didn't know what was there. We could have died."

"You never find out unless you look." If I didn't know him better, I may have imagined mockery in his smile.

"You said you'd found a city," I said. "A city of ghosts?" He glanced across at me, handed over a bottle of water, looked ahead again.

The road had effectively ended as we left town, cross-country evidently being a more comfortable ride. This desert was not as I had always imagined it to be—the high, sharp-ridged dunes of *Lawrence of Arabia*—but rather flat, hard-packed, supporting sparse oases of vegetation that seemed to sprout from the bases of rocky mounds or in shallows in the ground. Leaves were dark green and thin, their ends sharp, threatening and unwelcoming. If these plants did flower, now was not their season. The sun was high, the heat intense, and mirage lakes danced across the horizon. Ghost water, I thought, and the idea made Scott's silence even more frustrating.

"What city could be hidden out here?" I asked. "It's the desert, but it's hardly wilderness."

"Hardly?" he repeated, raising his eyebrows. "What's wilderness?"

"Well . . . the wilds. Somewhere away from civilization."

Scott lifted a hand from the wheel and swept it

13

ahead of him, as if offering me everything I could see. "This is as wild as it gets," he said. "Civilization? Where? Out here there are scorpions and snakes and spiders and flies, and other things to do you mischief. It's easy to die in the desert."

"And?" I asked. There had been no feeling to his words, no sense that he meant it. Spiders and snakes did not frighten him, or turn his desert into a wilderness. There was something else here for him.

"And history," he said. The jeep began to protest as we started up a shallow, long rise. Scott frowned down at the bonnet, cursing under his breath, and then with a cough the engine settled into its old rumble once more.

I looked around, searching for ruins or some other evidence of humanity, of history. But I saw only compacted sand and plants, and a shimmering mirage that made me ever more thirsty.

"The sands of time," Scott said. "Blown around the world for the last million years. Parts of every civilization that has ever existed on Earth are here. Shards of the pyramids. Flecks of stone from the hanging gardens of Babylon. Dust from unknown obelisks. Traces of societies and peoples we've never known or imagined. All here."

I looked across the desert, trying to perceive anything other than what my eyes told me were there. Yet again I envied Scott his sense of wonder. He could take a deep breath and know that a million people before him had inhaled part of that lungful. I could see or feel nothing of the sort.

"Time has ghosts," he said. "That's what time is: the

ghost of every instant passed, haunting the potential of every moment to come. And sometimes, the ghosts gather."

"The city of ghosts?"

Scott drew to a halt atop a low ridge. Ahead of us lay a staggering expanse of nothing: desert forever, the horizon merging with the light blue sky where distance blurred them together. Heat shimmered everything into falseness.

"Farther in," he said quietly. "A couple of hours' travel. I have plenty of water, and there's a spring at my camp. But here. I found this. Take a look. Gather your thoughts, and when you're ready, tell me what you think."

He dug down under his seat and handed me something. For a couple of seconds I drew back and kept my hands to myself, afraid that it would be deadly. Not an insect, nothing poisonous, nothing so banal; something *dangerous*. Something that, were I to accept it from Scott, would have consequences.

"Here," he said, urging me. "It won't hurt you. That's the last thing it'll do."

I took in a deep breath and held out my hand.

The bundle of cloth was small, and it had no weight whatsoever. I was holding a handful of air. It was old, crumbled, dried by the intense heat until all flexibility and movement had been boiled away. It lay there in my hand, a relic, and as I turned it this way and that I saw what was inside.

Bones. Short and thin, knotted, disjointed. Finger bones. One of them had a shred of mummified flesh still hanging on for dear, long-departed life.

I gasped, froze in my seat, conscious of Scott's gaze upon me. I hefted the bundle, still amazed at how light it seemed, wondering if the climate had done something to my muscles or sense of touch. And for a moment so brief I may have imagined it in a blink, I saw this person's death.

Cold. Wet. Alone. And a long, long way from here.

"It's old," Scott said. "Very old. Before Christ. Before the Minoans, the Egyptians, Mesopotamia."

"How do you know?" I whispered.

"It's hardly there," he said. "Touch it."

I pointed a finger and reached out, aiming between the folds of ancient cloth at the dull gray bone wrapped inside. Closer, closer, until my finger felt as though it had been immersed in water of the exact same temperature as our surroundings. But that was all.

I pushed farther, but there was no sense of the bone being there. It was not solid.

"Mirage?" I said. But I knew that was wrong. "What is this?" I hefted the package again, squeezed it, watched as it kept its shape and did not touch my skin. "What the bloody hell . . . ?"

"Sometimes I guess even ghosts fade away," Scott said. He started the jeep again and headed down the slope, out into the great desert.

I dropped the cloth bundle and kicked it away from my feet, watching, waiting for it to vanish or change. It did neither. But by the time we reached Scott's encampment, I thought perhaps it had faded a little more.

* * *

There were six tents scattered around a boggy depression in the ground. This was Scott's "spring." As we pulled up in the jeep a flock of birds took off from the watering hole, darting quickly between the tents, moving sharply like bats. There was movement on the ground too; lizards shimmied beneath rocks, and a larger creature on four legs—too fast to see, too blurred for me to make out—flickered out of sight over the lip of the depression and into the desert.

"Quite a busy place," I said.

"It's the only spring for miles in any direction. I don't mind sharing it."

"You have others on the dig?" I asked. The tents looked deserted, unkempt, unused, but there was no other reason for them to be there.

"I used to," he said. "The last one left three weeks ago."

"You been skimping on their wages again?" I was trying to be jolly, but it could not reach my voice, let alone my smile.

"Frightened off," he said casually. He jumped from the jeep, slammed the door and made for one of the tents.

I sat there for a while, trying to make out just what was different about this place compared to the other camps I had visited over the past two decades. The sun scorched down, trying to beat sense out of me. I closed my eyes, but still it found its way through, burning my vision red.

There were no people here, but that was not the main difference. There were fewer tents than at most digs. Those that were here looked older, more bedraggled, as if they had been here for a lot longer than usual.

Scott stood staring back at me, hands on his hips. "I have a solar fridge," he said. "I have beer. We need to wash up, catch up and then talk some about what I've found out here. You ready for some wonder, Pete?"

You ready for some wonder, Pete? He could have been reading my mind. And yet again, only my closeness to Scott prevented me from taking his comment as ridicule.

"Where's the dig?" I asked. "Where's the equipment? The washers, the boxed artifacts, the tools?"

"Ah," Scott said, throwing up his hands as if he'd been caught cheating at cards. "Well . . . Pete, please mate, I'm not trying to deceive you or catch you out. I just wanted you here to *share* something with me. Come on, into my tent. We'll crack a few, and then I'll tell you everything. The time needs to be right."

"Matthew," I said. It was the first time I had mentioned Scott's most baffling e-mail since my arrival.

His face dropped and he looked down at his feet. We stayed that way for some time—me sitting in the jeep, slowly frying in the sun; Scott standing a few steps away examining the desert floor—and then he looked up.

"I haven't found him yet, but he's here."

I shook my head, frowned.

"I just need to look farther . . . deeper . . ."

"Scott, has the sun—?"

"No, it hasn't. The sun hasn't touched me!" He almost became angry, but then he calmed, relaxed. "Pete, Matthew is here somewhere, because every dead person who has ever been wronged is here.

Somewhere. Under our feet, under this desert. I've found the City of the Dead."

He turned and walked into one of the larger tents, leaving me alone in the jeep. *The City of the Dead.* "A real city?" I said, but Scott seemed not to hear. I may have been alone. Tent flaps wavered for a few seconds in a sudden breeze, snapping angrily at the heat. I looked around and felt the immensity of the place bearing down, crushing me into the small, insignificant speck of sand that I was. I was lost here, just as lost as I was at home, and though it was a feeling I had never grown used to, at least here I could find justification. Here, I was lost because the desert made light of so many aspects of life I took to be important. Here there was only water, or no water. Here too there was life, or death . . . and perhaps, if Scott's weird story held any trace of truth, something connecting the two.

But I could not believe. I did not have the *facility* to believe.

The sun must have driven him mad.

I jumped from the jeep and followed him into his tent. Its interior was more well-appointed than it had any right to be, being compartmented into four by hanging swirls of fine material, and carpeted with an outlandish collection of rugs and throw cushions. In one quarter there was even some rudimentary furniture: a cot, a couple of low-slung chairs and the solar fridge. He was pulling out two bottles of beer, their labels beaded with moisture.

He popped the caps and offered me a bottle. "To us!" he said. "Nice fuckin' life!"

"Absolutely," I said. We clinked bottles and drank.

Only he could use that phrase and sound like he actually meant it.

"So tell me," I said. "This city? A real city? Why have you dragged me a million miles from home? Other than to sit and drink beer and see if you're still a pansy when it comes to booze."

"Three bottles and I'm done," he said, slurping noisily, wiping his chin, sighing in satisfaction. "I wonder if the dead spend their time mourning their senses?"

"The dead."

"Wouldn't you? If you died and could still think, reason, wouldn't you miss the sound of a full orchestra or a child's laugh? Miss the taste of a good steak or a woman's pussy? Miss the smell of fresh bread or a rose garden?"

I shrugged, nodded, not knowing quite how to respond.

"I would," he said. "Life is so lucky, you just have to wonder at it, don't you? Even thinking about it makes everything sound, taste and smell so much better." He looked at me. "Apart from you. Didn't you shower before you left home? Stinking bastard."

"And I suppose the showers are out of action," I said.

"Yes, but the Jacuzzi is in the next tent, and the Jacuzzi maids have been told to treat you special."

We shared a laugh then, for the first time this visit, and we sank wearily into the low chairs.

"The city," I said again. For someone so keen to drag me out here, he was being infuriatingly reticent about revealing his discovery.

"The city." He nodded. "I don't know if it's a real city, Pete. It's really here, really under our feet, and later I'll show you how I know that. The relic I handed you in the car is one of a few I've found, all of them . . . the same. Distant."

"It didn't feel all there."

"I think it was a ghost," he said, frowning, concentrating. "I think it was a part of someone who died a long time ago, but a piece that was buried or lost to the ages. The other things I've found point to that too."

"But have you actually *found* this place? Or are you surmising?"

"I've found enough to tell me that it's really here. For sure."

"These bits of ghosts?" I felt slightly foolish verbalizing what Scott had said. It was patently wrong, there was some other explanation, but he could state these outlandish ideas comfortably. They did not sound so real coming from my skeptical self.

"Them, and more. I saw a part of the city revealed by a sinkhole. Haven't been able to get close yet—the sand is too fluid. But there's nothing else it can be other than a buried ruin. Blocks, joints. I'll show you soon." He stared at me, challenging me to doubt.

"But why hasn't anyone else ever come here, found this stuff?"

Scott took another long drink from his bottle, emptying it, and then tilted his chair back and stared up at the tent ceiling. The sun cast weird shapes across the canvas, emphasizing irregularities in its surface and casting shadows where sand had blown and been trapped, gathered in folds and creases. Scott looked as though he was trying to make sense.

"Scott?"

"I don't know," he said. "I don't know why no one has found those scraps of things before, or seen the ruin, or pieced together the evidence that's just lying around for me to find. And for a while, this made me doubt the truth of what I'd discovered. It couldn't be so easy, I thought. I couldn't have just stumbled across it. The evidence was so *real,* and the existence of the city here is so *right,* that others must have come to the same conclusions. A hundred others, a thousand."

"Are you quite sure no one has?"

"No," he said. "Not positive. Perhaps others have found the place, but never had a chance to reveal any of their findings."

I drank my beer and glanced around the tent. The closer I looked, the more I saw Scott's identity and personality stamped on the interior. A pile of books stood in one corner, all of them reference, no fiction. *What's the point of reading something that isn't true?* he'd once said to me, and I'd hated myself for not being able to come up with a good reason. Me, someone who worked in publishing, incapable of defending the purpose of my life. A belt lay carelessly thrown down on the rugs, various brushes, chisels and other implements of his trade tied to it. And the rugs themselves, far from being locally made, seemed to speak a variety of styles and cultures. Some told stories within their weaves, others held only patterns, and one or two seemed to perform both tasks with deceptive simplicity. The realization that this man, my friend, did not actually have a home hit me then, strong and hard. He carried his home with him. After all these years, all this time, I guessed that I had assumed Scott would "come home" one day, not realizing that he lived there every day of his life.

I missed my wife and kids then, sharply and brightly. But the feeling, though intense, was brief, and it soon faded into a background fog as Scott opened another bottle for each of us.

"I think I found this place for a reason," he said at last. "I can't say I was led here—I led myself if anything, looking, delving, searching into old histories and older tales—but I think it was meant to be."

"Don't tell me you've started to believe in fate."

"Only if it's self-made," he said, grinning. "I was fated to find this place, and you were fated to join me here, to search more fully. But only because that's what both of us wanted. Me to find Matthew, and you to give your life an injection of *life.*"

I felt slighted, but I knew that he was right. In what he said about me, at least. As to Matthew, I could not begin to imagine.

"Where better for the city of the dead than nestling in the cradle of humanity?" he said. "Ethiopia is where the first people walked, where Homo sapiens came into being. What better place?"

Something slammed against the side of the tent, sending the canvas stretching and snapping against the poles. I jumped to my feet and Scott glanced up, bottle poised at his mouth. "Sounds like we're in for a bit of a blow," he said.

"What the hell was that?"

"Wind. Storm coming in. You'd best get your things inside. We'll share this tent. Sand storms can be a bit disconcerting the first time you're caught in one, especially in a tent. Magnifies sound."

"You never said anything about sand storms." I felt the familiar fear rising inside, the one that hit me keen and hard when I was removed from my normal place, the company of my normal people. The fear that said I was lost.

"Didn't say much at all," he said. "If I had, would you have come?"

"Of course!" I said. "Of course I would."

"Even though you think I've lost the plot?"

I considered lying to my friend then, but he would have known. He already knew the truth. "That was the main reason."

He smiled. "You're a good mate. I'm a lucky man. I may only have a few possessions to my name, but I'm rich in friends."

I was unfeasibly flattered by his comment, and I went on to say something trite in response—*thanks,* or *so am I*—when another gust of wind hit the tent. It seemed to suck the air from inside, drawing in the tent walls, pulling down the ceiling, shrinking the canopy as if to allow the desert sand and air to move closer. The whole structure leaned and strained for a few seconds that seemed like minutes, and then the gale lessened, the tent relaxed and I glared down at Scott.

"Are we likely to be left homeless by this?" I said.

"Nope. Tent's meant to move and shift with the wind." His eyes were wide, seeing something far more distant than I knew, and I saw the familiar excitement there, the knowledge that there was more going on than we could ever hope to understand. That kind of ignorance never offended Scott. It merely gave him more cause to wonder.

I ducked outside to drag in my luggage, squinting against the sand being blown around by the rising wind. I stood there for a while, hand shielding my eyes, looking out toward the horizon to see whether I could spot the storm. All around, the skies seemed to have darkened from light blue to a grubby, uniform gray. The sun was a smudge heading down to the western horizon, a smear of yellow like a daffodil whipped in the wind. Out past the camp I could see dust dancing above the ground, playing in spirals across the plain where the wind was being twisted by the heat. They flicked to and fro. Snapping at the ground. Whipping up more dust and sand to add to their mass.

And then, in the distance, floating above the horizon, there was a ghastly flash of light that lit the insides of the gray mass.

I gasped, felt grit on my teeth and in my eyes, and a few seconds later a long, low roar rolled in across the desert. It started as subdued as a rumbling stomach, but increased in volume until it shook the ground beneath my feet and smashed my ears. Another flash displayed just how dark it had suddenly become. The resultant thunder merged with the first. The sky was screaming at me.

Just as I turned to go back into the tent the wind came down with a vengeance. What I had thought a gale was only a precursor to this onslaught. Sand was ripped up and blasted into my face, my ears, my hair and eyes and mouth. The sound was tremendous; wind, thunder, and grit coursing across the tent walls.

25

Inside, Scott had stood up and was opening two more bottles of beer. "Bit of a howler!"

"Is it always like this?" I had to shout just to be heard, and even then I could have been mumbling.

"Never seen one like this before! Here. More beer!" He held out the bottle and I went to him, accepting it, grateful for the dulling effect of the alcohol.

The storm came down. It was so loud that we could not hear ourselves talk, let alone each other, so we sat together and listened. I was terrified. The aural onslaught was so extreme that I wanted to scream, challenge its ferocity with some of my own. It beat into the tent, seemingly increasing in volume all the time, and it was all for me, aimed at me, targeted at me and me alone.

Scott sat wide-eyed and astonished, an inscrutable smile on his face as he stared at the canopy shifting above us.

It went on for a long time, becoming more fearsome with each passing minute. The roar turned into something that sounded alive, a snarling thing, crunching down into the ground in a hideous rhythm. The storm was running toward us across the desert, legs so long that the footfalls were minutes apart. It was not an image that I relished, but deep down I found some satisfaction in the stirring of my mostly dormant imagination. Thousands of tons of sand picked up by the storm abraded the whole landscape. It was powered against the canvas, setting the whole structure vibrating into a blur.

Something hit the tent. It slid slowly across the surface, visible as a dark shadow against the slightly lighter background. Its edges shimmered in the wind, and it took several long seconds to pass over the tent's domed roof, finally being sucked away into the storm with a whiplike crack.

"What the hell was that?" I shouted

"One of the other tents, I guess."

"I thought you said they were meant to bend, could withstand this?"

"We weren't in that one." His comment made no sense. I guessed I had misheard.

We attempted some more shouted conversation, but two out of every three words were stolen by the storm. I imagined these lost thoughts blown together, mixed and matched into things neither of us had ever meant to say. Scott's tent seemed to be withstanding the battering, its poles bending and twisting just as he'd said they were designed to, though I never once felt safe. As far as I was concerned we were forever on the verge of doom. The tent would be whipped away into the gray storm and we would be left bare, exposed, tumbling across the desert in a cloud of rugs and cushions and clothes, sand scoring our skin until the flesh showed through, blinded, deafened, eventually buried wherever the storm chose to dump us.

Scott never looked anything less than amazed. His excitement did not flicker. He continued drinking, and to my surprise so did I, still able to enjoy the beer even in such desperate circumstances. Part of it was the lulling effect of the alcohol, but perhaps I was also taking on some of Scott's awe through our companionable silence.

The lightning flashes continued, shimmering across

the tent's outer walls and casting strange shadows, swirling, dancing dust devils celebrating the wind. The thunder came almost immediately. It was a long time before the period between lightning and thunder began to grow again. I imagined the storm waiting above our tent, examining us, interested in these petty humans who had decided to pitch against its power.

Still the sands scoured the tent, driven by the horrendous gales. I shouted at Scott several times to ask whether the canvas could withstand such a battering, but he did not answer. He knew I was asking something, but he merely smiled, eyes sparkling, bringing the bottle to his lips once more. He existed in his own little space.

There was no point in trying to sleep. I checked my watch regularly, but day and night had become confused, and when the time began to make no sense I stopped checking. Perhaps night fell, because the dark storm became that much darker, but lightning gave us brief moments of illumination here and there. Scott lit some electric lanterns around the tent, solar batteries charged during the day to keep the day with us through the long, dark desert nights. And it grew perceptibly cooler. I opened my luggage and rummaged around for a shirt and a pair of combat trousers, standing to change with my head only inches from the convex canvas ceiling. For some reason it seemed so much louder than when I was sitting down.

Eventually, after hours that felt like days, the storm began to abate. We only realized how much it had lessened when we found that we could converse comfortably by raising our voices only slightly.

"How long do these usually last?" I asked.

Scott shrugged. "As I said, never seen one like this before. But I think that was short."

I looked at my watch, but still it made no sense.

"Hours," he said. "Maybe six." He glanced at the empty beer bottles strewn around the floor of his tent. "Maybe more."

I suddenly realized how much I needed to urinate. I looked around the tent, but there was no sign of a bucket or a partitioned toilet area.

"Two tents along," Scott said. "If it's still there." He pointed the way without standing. He suddenly looked very drunk, even though minutes before he had been alert and observant.

I stared at him. I was scared, terrified of the desert and the prospect of leaving the tent on my own, but I could not articulate that idea.

He knew. "Come on," he said, standing and swaying slowly toward me. "Shit, listen to that. Like it never was."

The storm had all but died down. There was a continuous, low hissing of sand slipping slowly from the dome tent. But even that faded away after only a few more seconds, and we were left with our own heavy breathing.

The silence was shocking. My stomach rumbled, and I was ridiculously embarrassed.

"Like it never was," Scott said again. "Let's go and see what it's left us."

We exited the tent into a bloodred dusk.

And we saw what the storm had left behind.

*   *   *

The landscape had changed beyond recognition.

Where the watering hole had been, a sand dune now lay. Where the neighboring tents had been pitched, there was now a wind-patterned expanse of loose sand. And the horizon that had once been apparent, viewed across packed sand and low, gentle mounds, was now hidden behind something new.

Rising out of the desert, a city.

I fell to my knees. I could not take in the immensity of what we were viewing. My mind would not permit it. It did not fit within the confines of my imagination, the limits of my understanding.

Scott was amazed, but not surprised. That was something that terrified me even more. He was not surprised.

"There it is," he said. "There it is, at last." He walked across the altered landscape, ignoring the fact that ours was the only tent left standing. There was no sign of the others. They could have been anywhere.

"Scott?" I whispered at last. He turned and looked, smiling, but not at me. "Scott, what's going on?"

"The City of the Dead," he said. "The storm gave it to us. Pete, you have to come and see it with me. Don't just stay here."

"I'm afraid. It shouldn't be there, it's too . . . big."

"Out of the desert, that's all. *Please,* Pete. You'll always regret it if you don't come. You'll think about it forever. It'll haunt you . . . *believe* me, I know. Live a little."

Live a little. Yes, that was what I wanted to do. Scott had lived a lot, and I only wanted to live a little. But still, I was terrified. I could conceive of no way that this could be happening. I looked past him at the ruins revealed by the storm. They seemed to begin just over a wide, low dune created at the western extremes of the old camp, and if they were as close as I believed they probably rose about twenty feet above the desert level. Only twenty feet.

But before the storm, there had been nothing there at all.

"They shouldn't be there. . . ." I said.

Scott shrugged. "The desert is deceiving. Messes with perspective. Come on."

He was lying. But somehow I stood and followed.

The sand underfoot was loose and treacherous; more than once we both slipped and slid several steps down the side of the new dune. I could not take my eyes from the ruin rising before me. I tried to convince myself that I had been misled by Scott's certainty; that the structure was naturally formed, carved from solid stone by millennia of scouring wind. But it could only be artificial. There were the joints between blocks, the blocks themselves huge and probably each weighing several tons. And the windows, squared at the base, curved inward at their head, like traditional church windows back home. Around the windows, still visible here and there, ornamentation. Scrolls. Patterned carvings that may have been some sort of writing. And in one place, staring out at us as we approached, guarding the ancient ruin it formed a part of, the face of a gargoyle.

I tried not to look, but my gaze was drawn there. It had three eyes, two mouths, and though its edges had

31

been worn by eons of erosion, still its teeth looked sharp.

"Scott," I whispered.

"I know!" he said, excitement to my fear. "Come on! I think this is just a part of it."

We walked slowly up the low slope of the new dune. I glanced back once or twice at the remains of the camp we left behind. Only the single large tent was visible now, with a few sand-covered mounds here and there that may have been scattered equipment. Ahead of us, the old ruin revealed itself more and more with each step.

I was afraid to reach the top. Afraid to see whether this was just a part of it, or if there was so much more beyond. I so wanted this to be a single tall wall.

When we crested the hill, the world became a different place. Everything I had held true shifted, much of it drastically. My beliefs, my faith took a gut-punch and reeled against the assault. Scott touched my shoulder and then held on; he knew what I was feeling. I looked at him, and his eyes were ablaze with the thrill of discovery.

The ruins lay in a wide hollow in the desert. There was not one high wall. There was not even a single building. Spread across the floor of the depression in the land, seemingly growing from the ground, lay the remains of several large and dozens of smaller buildings. Sand and grit were skirted around bases and against walls, had drifted up and through openings that may have been windows, may have been wounds. Some of the ruins rose above the level of the desert floor, but many more had been revealed below, shown the sunlight for the first time in eons when the terrible sand storm had opened them up to view. The hollow must have been a mile across.

"Let's go down," Scott said.

"Why?"

"I want to see. I want to know where the dead live. Look, over there!" He pointed to our left, and before the dark stone of the first tumbled building there was something in the sand, something dark, moving.

At first I thought it was a scorpion or small lizard. But as we moved closer I saw the reality. It was a foot, still clad in the remains of a sandal, bones stripped of flesh and dangling with scraps of skin, snapped or broken at the ankle. The illusion of movement stopped as we came closer, but I blinked several times and wiped sand from my eyes, waiting for it to move again.

Scott hesitated momentarily before picking it up. "Here," he said, offering me the relic. "Touch something timeless."

Before I could refuse he grabbed my hand and placed the skeletal foot there. It had no weight. Lighter than a feather, little more than a memory, it lay across my palm and fingers, yet seemed not to touch them. It felt warm, though that may have been the sun beating through its nothingness—

And the sun struck down as this person walked, endlessly, herded with a thousand more, driven from one old land and taken toward another. Soldiers and settlers accompanied them on their way, using guns and boots if any of the ragged tribe lagged behind. This person was old by now, crying, leaving a trail of tears as she was torn away from her own lands for the first time ever, and she died from thirst and sorrow on strange soil—

I dropped the thing back into the sand and it landed with a thud. It sat there motionless, and at any second I expected it to strike out.

"There's more," he said. "Signs of habitation."

I shook my head, trying to dispel whatever it was I had imagined. *Hallucination? Vision?* "You really believe this place is what you said it is?"

"Of course!" he said. "And there's more, much more. This is just the surface. I want to go down inside. Matthew is inside!"

"If that's true—if everything you're saying, all this madness, has an ounce of truth—do you know what this would do to the world? To religion, belief, faith?"

"I don't care," Scott said.

"Why?"

"Because caring can't change the truth."

I stared over Scott's shoulder at the ruined city risen from the sands.

"I want to go *deeper,*" Scott said, and he turned and walked down toward the ruins.

I followed, sliding once or twice, starting a small avalanche that preceded us both down the slope. There were several more dark shapes in the sand, shapes with glimpses of white within, old bones, ready to crumble in the heat. I wondered if they were light and insubstantial like the foot. Light, but filled with memories waiting to be relived. I had no wish to touch them.

Scott reached the first ruin. He stood very close, hand held up in front of him, palm out, almost touching the wall. The stone sported some elaborate designs, letters or images, numbers or figures.

"Old," Scott said. "These are so old."

"What language is that? Is that hieroglyphics?"

"An earlier form, perhaps. Though initiated separately. I've seen variations of this before, many times all across the world. I've been searching for so long, it's almost my second tongue."

"What does it say?"

Scott turned to me and smiled, and his hand touched the rock for the first time. He sighed and blinked heavily, as if suddenly tired or drunk. "You don't want to know," he said. "Come on."

Scott and I circled the stone ruin. It was built from huge flat blocks, far too large to possibly be moved by hand, and old though it was, burial in the sands must have protected it from erosion by the winds of time. In addition to the strange markings there were several more of the gruesome gargoyles at various points on its upper surface, not corresponding at all with any opening or any particular spacing. I glanced back, and our footprints seemed to have disappeared into the desert. The sand was so smooth, so fine that it had flowed back in to fill the depressions, leaving little more than dents in the surface. It was as though the buried city were swallowing our presence. Or wiping it away.

"I think this may be a temple," he said.

"May *have* been," I said.

"No." He shook his head, frowning and smiling at me at the same time. "This may be the City of the Dead, but it can never be deserted."

"What do you mean?"

"Come on," he said. "Deeper."

Farther down in the depression stood the remains of more buildings. They looked ruined to me, ancient and ruined, but what Scott had said stuck with me, forced me to view them in a different light. So there was no roof on these four tumbled-down walls, but what need of a roof buried in the sands? The doorway was blocked with the tumbled stone arch that had once held it open, but do the dead need true doorways? I looked around at our feet and saw more of the scattered remains, some of them still wrapped in old cloth, some of the bones white in the glaring sun, bleached and seemingly brittle as if they had been exposed for eons, not hours. The wind must have danced and spun between these barely standing walls, because the stone floor was revealed in places, sand swept aside. It held patterns, colored rocks inlaid in the stone so perfectly that their edges seemed to merge, offering no cracks for time to pry apart. Scott tried to brush away more sand, reveal a larger pattern, but the more that was on display the less sense it made.

He revelled in the mystery, while it made me more nervous.

"Is that a language?" I asked. "Same as the wall markings?"

Scott shook his head. "Not a language as we know it," he said. "I think it's meant to inspire feelings. True art. We could carry on, uncover it all. Find out *which* feelings."

I shook my head. "Let's move on."

"Good man!" Scott said, slapping my shoulder and hurrying on ahead.

There was a maze of long, low walls at the base of the depression, spreading maybe three hundred feet from side to side. Scott paused at its perimeter for a few moments, looking around, kicking at the sand. He stooped and picked up a badly eroded bone. It may have been a skull, but it was full of unnatural holes. He closed his eyes.

The air around us seemed to shimmer, as if stirred by an invisible breeze. I felt no breath against my sweating skin, but the ruined walls and the high ridge of sand around us flickered as if through a heat haze. And though I felt no breath, I seemed to hear a whisper.

Scott dropped the relic, glancing back at me. "Murder," he said.

I looked at the tangled mess of cloth and bone. And then I surprised myself. I must have shocked Scott as well, because he raised his eyebrows and took a step back.

I reached out and picked up the skull—

And it was dark by the sea, windy and wet, stinking of rotting sea life as beaches always do. This person stood with his back to the cliffs, staring out, watching the bursts of effervescence as waves broke and captured the moonlight. In one hand there was a gun, in the other a torch, and when the small rowboat came ashore both would be pointed outward this night, and both used. But that chance did not arrive. The waves hid the sound of the shape creeping up behind him, out of the cave where it must have been waiting all day. When the knife curled around his throat and slid through his skin, the moon caught the spurting blood, bright as breaking waves, and the betrayal tasted of salt—

I dropped the bundle and watched it sink into the sand. The sudden change from vision to real life—darkness and wet, to dryness and blazing sun—startled me, but not as much as it should have. I squinted at Scott, and for the first time I saw a fleck of fear in his eyes, a dark, fiery look that floated there like the sun reflected in negative.

"Did you see?" he whispered.

I nodded.

"You saw what ties that person to this city," he said. "Why they can't let go."

"Murder?"

"Unfinished business."

I looked down at where the old skull had fallen and sunk. I felt observed.

"I'm going down," Scott said,

"What?"

"I'm going down into the city. For every ghost with unfinished business, there's someone accountable."

"Matthew," I said, but Scott chose not to answer. He was already walking away, across the boiling sand, past ruins that should not be, past the mysterious language carved into these stone walls, his footprints being swallowed by the desert behind him, eschewing the sun for darker depths. When he reached another pile of stone protruding from the ground he turned and looked back at me.

"I'd like you to come," he said. Perhaps he feigned

the fear. Maybe he was playing me even then, luring me to his own ends. But I was his friend, and the fear I thought I heard in his few words somehow enabled me to better my own.

I followed him into the ground.

The way down should never have been there. After the storm, and after the eons that the desert had had to fill this place with its own, there should have been no clear route underground. The fluid sand should have seen to that. It was as if while the gale thundered above, so too had a storm raged down below, powerful enough to expel the sand like the cork from a shaken bottle of champagne. And Scott had found the way.

"Down there," he said. "Down there we'll find ghosts, Pete. Wraiths never given a chance to rest. Are you sure you want to come with me?"

"I've come all this way," I said, failing to understand my own skewed logic.

"I knew I could count on you. Say goodbye to the sun!" He looked up and squinted at the sun, blazing and hot, even though it was dipping into the west.

I looked as well, but not for long. I did not want to imbue the moment with too much ceremony. That would be admitting that I may never see the sun again.

The hole was just wide enough for our entry. It opened beneath a wall, smashed through the buried foundations by some ancient cataclysm, leading in and down like an opened throat waiting to swallow us whole. Scott slipped quickly inside on his stomach, but I lay there for a while in the hot sand, looking at the perimeter of the hole and wondering just what was holding it up. It looked like compacted sand, little more. The wall passed above it and pressed down, but there was no lintel, no supporting stone. A trial of danger before entering the City of the Dead.

I squeezed through, scraped my back against the edge, felt sand crumble down the neck of my shirt, and then I was inside.

Scott was rummaging around at the base of a wall, cursing and shaking his head. Enough light filtered in for me to see him there, moving stuff aside with his foot, bending, grabbing something, dropping it again. He groaned and sighed, spat and whimpered.

"Scott!"

"We need a torch," he said. "We need some light." And I saw what he was doing. There were more segments of skeletons piled against the wall, as if blown there by some subterranean wind, and Scott was sorting them until he found a bone long enough to use as a torch. And every time he touched a bone . . .

"Here," he said. "Not so bad. Love rejected. Hell of a reason to miss out on Heaven." He held a long thigh bone, knotted a wad of material about its smashed joint, twisting and tying it hard so that the fire would take its time eating through. He slipped a lighter from his pocket and gave us light.

We were in a long corridor, its floor sloping down quite steeply, its far end lost in darkness.

"I guess we go down," he said.

"No other way. Scott, do you really think—"

"Shhh!" he hissed. "Hear that? Do you *hear that?*"

I listened intently, breathing out slowly through my

nose, and perhaps I heard the echoes of his voice. They seemed to go on for a long time, and they grew closer again before fading away into the stone walls.

"Let's go," he said. "They know we're here."

He headed off into the corridor and I could only follow. The light from his makeshift torch was very weak, but it bled back far enough to touch the ground around my feet, casting sad reflections from the bones Scott had rooted through. They were mixed, but I was sure they would not match. A dozen remains here, two dozen, and I accidentally kicked one aside with my sandaled foot—

The ship was going, sinking quickly, and this person was trapped inside, searching for an air pocket, trying to force his way through the deluge, pushing aside floating things, food, ropes, bodies, cursing at those who had shut them down here, cursing until his mouth opened and emitted a final bubbling gasp that no one would ever hear—

Scott would have felt every one of those remains. Every death, each betrayal or sin or deceit, telling its story as he shuffled the remains.

"It's all so unfair." I had no idea what I was seeing, and no idea why.

"It's life," he said. "Or death."

Scott went on, and the slope began to dip down even steeper than before. I glanced back frequently, just to reassure myself that the glow of sunlight was still behind us. That small entrance grew smaller and fainter, from a false sun into little more than a smudge in the dark. And then, as I knew had to happen, we turned a bend in the corridor and the daylight vanished.

I stopped and called out to Scott. "We're alone."

He paused and looked back over my shoulder. The torch he carried was growing fainter as the fire consumed the ancient material. I reached out to take it from him, but there was nothing there. No bone to touch, no friction, no heat when I held my hand in the guttering flames. Nothing.

"Scott," I said. "Just where the hell are you taking us?"

"There'll be light," he said. "Every place I've read of this, there's the light of the dead. We just have to get there. This is the route to the city, not the city proper. We should find it soon, Pete. Soon! And then perhaps I can lay Matthew to rest."

"This is madness," I said. Our voices were peculiarly dead in that subterranean place, consumed by the rock walls and the weird hieroglyphs. The etchings writhed in the weak light from Scott's insubstantial torch, given a life of their own.

"Stay with me, Pete," he said. He turned away and continued along the tunnel, heading down and away from the vanished light, perhaps leading us into places and dangers neither of us could truthfully imagine. "You're my best friend."

I followed because it was the only thing I could do. I like to think I stayed on his tail because of my devotion to my friend, my burgeoning sense of adventure, my excitement at what we might have discovered around the next curve in the corridor, or the next. But in reality I think I was simply scared. I could not face the walk back out on my own. Uphill. Past those strange markings on the wall, those bones that had no weight or touch.

I had no choice but to follow. We walked for what felt like hours. Scott's torch had guttered down to little more than a blue smudge in the utter darkness. The new light that manifested came so slowly, so gradually, that for a while I could not understand how that failing torch was throwing out so much illumination. But this new light was growing and expanding, dusty and blue, originating from no single source. The walls of the passage began to glow, as if touched by the early morning sun, and the shapes and tales carved there told differing stories as the shadows writhed and shifted. None of them was clear to me.

"Scott," I said, afraid, more afraid than I had been since those first blasts of the storm had assaulted the tent walls.

"The light of the dead," he said. "They need it to see. I guess they don't like the dark. We're almost there, Pete."

Ahead of us the passage narrowed, walls closing in and ceiling dipping until we had to stoop to pass by. The ceiling touched my head once, and I didn't like the sensation; the rock was smooth and as warm as living flesh. I could not shake the idea that we were walking willingly into the belly of a beast, and now here we were at the base of its esophagus, deep deep down, about to enter its stomach and submit ourselves to digestion.

There were more remains around our feet here, scattered across the ground, offering no resistance as we waded through. The bones tumbled aside, clanking silently together, some falling into dust as soon as they were disturbed and others rolling together as if coveting their former cozy togetherness. I could not feel them. It was like kicking aside wafts of smoke. I wondered if they could feel me.

Scott was ahead of me. When I heard him gasp, and I walked into him, and his gasp came again as a groan, I knew that things were about to change. The claustrophobic passage opened out onto a small ledge strewn with skeletal parts that seemed to dance away as we both came to a stunned standstill, looking out at the place we had come down here to find.

I once stood on the viewing platform at the top of the Empire State Building in New York, looking down at the city surrounding me, the myriad streets and blocks crawling with people and cars, the mechanical streams spotted yellow with frequent taxis, sirens singing up out of the city like wailing souls long-lost, other high buildings near and far speckled with interior lights, the city rising in three dimensions, not just spread out like the carpet of humanity I had imagined. I could look east toward the river and see a hotdog vendor's stand at a road junction, and then south toward Greenwich Village, where through one of the telescopes I could just make out someone hurrying across a street with a dog tugging them along, and I knew that these two people may never meet. In a city of that size, there was a good chance that they would pass their lives without ever exchanging glances. And I, at the top of this huge tower, could see it all. I could see a fire to the east of Central Park, follow the course of fire engines screeching intermittently through the traffic, but wherever the owners of the burning building were I could not tell them. I had a strange feeling of being lifted way above the city, an observer rather than a player, and as I descended in the express elevator and exited once more onto the streets, I experienced a dislocation that lasted for the rest of the day. I glanced back up at the tower, and wondered just who was looking down at me right then.

What I saw in this place way below the desert was larger, older and far less explicable.

The City of the Dead lay spread out before us. It was flat and utterly without limit, stretching way out farther than I could see, and it was sheer distance rather than anything else that faded it into the horizon. No hazy atmosphere, no darkening of the air—the light of the dead was rich and pure and all-encompassing, much more revealing and honest than mere sunlight—but pure, unbelievable distance. The city went on forever, and I could see only at the speed of light. It spread out left and right and ahead, the only visibly defined border being the high cliff from which we had emerged. The wall fell down to the city and rose higher than I could see, and it faded similarly as I looked left and right. It did not seem to curve around, perhaps enclosing the city, but stood in a straight line, and here and there I spied other ledges and darker smudges that may have been the mouths of other tunnels. In the distance I thought I saw another shocked individual standing on one of these ledges, but I blinked and the image was taken away.

I looked down, trying to judge how far below the ground lay. *Too far to climb but close enough to fall,* I thought, and though I had no idea where the idea came from I looked at Scott, caught his eye, knew that he was thinking the same awful thing.

Together we stepped forward and tipped slowly over the lip of the ledge, leaning into space, somehow welcoming the plunge that would immerse us in this city.

The fall lasted long enough for me to make out plenty more detail. I did not dwell upon the strangeness of what was happening—right then, it did not seem important—and though I knew that things had changed irrevocably as Scott and I had set foot on that ledge, I took the opportunity to view this place. Here was the supposed City of the Dead. The buildings were hugely diverse, ranging from small shacks made of corrugated tin spread across branch uprights, to golden-domed offerings of love; steel and glass towers, to complex timber-clad settlements; frosty ice-sculptured homes, to hollows in the ground, caves, deep holes heated by the boiling insides of the hot earth itself. There was no order, no design to the city, no blocks or arrangement, merely buildings and the spaces in between. Here and there I saw wider areas that may have been parks, though there was no greenery to be seen. The things in these parks may have been dead trees, or simply much taller skeletons than any I had seen before. Some buildings had windows and some did not, and only some of those with windows retained their glazing. It was only as we fell closer to the city— and that fall, that plunge, was still accepted by both of us—that my attention was drawn more to the spaces in between the buildings.

In those spaces, things moved.

Until now I had seen this as the City of the Dead, and I was falling toward it, and that did not matter.

Now, seeing this movement in the streets and roads and alleys and parks—seeing also the flittering movements behind the windows of the taller buildings, shadows denying the strange, level light that this place possessed—I came to dwell upon exactly what was happening to us. We fell, though there was no sensation of movement; no wind in my ears, no sickness in my stomach, no velocity. And soon, looking down, I knew that there was an impact to come. Directly below us was a collection of smaller, humped buildings, rising from the ground like insect hills, surrounded by taller constructions that even now we began to fall past.

"Scott!" I yelled, but even though I felt no breeze, my voice was stolen away. He was next to me, spread-eagled in the air, and when he caught my eye he looked quickly away again. What that signified, I did not know.

The impact came closer, and then it was past. It did not hurt, and I had no memory at all of having landed. One second we were falling by tall buildings, flitting past windows that each seemed to hold a shadowy face observing our descent, and the next we were on the ground. Dust rose around us and floated in the still air, drifting up, up, as if eager to trace the paths of our recent descent. We lay there, watching the dust form ghostly shapes around us. Somehow, at the end of our fall, we had flipped over to land on our backs.

"We're here," Scott whispered. "Look."

He did not point and I did not turn my head to see where he was looking. I did not need to. Because one of those ambiguous shapes suddenly became more real, emerging from the dust like a sunbeam bursting through cloud cover, carrying a bluish light and forming a very definite shape as it passed first over Scott's body, and then my own. The shape of a woman in long, flowing robes, her hair short, her hands held out before her as if forever warding off some horrible fate. Her foot touched my arm—

She saw it coming at her, the dog, the animal, whatever it is, she saw it and she saw the faces of those behind it, and they could have been grimacing or laughing. She brought up her hands, as if that would do any good, and before the thing crashed into her in a rage of teeth and claws, she caught sight of the face of someone she had once loved in the gleeful crowd—

I scurried back, pushing with my feet until I was leaning against a stone wall, shaking my head to loosen the image. The wraith drifted away down the street and eventually faded into the uniform blue light that smothered this place. The wall at my back should have felt good, but it was merely more confirmation this was somewhere that should not be, as was the solid ground, the ground I had hit after minutes of falling. I glanced up, but the cliff wall was nowhere to be seen. Only that blue light.

"Are we alive?" I said, a sick fear suddenly making me cold.

"Of course," Scott said. "Do you remember dying?"

"No. But that doesn't mean we didn't. We fell!"

"Everyone here remembers dying," he said. "That's why they're here."

"But why—"

"No more questions, Pete," he said. "Just open your eyes to it all."

"I'm not sure I want to."

Scott reached down to help me up. His firm grip was comforting, and we held on to each other for a second or two as we stood there together, looking around. He was real to me and I was real to him, and right then that was very important. These buildings were real too. I kicked at the stone wall I had been leaning against. There was a dull *thud* and dust drifted from my tatty shoe. And I realized then, for the first time, how utterly silent it was.

Wherever we were, however deep below the ground or submerged in disbelief, there were no voices, no gusts of air, no sounds of a city, no movements, no breaths. My own heart started to sound excessively loud as it continued on its startled course, busy pumping oxygen through veins to dilute my fear and cool the heat of my distress. I was not used to existence without noise of some kind. At home, with a wife and two children sharing the house, there was always a raised voice or a mumbled dream, music or television adding a theme, toys being crashed or musical instruments adding their tone-deaf lilt to the air. Even at work, reading and editing, the voices in my mind were loud enough to be audible. Here, in this city larger than any I had ever seen or imagined, the complete silence was incongruous and unfair. And it made things so obviously false.

"We're not really here," I said. Scott ignored me. Perhaps in silence he was dealing with this in his own way.

There was an opening in the stone wall a few meters along, and I went to it and looked inside. I saw a room, large and high-ceilinged, bereft of anything—furniture, character, life. Four walls, a floor, a ceiling, nothing more. There were no signs of it ever having been used. There was a doorway in the far wall without a door, no glass in the window I looked through, no light fixture in the ceiling; the same uniform blue light lit every corner of the room, top and bottom, revealing nothing but slight drifts of dust. Shadows had no place here. I stood back slightly and looked up, realizing that the building was maybe fifteen stories tall, all of them identically holed with glassless windows, and I was certain that each room and floor was the same sterile, deserted emptiness.

Scott nudged against me as he walked by, and when I glanced down I realized that he had done so on purpose.

There were several more wraiths moving along the street. Two of them walked, strutting purposefully together, their expressions and facial features similar. They wore bathing shorts and nothing else, their torsos and limbs dark with suntan, faces young and strong and long, long dead. They did not touch each other as they strode by, and they exuded contempt, staring straight ahead and doing nothing to acknowledge the other's closeness. Another shape seemed to float and spin through the air, but as she passed by I realized that she was falling horizontally, clothes ripped from her body by the invisible wind that whipped her hair around her head, face and shoulders. She may have been beautiful, but the forces crushing her this way and that were too cruel to tell. She passed over the heads of the striding brothers and cornered at the end of the street, her fall unimpeded. Two more shapes came by separately, neither of them appearing to notice us. One shouted silently and waved fists at the sky, and the other struggled on footless legs, stumping his way along and swinging his arms for balance, as if pushing through mud. One of his hands brushed mine, I saw it but did not feel it—

He was in the sea, trapped by a giant clam that had closed around both feet, his muscles burning acid into his bones as he struggled to keep his nose high enough to snort in a desperate breath between waves, and even though the salt water was doing its best to blind him, he could see the boat bobbing a few feet away, the faces peering over the edge, laughing so much as their tears of mirth fell to quicken his fate—

I gasped and pressed myself back against the wall, watching the dead man hobble away.

Scott had remained in the center of the narrow street, staring about him as the new shapes breezed by. Perhaps they touched him, but he seemed not to have noticed. With the taste of brine still on my lips I went to him, desperate to feel someone real again. I clapped my hand to his shoulder, held on hard, followed his gaze. High buildings, that blue light, no sign of where we had come from . . . and high up, sometimes, darker blue shapes sweeping by.

"What are they?" I asked.

"I don't know. But Pete, Matthew is here. He has to

51

be! I have to find him, and however long it takes . . ." He left the sentence unfinished, ominous with possibilities.

"These aren't just ghosts," I said.

"Not ghosts, no!" He shook his head as if frustrated at my naïveté. "Dead people, Pete."

"There's nothing to them!"

"Do you have to feel something for it to be real or mean anything? Can you touch your dreams, taste your imagination? They're as real as we are, just not in quite the same place, the same way. And they're here because they were wronged."

"How could you know all this?"

"You think I haven't been looking for this place?" he said. "Poring over every scrap of ancient script I've discovered, or uncovered in some godforsaken old library somewhere? Tearing apart whole digs by hand to find a fragment of writing about it, a shred of evidence? Ever since I first got wind of this place the year Matthew died, it's been my only reason to keep on living."

"Matthew? Why . . . ?"

He looked at me then, a quick glance, as if he was unwillingly to relinquish the sight of our unbelievable surroundings. "I wasn't there when he died."

"He died of leukemia, Scott," I said.

"I should have been there."

"You couldn't have done anything! He died of leukemia. Just tell me what you could have done?"

He stared at me, but not for effect. He really could not understand why I was even asking. "I could have held his hand," he said.

"You think your young son could hold that against you?"

"No, but I could. And that's enough to keep him here."

"You can't know any of this!" I said, shaking my head, looking around at the impossible buildings with the occasional impossible shape floating, striding or crawling by. "You might think you do, but you've been—"

"Misled?" He said it mockingly, as if anyone could draw a sane idea from this place.

"No," I said. "Not misled. Maybe just a little mad."

"Do you see all this?" he asked.

"I don't know *what* I see. It's madness. My eyes are playing tricks, I'm drunk, I'm dreaming, I'm drugged. All this is madness and—"

"You see the City of the Dead!" He grabbed my lapels and propelled me back against a wall, dust puffing out around me in an uneven halo. His shout tried to echo between the buildings, but it was soon swallowed or absorbed, and it did not return. He did not shout again.

"Scott, please . . ." I felt a little madness closing in myself. Some vague insulating layer of disbelief still hung around me, blurring the sharp edges and dangerous points of what I saw and what I could not believe. But beyond that layer lay something far more dangerous. I wondered if Scott was there already.

"Don't 'please' me!" he said. "Matthew is here, *trapped* here, because of *me!* He could be there!" He pointed along the street at a large domed building, ran there, peered in through one of several triangular openings. I followed after him and looked inside. There were shadows moving about, writhing across the floor like the dark echoes of snakes, passing through the blue light and somehow negating it with themselves.

"There's only—"

"He could be there!" Scott said, running away from me again, dodging around a gray shape that stood wringing its hands. He passed by a row of squat-fronted buildings and ducked into a gap in the block, disappearing from view. I followed quickly and found him leaning over a low wall, looking down into the huge basement rooms that it skirted. "Down there, see?" Scott said. "He could so easily be down there!" I saw several shapes sitting on rough circular seats, each of them gesticulating and issuing silent shouts and pleas.

"Is he?" I asked.

"No," Scott said, "not there. But there! He could be there!" Yet again he ran, heading between two buildings. The lonely pad of his footsteps sounded like a riot in that silent place.

I ran after him, terrified that he would lose me in a maze of alleys and streets, parks and squares. "Matthew!" he called, still running, calling again. His voice came back to me and guided me on.

I did not want to be lost. I'd spent my whole life being lost and found, lost and found again, sometimes the same day, emotionally tumbled and torn down by the doubt and fear that time was running away from me. My mind could not cope with the complexity of life, I had often thought, and while others found their escape in imagination and wonder, I wallowed, lost in a miserable self-pity. Now, in this place, lost was the last place I wanted to be.

I spun around a corner and straight into the figure of a lady of the night standing against a wall, smiling at me, making some silent offer as I ducked by. Her fingers snagged my sleeves and brushed against my skin, and in that brief instant I saw abuse more terrible than I could have imagined. I gasped, fell to my knees and crawled forward, desperate to escape this dead woman's cursed touch. I turned and glanced back at her. She was laughing, pointing at me as if that could touch and show me again. I stood and ran, wondering just how mad a dead person could become.

Scott's shouts drew me on. I was darting around corners blindly, not knowing what would be revealed beyond. A long alley once, the blue light of the dead faded here as if swallowed by the walls. Then a square courtyard, filled with so many wandering shapes that I could not help touching several of them as I ran by, sensing them stroke my skin but unaware of any weight, any substance to their presence. At each touch, I saw something of their reason for being here. This place was an unbalanced concentration of pain and suffering, I knew, but before long I began to despair that there was any good left anywhere in the world.

I wondered what these dead things saw or felt when *I* touched *them*.

"In here!" Scott called. "Or over there!" His voice angled in from several directions at once now, the city juggling it to confuse me. I passed from the courtyard into another narrow alley, this one turning and bearing downward, no square angles, only curved walls to enclose its sloping floor. There were shapes sitting in doorways like black-garbed Greek women, but they all looked up at me with pale, dead faces. Some reached out to show me their stories; most did not. One of them turned at my approach and passed through a doorway into the building behind it, and I could not help stopping and looking inside. There were things apparently growing in there, strange dark fungi breaking from the floor and reaching for the ceiling, but when one of them moved and cast its dead gaze upon me, I turned and fled.

Some dead people walked, and some ran. Some stood still or sat down, forgetting to move at all.

Scott's voice rang in again, and for the first time I realized that it was only his voice. Footsteps no longer accompanied his cries. He had either stopped running, or he was too far away for me to hear them. Yet still he was crying out for Matthew, and somewhere he looked upon ghosts and did not see his dead son's face, because his call came again and again. I ran on, but with every step, and whichever direction I took, his voice grew fainter.

I came across a district of timber buildings, most of them squared and severe looking with their ancient saw marks, a few seemingly made from the natural shapes of cut trees; curved roofs, irregular walls, windows of bare branches where leaves may have grown once.

There was no greenery, only dead wood.

I wondered who had built this place.

The ground was scattered with fine sawdust, ankle deep in places, and I saw no footprints of any kind. My own were the first, and I imagined them as prints on the moon, no air movement to take them away, destined to remain for as long as time held them. Yet the dead were here too, though leaving no trace. Remains were scattered against the timber walls, just as they had been in the caves and tunnel leading down from the surface, and as I accidentally kicked a skull out of my way, I had a brief inkling of its owner's fate—

Standing in the woods as strange sounds came in, weird visions lighting their way between the trees as the hunt drew closer, the air grew warmer, and the fear became an all-encompassing thing as the first of the arrows *twanged* into trees and parted the air by his head. The voices called in a language he could not know, though he recognized the universal sound of laughter, vicious laughter, and that made him turn to run. The knowledge of his own death was there already, as if he had seen what I was seeing many times over—

I kicked the holed skull away just as I heard the sound of an arrow parting the air.

The place was utterly silent once more as I looked down into the sightless sockets. *Where was his ghost?* I wondered. *Is this it? Do even ghosts fade away in the end?* And as I mused on this, wondering where I was and why and just how I would ever escape, I realized that Scott's voice had bled away to nothing, and that I was alone and lost.

*   *   *

I despaired. My breath came heavy and fast, and the air tasted of the blue light, cool and devoid of life. I could not be here, or anywhere like this, because cities like this did not exist. I saw and smelled this place, but I was lying to myself. In fleeing, Scott had taken his open mind with him, leaving me with my own weak, insipid perception of things.

I found a small courtyard, the fossilized remains of plants clinging solidly to the walls. The well at the center was dry as my mouth. There were no dead here and no remains on the ground, so for a time I could pretend that I was alone. I sat beneath an overhanging balcony. There was no shade from the unvarying bluish light, but the balcony gave me the psychological impression of being hidden away from prying eyes. So I sat there, held my head in my hands and looked down at my feet, striving to forget that the dust around them was in a place that could not be.

There were dead people all around me. And the blue light, the light of the dead, giving me no day or night, brightness or darkness, cold or heat. . . .

I believed none of it, because I *could* not. I was more willing to accept that I was mad, or dead myself.

My breathing became slower, gentler and more calmed, and eventually I fell asleep.

Upon waking there was no telling how much time had passed. I was still not hungry or thirsty. I had not dreamed. I was in the same position in which I had dropped off. Time eluded me.

"Scott!" I shouted once, loud, but the sound terrified me more than being alone. It felt so wrong. Even though my voice sailed away, I had the distinct sense that it was ricocheting from walls and angles I could not see, not from these buildings that stood around me. The resonance sounded wrong.

My old friend did not answer. Perhaps he'd been as dead as this place all along.

I leaned back and closed my eyes, and a sudden breeze blew a handful of dust across my face, a hundred images screaming and destroying the relative peace of the moment, assaulting my senses with smells and sounds and views from too many different places and times to take in. Each scrap of dust stung, and each sting was a past life striving to make itself and its suffering known. I opened my mouth to cry out and felt grit on my tongue and between my teeth. Held there by my saliva, these old ghosts had time to make themselves and their reasons for being here known—

She ran along the dock, the animals chasing her, jeering and laughing and tripping as they tried to drag their trousers down, readying themselves—

Where had that breeze come from?—

A man stood against a wall and stared down the barrel of a dozen guns, hating them, hating what they were doing, hating their uncaring eyes as they saw a rat in front of them, not a man, not a human being—

Something must have caused it!—

She should never have left him, never, not when he could do this, not when he could stroke his wrists this way and open the skin, the flesh, the veins, she should never have left him, never—

There had been no movement before, nothing, and now a wind to blow the dust over me?—

The rattle of machine-gun fire tore the air above him, just as his stomach had been torn asunder, and the sand was soaking up his life as he cried out for help that would not come—

There were more, more, so many images crowding in and flooding my mind that for some time, seconds or days, I forgot just who I was. I stood and ran and raged, shaking my head, running blind, and each impact with a wall only gave me more painful deaths to see, more wronged lives ripped away by unfairness at best, evil at worst. I remember faces watching me, and for a time these faces seemed even more alive than I felt, true observers rather than mere echoes of who and what they had once been.

For a while, I was just like them.

Perhaps that was their way of trying to chase me away.

I walked. Through the city, past the barren buildings, dodging fleeting shapes of dead people where I could. Some of them glanced at me, and one even smiled. I always tried to look the other way.

Eventually, after hours spent walking, I found myself at the base of a cliff, and without thinking I began to climb. Up must be good, I reasoned. If we had come *down* here then *up* must be good. Hand over hand, feet seeking purchase, fingers knotting with cramps, muscles twisting and burning as I heaved myself higher, higher. I refused to look back down, because I knew that silent city was below me, watching, and that somewhere Scott still pursued his own wronged ghost. I could not bear to see him.

I had no thoughts of trying to find him in a place so endless.

Time lost its meaning. The blue light of the dead lit my way. I went up and up, and though I once thought of sleep, there was nowhere to rest. I moved on, never pausing for more than a few seconds to locate the next handhold or footrest, weightless. I did not tire. My heavy breathing fled into the massive space behind me, swallowed away without echo. I wondered how far the sound would travel before fading away. Perhaps forever.

I was hardly surprised when I tumbled onto the same ledge Scott and I had fallen from. I had no idea how long had passed since then. I was not hungry or thirsty and did not need to urinate, but I was certain that I had been in the city for days. Its grime seemed to cling to my skin, giving glimpses of the multifarious fates its inhabitants had suffered. And much as I thought of my wife and children right then, they seemed like memories from ages ago, the past lives of someone else entirely. It was the city that had taken the bulk of my life.

I plunged into the tunnel without a backward glance. If I turned I may have seen something impossible to ignore, a sight so mind-befuddling that it would petrify me, leaving me there to turn slowly to stone or a pillar of salt. I simply ducked away from that impossible place and entered the real world of darkness once again.

The blue light abandoned me immediately. I was in pitch blackness. I must have kicked through the shapes at my feet, though I could only visualize them.

I kept one hand held out, fingertips flitting across the stone wall to my right. Perhaps it was because I could imagine nothing worse than that place I was leaving behind—and the fate that must surely await Scott there, given time—but I walked forward without fear, and with a burning eagerness to see the sun once more.

I walked, and walked, and all the time I thought back to Scott running from me, wondering what had made him do so, why he had not turned to say goodbye.

He should never have left me like that. Never. Not on my own down there.

The tunnel seemed far longer than it had on the way down. The slope was steeper, perhaps, or maybe I had taken a branch in the darkness, a route leading somewhere else. I walked on because that was all I could do.

As light began to bleed in, its manifestation was so subtle that it took me a while to notice. I could not see and then I could see, and I did not discern the moment when that changed. My fear was dwindling, fading away with the darkness. We are all energy after all, I thought. There's nothing to us but space and power. Our thoughts are an illusion, and the world around us even more so.

An illusion . . .

"Where is *that* coming from?" I whispered, and my voice was curiously light. Those ideas, those images and concepts, all so unlike me. Given time perhaps I could have thought them, but it had only been a while since I had left the city, only a while.

He should have never left me alone. . . .

I heard Scott calling my name. His voice floated to me from afar, nebulous and ambiguous, and it could have been a breeze drifting through the tunnels from above. I made out carved symbols on the walls, recognized them from our journey down here. In the bluish light issuing from my skin, eyes and mouth, the ancient words were beginning to make some kind of sense.

I heard Scott again from up ahead, but his voice was fainter now, fading, retreating somewhere and some place lost to me forever.

Voices rose behind me to call me back, and sounds, and the noises of a city coming to life.

At last I could hear the dead.

White

one

the color of blood

We found the first body two days before Christmas.

Charley had been out gathering sticks to dry for tinder. She had worked her way through the wild garden and down toward the cliffs, scooping snow from beneath and around bushes and bagging whatever dead twigs she found there. There were no signs, she said. No disturbances in the virgin surface of the snow, no tracks, no warning. Nothing to prepare her for the scene of bloody devastation she stumbled across.

She had rounded a big boulder and seen the red splash in the snow, which was all that remained of a human being. The shock froze her comprehension. The reality of the scene struggled to imprint itself on her mind. Then, slowly, what she was looking at finally registered.

64

She ran back screaming. She'd only recognized her boyfriend by what was left of his shoes.

We were in the dining room trying to make sense of the last few weeks when Charley burst in. We spent a lot of time doing that: talking together in the big living rooms of the manor; in pairs, crying and sharing warmth; or alone, staring into darkening skies and struggling to discern a meaning in the infinite. I was one of those more usually alone. I'd been an only child and contrary to popular belief, my upbringing had been a nightmare. I always thought my parents blamed me for the fact that they could not have any more children, and instead of enjoying and revelling in my own childhood, I spent those years watching my mother and father mourn the ghosts of unborn offspring. It would have been funny if it were not so sad.

Charley opened the door by falling into it. She slumped to the floor, hair plastered across her forehead, her eyes two bright sparks peering between the knotted strands. Caked snow fell from her boots and speckled the timber floor, dirtied into slush. The first thing I noticed was its pinkish tinge.

The second thing I saw was the blood covering Charley's hands.

"Charley!" Hayden jumped to his feet and almost caught the frantic woman before she hit the deck. He went down with her, sprawling in a sudden puddle of dirt and tears. He saw the blood then and backed away automatically. "Charley?"

"Get some towels," Ellie said, always the pragmatist, "and a fucking gun."

I'd seen people screaming—all my life I'd never forgotten Jayne's final hours—but I had never seen someone actually *beyond* the point of screaming. Charley gasped and clawed at her throat, trying to open it up and let out the pain and the shock trapped within. It was not exertion that had stolen her breath; it was whatever she had seen.

She told us what that was.

I went with Ellie and Brand. Ellie had a shotgun cradled in the crook of her arm, a bobble hat hiding her severely short hair, her face all hard. There was no room in her life for compliments, but right now she was the one person in the manor I'd choose to be with. She'd been all for trying to make it out alone on foot; I was so glad that she eventually decided to stay.

Brand muttered all the way. "Oh fuck, oh shit, what are we doing coming out here? Like those crazy girls in slasher movies, you know? Always chasing the bad guys instead of running from them? Asking to get their throats cut? Oh man . . ."

In many ways I agreed with him. According to Charley there was little left of Boris to recover, but she could have been wrong. We owed it to him to find out. However harsh the conditions, whatever the likelihood of his murderer—animal or human—still being out here, we could not leave Boris lying dead in the snow. Apply whatever levels of civilization, foolish custom or superiority complex you like, it just wasn't done.

Ellie led the way across the manor's front garden and out onto the coastal road. The whole landscape was hidden beneath snow, like old sheet-covered furniture awaiting the homecoming of long-gone owners.

I wondered who would ever make use of this land again—who would be left to bother when the snow finally did melt—but that train of thought led only to depression.

We crossed the flat area of the road, following Charley's earlier footprints in the deep snow; even and distinct on the way out, chaotic on the return journey. As if she'd had something following her.

She had. We all saw what had been chasing her when we slid and clambered down toward the cliffs, veering behind the big rock that signified the beginning of the coastal path. The sight of Boris opened up and spread across the snow had pursued her all the way, and was probably still snapping at her heels now. The smell of his insides slowly cooling under an indifferent sky. The sound of his frozen blood crackling under foot.

Ellie hefted the gun, holding it waist high, ready to fire in an instant. Her breath condensed in the air before her, coming slightly faster than moments before. She glanced at the torn-up Boris, then surveyed our surroundings, looking for whoever had done this. East and west along the coast, down toward the cliff edge, up to the lip of rock above us, east and west again; Ellie never looked back down at Boris.

I did. I couldn't keep my eyes off what was left of him. It looked as though something big and powerful had held him up to the rock, scraped and twisted him there for a while, and then calmly had taken him apart across the snow-covered path. Spray patterns of blood stood out brighter than their surroundings. Every speck was visible and there were many specks, thousands of them spread across a ten-meter area. I tried to find a recognizable part of him, but all that was even vaguely identifiable as human was a hand, stuck to the rock in a mess of frosty blood, fingers curled in like the legs of a dead spider. The wrist was tattered, the bone splintered. It had been snapped, not cut.

Brand pointed out a shoe on its side in the snow. "Fuck, Charley was right. Just his shoes left. Miserable bastard always wore the same shoes."

I'd already seen the shoe. It was still mostly full. Boris had not been a miserable bastard. He was introspective, thoughtful, sensitive, sincere—qualities Brand would never recognize as anything other than sourness. Brand was as thick as shit and twice as unpleasant.

The silence seemed to press in around me. Silence, and cold, and a raw smell of meat, and the sea chanting from below. I was surrounded by everything.

"Let's get back," I said. Ellie glanced at me and nodded.

"But what about—" Brand started, but Ellie cut in without even looking at him.

"You want to make bloody snowballs, go ahead. There's not much to take back. We'll maybe come again later. Maybe."

"What did this?" I said, feeling reality start to shimmy past the shock I'd been gripped by for the last couple of minutes. "Just what the hell?"

Ellie backed up to me and glanced at the rock, then both ways along the path. "I don't want to find out just yet," she said.

Later, alone in my room, I would think about exactly

what Ellie had meant. *I don't want to find out just yet,* she had said, implying that the perpetrator of Boris's demise would be revealed to us soon. I'd hardly known Boris, quiet guy that he was, and his fate was just another line in the strange composition of death that had overcome the whole country during the last few weeks.

Charley and I were here in the employment of the Department of the Environment. Our brief was to keep a check on the radiation levels in the Atlantic Drift, since things had gone to shit in South America and the dirty reactors began to melt down in Brazil. It was a bad job with hardly any pay, but it gave us somewhere to live. The others had tagged along for differing reasons; friends and lovers of friends, all taking the opportunity to get away from things for a while and chill out in the wilds of Cornwall.

But then things went to shit here as well. On TV, minutes before it had ceased broadcasting for good, someone called it the ruin.

Then it had started to snow.

Hayden had taken Charley upstairs, still trying to quell her hysteria. We had no medicines other than aspirin and cough mixtures, but there were a hundred bottles of wine in the cellar. It seemed that Hayden had already poured most of a bottle down Charley's throat by the time the three of us arrived back at the manor. Not a good idea, I thought—I could hardly imagine what ghosts a drunken Charley would see, what terrors her alcohol-induced dreams held in store for her once she was finally left on her own—but it was not my place to say.

Brand stormed in and with his usual subtlety painted a picture of what we'd seen. "Boris's guts were just everywhere, hanging on the rock, spread over the snow. Melted in, like they were still hot when he was being cut up. What the fuck would do that? Eh? Just what the fuck?"

"Who did it?" Rosalie, our resident paranoid, asked.

I shrugged. "Can't say."

"Why not?"

"Not won't," I said. "Can't. Can't tell. There's not too much left to tell by, as Brand has so eloquently revealed."

Ellie stood before the open fire and held out her hands, palms up, as if asking for something. A touch of emotion, I mused, but then my thoughts were often cruel.

"Ellie?" Rosalie demanded an answer.

Ellie shrugged. "We can rule out suicide." Nobody responded.

I went through the kitchen and opened the back door. We were keeping our beer on a shelf in the rear conservatory now that the electricity had gone off. There was a generator, but not enough fuel to run it for more than an hour every day. We agreed that hot water was a priority for that meager time, so the fridge was now extinct.

I surveyed my choices: Stella, a few final cans of Caffreys, Boddingtons. That had been Jayne's favorite. She'd drunk it in pints, inevitably doing a bad impression of some mustachioed actor after the first creamy sip. I could still see her sparkling eyes as she tried to think of someone new. . . . I grabbed a Caffreys and shut the back door, and it was as the latch clicked home that I started to shake.

I'd seen a dead man five minutes ago, a man I'd been talking to the previous evening, drinking with, chatting about what the hell had happened to the world, making inebriated plans of escape, knowing all the time that the snow had us trapped here like chickens surrounded by a fiery moat. Boris had been quiet but thoughtful, the most intelligent person here at the manor. It had been his idea to lock the doors to many of the rooms because we never used them, and any heat we managed to generate should be kept in the rooms we did use. He had suggested a long walk as the snow had begun in earnest and it had been our prevarication and, I admit, our arguing that had kept us here long enough for it to matter. By the time Boris had persuaded us to make a go of it, the snow was three feet deep. Five miles and we'd be dead. Maximum. The nearest village was ten miles away.

He was dead. Something had taken him apart, torn him up, ripped him to pieces. I was certain that there had been no cutting involved as Brand had suggested. And yes, his bits did look melted into the snow. Still hot when they struck the surface, bloodying it in death. Still alive and beating as they were taken out.

I sat at the kitchen table and held my head in my hands. Jayne had said that this would hold all the good thoughts in and let the bad ones seep through your fingers, and sometimes it seemed to work. Now it was just a comfort, like the hands of a lover kneading hope into flaccid muscles, or fear from tense ones.

It could not work this time. I had seen a dead man. And there was nothing we could do about it. We should be telling someone, but over the past few months any sense of "relevant authorities" had fast faded away, just as Jayne had two years before; faded away to agony, then confusion and then to nothing. Nobody knew what had killed her. Growths on her chest and stomach. Bad blood. Life.

I tried to open the can, but my fingers were too cold to slip under the ring-pull. I became frustrated, then angry, and eventually in my temper I threw the can to the floor. It struck the flagstones and one edge split, sending a fine yellowish spray of beer across the old kitchen cupboards. I cried out at the waste. It was a feeling I was becoming more than used to.

"Hey," Ellie said. She put one hand on my shoulder and removed it before I could shrug her away. "They're saying we should tell someone."

"Who?" I turned to look at her, unashamed of my tears. Ellie was a hard bitch. Maybe they made me more of a person than she.

She raised one eyebrow and pursed her lips. "Brand thinks the army. Rosalie thinks the Fairy Underground."

I scoffed. "Fairy-fucking-Underground. Stupid cow."

"She can't help being like that. You ask me, it makes her more suited to how it's all turning out."

"And how's that, exactly?" I hated Ellie sometimes, all her stronger-than-thou talk and steely eyes. But she was also the person I respected the most in our pathetic little group. Now that Boris had gone.

"Well," she said, "for a start, take a look at how we're all reacting to this. Shocked, maybe. Horrified. But it's almost like it was expected."

"It's all been going to shit. . . ." I said, but I did not need to continue. We had all known that we were not immune to the rot settling across society, nature, the world. Eventually it would find us. We just had not known when.

"There is the question of who did it," she said quietly.

"Or what."

She nodded. "Or what."

For now, we left it at that.

"How's Charley?"

"I was just going to see," Ellie said. "Coming?"

I nodded and followed her from the room. The beer had stopped spraying and now fizzled into sticky rivulets where the flags joined. I was still thirsty.

Charley looked bad. She was drunk, that was obvious, and she had been sick down herself, and she had wet herself. Hayden was in the process of trying to mop up the mess when we knocked and entered.

"How is she?" Ellie asked pointlessly.

"How do you think?" He did not even glance at us as he tried to hold on to the babbling, crying, laughing and puking Charley.

"Maybe you shouldn't have given her so much to drink," Ellie said. Hayden sent her daggers but did not reply.

Charley struggled suddenly in his arms, ranting and

73

Tim Lebbon

shouting at the shaded candles in the corners of the room.

"What's that?" I said. "What's she saying?" For some reason it sounded important, like a solution to a problem encoded by grief.

"She's been saying some stuff," Hayden said loudly, so we could hear above Charley's slurred cries. "Stuff about Boris. Seeing angels in the snow. She says his angels came to get him."

"Some angels," Ellie muttered.

"You go down," Hayden said. "I'll stay here with her." He wanted us gone, that much was obvious, so we did not disappoint him.

Downstairs, Brand and Rosalie were hanging around the mobile phone. It had sat on the mantelpiece for the last three weeks like a gun without bullets, ugly and useless. Every now and then someone would try it, receiving only a crackling nothing in response. Random numbers, recalled numbers, numbers held in the phone's memory, all came to naught. Gradually it was tried less—every unsuccessful attempt had been more depressing.

"What?" I said.

"Trying to call someone," Brand said. "Police. Someone."

"So they can come to take fingerprints?" Ellie flopped into one of the old armchairs and began picking at its upholstery, widening a hole she'd been plucking at for days. "Any replies?"

Brand shook his head.

"We've got to do something," Rosalie said. "We can't just sit here while Boris is lying dead out there."

Ellie said nothing. The telephone hissed its amusement. Rosalie looked to me. "There's nothing we can do," I said. "Really, there's not much to collect. If we did bring his . . . bits . . . back here, what would we do?"

"Bury . . ." Rosalie began.

"Three feet of snow? Frozen ground?"

"And the things," Brand said. The phone crackled again and he turned it off.

"What things?"

Brand looked around our small group. "The things Boris said he'd seen."

Boris had mentioned nothing to me. In our long, drunken talks, he had never talked of any angels in the snow. Upstairs, I'd thought that it was simply Charley drunk and mad with grief, but now that Brand had said it too I had the distinct feeling I was missing out on something. I was irked, and upset at feeling irked.

"Things?" Rosalie said, and I closed my eyes. *Oh fuck, don't tell her,* I willed at Brand. She'd regale us with stories of secret societies and messages in the clouds, disease-makers who were wiping out the inept and the crippled, the barren and the intellectually inadequate. Jayne had been sterile, so we'd never had kids. The last thing I needed was another one of Rosalie's mad ravings about how my wife had died, why she'd died, who had killed her.

Luckily, Brand seemed of like mind. Maybe the joint he'd lit had stewed him into silence at last. He turned to the fire and stared into its dying depths, sitting on the edge of the seat as if wondering whether to feed it some more. The stack of logs was running low.

"Things?" Rosalie said again, nothing if not persistent.

"No things," I said. "Nothing." I left the room before it all flared up.

In the kitchen I opened another can, carefully this time, and poured it into a tall glass. I stared into creamy depths as bubbles passed up and down. It took a couple of minutes for the drink to settle, and in that time I had recalled Jayne's face, her body, the best times we'd had together. At my first sip, a tear replenished the glass.

That night I heard doors opening and closing as someone wandered between beds. I was too tired to care who.

The next morning I half expected it to be all better. I had the bitter taste of dread in my mouth when I woke up, but also a vague idea that all the bad stuff could only have happened in nightmares. As I dressed—two shirts, a heavy pullover, a jacket—I wondered what awaited me beyond my bedroom door.

In the kitchen Charley was swigging from a fat mug of tea. It steamed so much, it seemed liable to burn whatever it touched. Her lips were red-raw, as were her eyes. She clutched the cup tightly, knuckles white, thumbs twisted into the handle. She looked as though she wanted to never let it go.

I had a sinking feeling in my stomach when I saw her. I glanced out the window and saw the landscape of snow, added to yet again the previous night, bloated flakes still fluttering down to reinforce the barricade against our escape. Somewhere out there, Boris's parts were frozen memories hidden under a new layer.

"Okay?" I said quietly.

Charley looked up at me as if I'd farted at her mother's funeral. "Of course I'm not okay," she said, enunciating each word carefully. "And what do you care?"

I sat at the table opposite her, yawning, rubbing hands through my greasy hair, generally trying to disperse the remnants of sleep. There was a pot of tea on the table, and I took a spare mug and poured a steaming brew. Charley watched my every move. I was aware of her eyes upon me, but I tried not to let it show. The cup shook, and I could barely grab a spoon. I'd seen her boyfriend splashed across the snow. I felt terrible about it, but then I realized that she'd seen the same scene. How bad must she be feeling?

"We have to do something," she said.

"Charley—"

"We can't just sit here. We have to go. Boris needs a funeral. We have to go and find someone, get out of this godforsaken place. There must be someone near, able to help, someone to look after us? I need someone to look after me."

The statement was phrased as a question, but I ventured no answer.

"Look," she said, "we have to get out. Don't you see?" She let go of her mug and clasped my hands; hers were hot and sweaty. "The village, we can get there. I know we can."

"No, Charley," I said, but I did not have a chance to finish my sentence (*there's no way out, we tried, and didn't you see the television reports weeks ago?*) before

Ellie marched into the room. She paused when she saw Charley, then went to the cupboard and poured herself a bowl of cereal. She used water. We'd run out of milk a week ago.

"There's no telephone," she said, spooning some soggy corn flakes into her mouth. "No television, save some flickering pictures most of us don't want to see. Or believe. There's no radio, other than the occasional foreign channel. Rosie says she speaks French. She's heard them talking of 'the doom.' That's how she translates it, though I think it sounds more like 'the ruin.' The nearest village is ten miles away. We have no motorized transport that will even get out of the garage. To walk it would be suicide." She crunched her limp breakfast, mixing in more sugar to give it some taste.

Charley did not reply. She knew what Ellie was saying, but tears were her only answer.

"So we're here until the snow melts," I said. Ellie really was a straight bitch. Not a glimmer of concern for Charley, not a word of comfort.

Ellie looked at me and stopped chewing for a moment. "I think until it does melt, we're protected." She had a way of coming out with ideas that both enraged me, and scared the living shit out of me at the same time.

Charley could only cry.

Later, three of us decided to try to get out. In moments of stress, panic and mourning, logic holds no sway.

I said I'd go with Brand and Charley. It was one of the most foolish decisions I've ever made, but seeing Charley's eyes as she sat in the kitchen on her own, thinking about her slaughtered boyfriend, listening to Ellie go on about how hopeless it all was . . . I could not say no. And in truth, I was as desperate to leave as anyone.

It was almost ten in the morning when we set out.

Ellie was right, I knew that even then. Her face as she watched us struggle across the garden should have brought me back straightaway: She thought I was a fool. She was the last person in the world I wanted to appear foolish in front of, but still there was that nagging feeling in my heart that pushed me on—a mixture of desire to help Charley and a hopeless feeling that by staying here, we were simply waiting for death to catch us.

It seemed to have laid its shroud over the rest of the world already. Weeks ago the television had shown some dreadful sights: people falling ill and dying in the thousands, food riots in London, a nuclear exchange between Greece and Turkey. More, lots more, all of it bad. We'd known something was coming—things had been falling apart for years—but once it began it was a cumulative effect, speeding from a steady trickle toward decline to a raging torrent. *We're better off where we are,* Boris had said to me. It was ironic that because of him, we were leaving.

I carried the shotgun. Brand had an air pistol, though I'd barely trust him with a sharpened stick. As well as being loud and brash, he spent most of his time doped to the eyeballs. If there was any trouble, I'd be watching out for him as much as anything else.

Something had killed Boris and whatever it was, animal or human, it was still out there in the snow. Moved on, hopefully, now it had fed. But then again, perhaps not. It did not dissuade us from trying.

The snow in the manor garden was almost a meter deep. The three of us had botched together snow shoes of varying effectiveness. Brand wore two snapped-off lengths of picture frames on each foot, which seemed to act more as knives to slice down through the snow than anything else. He was tenaciously pompous; he struggled with his mistake rather than admitting it. Charley had used two frying pans with their handles snapped off, and she seemed to be making good headway. My own creations consisted of circles of mounted canvas cut from the redundant artwork in the manor. Old owners of the estate stared up at me through the snow as I repeatedly stepped on their faces.

By the time we reached the end of the driveway and turned to see Ellie and Hayden watching us, I was sweating and exhausted. We had traveled about fifty meters.

Across the road lay the cliff path leading to Boris's dismembered corpse. Charley glanced that way, perhaps wishing to look down upon her boyfriend one more time.

"Come on," I said, clasping her elbow and heading away. She offered no resistance.

The road was apparent as a slightly lower, smoother plain of snow between the two hedged banks on each side. Everything was glaring white, and we were all wearing sunglasses to prevent snow-blindness. We could see far along the coast from here as the bay swept around toward the east, the craggy cliffs were spotted white where snow had drifted onto ledges, an occasional lonely seabird diving to the sea and returning empty-beaked to sing a mournful song for company. In places the snow was cantilevered out over the edge of the cliff, a deadly trap should any of us stray that way. The sea itself surged against the rocks below, but it broke no spray. The usual roar of the waters crashing into the earth, slowly eroding it away and reclaiming it, had changed. It was now more of a grind as tonnes of slushy ice replaced the usual white horses, not yet forming a solid barrier over the water but still thick enough to temper the waves. In a way it was sad; a huge beast winding down in old age.

I watched as a cormorant plunged down through the chunky ice and failed to break surface again. It was as if it were committing suicide. Who was I to say it was not?

"How far?" Brand asked yet again.

"Ten kilometers," I said.

"I'm knackered." He had already lit a joint and he took long, hard pulls on it. I could hear its tip sizzling in the crisp morning air.

"We've come about three hundred meters," I said, and Brand shut up.

It was difficult to talk; we needed all our breath for the effort of walking. Sometimes the snowshoes worked, especially where the surface of the snow had frozen the previous night. Other times we plunged straight in up to our thighs and we had to hold our arms out for balance as we hauled a leg out, just to let it sink in again a step along. The rucksacks did not help. We each carried food, water and dry clothing, and Brand especially seemed to be having trouble with his.

The sky was a clear blue. The sun rose ahead of us as if mocking the frozen landscape. Some days it started like this, but the snow never seemed to melt. I had almost forgotten what the ground below it looked like; it seemed that the snow had been here forever. When it began our spirits had soared, like a bunch of school kids waking to find the landscape had changed overnight. Charley and I had still gone down to the sea to take our readings, and when we returned there was a snowman in the garden wearing one of her bras and a pair of my briefs. A snowball fight had ensued, during which Brand became a little too aggressive for his own good. We'd ganged up on him and pelted him with snow compacted to ice until he shouted and yelped. We were cold and wet and bruised, but we did not stop laughing for hours.

We'd all dried out in front of the open fire in the huge living room. Rosalie had stripped to her underwear and danced to music on the radio. She was a bit of a sixties throwback, Rosalie, and she didn't seem to realize what her little display did to cosseted people like me. I watched happily enough.

Later, we sat around the fire and told ghost stories. Boris was still with us then, of course, and he came up with the best one, which had us all cowering behind casual expressions. He told us of a man who could not see, hear or speak, but who knew of the ghosts around him. His life was silent and senseless save for the day his mother died. Then he cried and shouted and raged at the darkness, before curling up and dying himself. His world opened up then, and he no longer felt alone, but whomever he tried to speak to could only fear or loathe him. The living could never make friends with the dead. And death had made him more silent than ever.

None of us would admit it, but we were all scared shitless as we went to bed that night. As usual, doors opened and footsteps padded along corridors. And, as usual, my door remained shut and I slept alone.

Days later the snow was too thick to be enjoyable. It became risky to go outside, and as the woodpile started to dwindle and the radio and television broadcasts turned more grim, we realized that we were becoming trapped. A few of us had tried to get to the village, but it was a half-hearted attempt and we'd returned once we were tired. We figured we'd traveled about two miles along the coast. We had seen no one.

As the days passed and the snow thickened, the atmosphere did likewise with a palpable sense of panic. A week ago, Boris had pointed out that there were no plane trails anymore.

This, our second attempt to reach the village, felt more like life and death. Before Boris had been killed we'd felt confined, but it also gave a sense of protection from the things going on in the world. Now there was a feeling that if we could not get out, worse things would happen to us where we were.

I remembered Jayne as she lay dying from the unknown disease. I had been useless, helpless, hopeless, praying to a God I had long ignored to grant us a kind fate. I refused to sit back and go the same way. I would not go gently. Fuck fate.

"What was that?"

Brand stopped and tugged the little pistol from his belt. It was stark black against the pure white snow.

"What?"

He nodded. "Over there." I followed his gaze and looked up the sloping hillside. To our right the sea sighed against the base of the cliffs. To our left—the direction Brand was now facing—snowfields led up a gentle slope toward the moors several miles inland. It was a rocky, craggy landscape, and some rocks had managed to hold off the drifts. They peered out darkly here and there, like the faces of drowning men going under for the final time.

"What?" I said again, exasperated. I'd slipped the shotgun off my shoulder and held it waist-high. My finger twitched on the trigger guard. Images of Boris's remains sharpened my senses. I did not want to end up like that.

"I saw something moving. Something white."

"Some snow, perhaps?" Charley said bitterly.

"Something running across the snow," he said, frowning as he concentrated on the middle distance. The smoke from his joint mingled with his condensing breath.

We stood that way for a minute or two, steaming sweat like smoke signals of exhaustion. I tried taking off my glasses to look, but the glare was too much. I glanced sideways at Charley. She'd pulled a big old revolver from her rucksack and held it with both hands. Her lips were pulled back from her teeth in a feral grimace. She really wanted to use that gun.

I saw nothing. "Could have been a cat. Or a seagull flying low."

"Could have been." Brand shoved the pistol back into his belt and reached around for his water canteen. He tipped it to his lips and cursed. "Frozen!"

"Give it a shake," I said. I knew it would do no good but maybe shut him up for a while. "Charley, what's the time?" I had a watch, but I wanted to talk to Charley, keep her involved with the present, keep her here. I had started to realize not only what a stupid idea this was, but what an even more idiotic step it had been letting Charley come along. If she wasn't here for revenge, she was blind with grief. I could not see her eyes behind her sunglasses.

"Nearly midday." She was hoisting her rucksack back onto her shoulders, never taking her eyes from the snowscape sloping slowly up and away from us. "What do you think it was?"

I shrugged. "Brand seeing things. Too much wacky baccy."

We set off again. Charley was in the lead, I followed close behind and Brand stumbled along at the rear. It was eerily silent around us, the snow muffling our gasps and puffs, the constant grumble of the sea soon blending into the background as much as it ever did. There was a sort of white noise in my ears: blood pumping, breath ebbing and flowing, snow crunching underfoot. They merged into one whisper, eschewing all outside noise, almost soporific in rhythm. I coughed to break the spell.

"What the hell do we do when we get to the village?" Brand said.

"Send back help," Charley stated slowly, enunciating each word as if to a naïve young child.

"But what if the village is like everywhere else we've seen or heard about on TV?"

Charley was silent for a while. So was I. A collage of images tumbled through my mind, hateful and hurtful and sharper because of that. Hazy scenes from the last day of television broadcasts we had watched: loaded ships leaving docks and sailing off to some nebulous sanctuary abroad; shootings in the streets, bodies in the gutters, dogs sniffing at open wounds; an airship, drifting over the hills in some vague attempt to offer hope.

"Don't be stupid," I said.

"Even if it is, there will be help there," Charley said quietly.

"Like hell." Brand lit another joint. It was cold, we were risking our lives, there may very well have been something in the snow itching to attack us . . . but at that moment I wanted nothing more than to take a long haul on Brand's pot, and let casual oblivion anesthetize my fears.

An hour later we found the car.

By my figuring we had come about three miles. We were all but exhausted. My legs ached, knee joints stiff and hot as if on fire.

The road had started a slow curve to the left, heading inland from the coast toward the distant village. Its path had become less distinct, the hedges having sunk slowly into the ground until there was really nothing to distinguish it from the fields of snow on either side. We had been walking the last half hour on memory alone.

The car was almost completely buried by snow, only one side of the windscreen and the iced-up aerial still visible. There was no sign of the route it had taken; whatever tracks it had made were long since obliterated by the blizzards. As we approached the snow started again, fat flakes drifting lazily down and landing on the icy surface of last night's fall.

"Do not drive unless absolutely necessary," Brand said. Charley and I ignored him. We unslung our rucksacks and approached the buried shape, all of us keeping hold of our weapons. I meant to ask Charley where she'd gotten hold of the revolver—whether she'd had it with her when we both came here to test the sea and write environmental reports that would never be read—but now did not seem the time. I had no wish to sound judgmental or patronizing.

As I reached out to knock some of the frozen snow from the windscreen, a flight of seagulls cawed and took off from nearby. They had been all but invisible against the snow, but there were at least thirty of them lifting as one, calling loudly as they twirled over our heads and then headed out to sea.

We all shouted out in shock. Charley stumbled sideways as she tried to bring her gun to bear and fell on her back. Brand screeched like a kid, then let off a pop with his air pistol to hide his embarrassment. The pellet found no target. The birds ignored us after the initial fly-past, and they slowly merged with the hazy distance. The new snow shower brought the horizon in close.

"Shit," Charley muttered.

"Yeah." Brand reloaded his pistol without looking at either of us, then rooted around for the joint he'd dropped when he'd screamed.

Charley and I went back to knocking the snow away, using our gloved hands to make tracks down the windscreen and across the bonnet. "I think it's a Ford," I said uselessly. "Maybe an old Mondeo." Jayne and I had owned a Mondeo when we'd been courting. Many was the time we had parked in some shaded woodland or beside units on the local industrial estate, wound down the windows and made love as the cool night air looked on. We'd broken down once while I was driving her home; it had made us two hours late and her father had come close to beating me senseless. It was only the oil on my hands that had convinced him of our story.

I closed my eyes.

"Can't see anything," Charley said, jerking me back to cold reality. "Windscreen's frozen up on the inside."

"Take us ages to clear the doors."

"What do you want to do that for?" Brand said. "Dead car, probably full of dead people."

"Dead people may have guns and food and fuel," I said. "Going to give us a hand?"

Brand glanced at the dark windscreen, the contents of the car hidden by ice and shadowed by the weight of snow surrounding it. He sat gently on his rucksack, and when he saw it would take his weight without sinking in the snow, he re-lit his joint and stared out to sea. I wondered whether he'd even notice if we left him there.

"We could uncover the passenger door," Charley said. "Driver's side is stuck fast in the drift, take us hours."

We both set about trying to shift snow away from the car. "Keep your eyes open," I said to Brand. He just nodded and watched the sea lift and drop its thickening ice floes. I used the shotgun as a crutch to lift myself onto the hood, and from there to the covered roof.

"What?" Charley said. I ignored her, turning a slow circle, trying to pick out any movement against the fields of white. To the west lay the manor, a couple of miles away and long since hidden by creases in the landscape. To the north the ground still rose steadily away from the sea, rocks protruding here and there along with an occasional clump of trees hardy enough to survive Atlantic storms. Nothing moved. The shower was turning quickly into a storm and I felt suddenly afraid. The manor was at least three miles behind us; the village seven miles ahead. We were in the middle, three weak humans slowly freezing as nature freaked out and threw weeks of snow and ice at us. And here we were, convinced we could defeat it, certain in our own puny minds that we were the rulers here, we called the shots. However much we polluted and contaminated, I knew, we would never call the shots. Nature may let us live within it, but in the end it would purge and clean itself. And whether there would be room for us in the new world . . .

Perhaps this was the first stage of that cleansing.

While civilization slaughtered itself, disease and extremes of weather took advantage of our distraction to pick off the weak.

"We should get back," I said.

"But the village—"

"Charley, it's almost two. It'll start getting dark in two hours, maximum. We can't travel in the dark; we might walk right by the village, or stumble onto one of those ice overhangs at the cliff edge. Brand here may get so doped he thinks we're ghosts and shoot us with his pop-gun."

"Hey!"

"But Boris . . ." Charley said. "He's . . . we need help. To bury him. We need to tell someone."

I climbed carefully down from the car roof and landed in the snow beside her. "We'll take a look in the car. Then we should get back. It'll help no one if we freeze to death out here."

"I'm not cold," she said defiantly.

"That's because you're moving, you're working. When you walk you sweat and you'll stay warm. When we have to stop—and eventually we will—you'll stop moving. Your sweat will freeze, and so will you. We'll all freeze. They'll find us in the thaw, you and me huddled up for warmth, Brand with a frozen reefer still in his gob."

Charley smiled; Brand scowled. Both expressions pleased me.

"The door's frozen shut," she said.

"I'll use my key." I punched at the glass with the butt of the shotgun. After three attempts the glass shattered and I used my gloved hands to clear it all away. I caught a waft of something foul and stale. Charley stepped back with a slight groan. Brand was oblivious.

We peered inside the car, leaning forward so that the weak light could filter in around us.

There was a dead man in the driver's seat. He was frozen solid, hunched up under several blankets, only his eyes and nose visible. Icicles hung from both. His eyelids were still open. On the dashboard a candle had burnt down to nothing more than a puddle of wax, imitating the ice as it dripped forever toward the floor. The scene was so still it was eerie, like a painting so lifelike that textures and shapes could be felt. I noticed the driver's door handle was jammed open, though the door had not budged against the snowdrift burying that side of the car. At the end he had obviously attempted to get out. I shuddered as I tried to imagine this man's lonely death. It was the second body I'd seen in two days.

"Well?" Brand called from behind us.

"Your drug supplier," Charley said. "Car's full of snow."

I snorted, pleased to hear the humor, but when I looked at her she seemed as sad and forlorn as ever. "Maybe we should see if he brought us anything useful," she said, and I nodded.

Charley was smaller than me, so she said she'd go. I went to protest, but she was already wriggling through the shattered window, and a minute later she'd thrown out everything loose she could find. She came back out without looking at me.

There was a rucksack half full of canned foods; a petrol can with a swill of fuel in the bottom; a novel frozen at page ninety; some plastic bottles filled with piss and split by the ice; a rifle, but no ammunition; a smaller rucksack with wallet, some papers, an electronic credit card; a photo wallet frozen shut; a plastic bag full of shit; a screwed-up newspaper as hard as wood.

Everything was frozen.

"Let's go," I said. Brand and Charley took a couple of items each and shouldered their rucksacks. I picked up the rifle. We took everything except the shit and piss.

It took us four hours to get back to the manor. Three times on the way Brand said he'd seen something bounding through the snow—a stag, he said, big and white with sparkling antlers—and we dropped everything and went into a defensive huddle. But nothing ever materialized from the worsening storm, even though our imaginations painted all sorts of horrors behind and beyond the snowflakes. If there were anything out there, it kept itself well hidden.

The light was fast fading as we arrived back. Our tracks had been all but covered, and it was only later that I realized how staggeringly lucky we'd been to even find our way home. Perhaps something was on our side, guiding us, steering us back to the manor. Perhaps it was the change in nature taking us home, preparing us for what was to come next.

It was the last favor we were granted.

Hayden cooked us some soup as the others huddled around the fire, listening to our story and trying so hard not to show their disappointment. Brand kept chiming in about the things he'd seen in the snow. Even Ellie's face held the taint of fading hope.

"Boris's angels?" Rosalie suggested. "He *may* have seen angels, you know. They're not averse to steering things their way, when it suits them." Nobody answered.

Charley was crying again, shivering by the fire. Rosalie had wrapped her in blankets and now hugged her close.

"The gun looks okay." Ellie said. She'd sat at the table and stripped and oiled the rifle, listening to us all as we talked. She illustrated the fact by pointing it at the wall and squeezing the trigger a few times. *Click click click*. There was no ammunition for it.

"What about the body?" Rosalie asked. "Did you see who it was?"

I frowned. "What do you mean?"

"Well, if it was someone coming along the road toward the manor, maybe one of us knew him." We were all motionless save for Ellie, who still rooted through the contents of the car. She'd already put the newspaper on the floor so that it could dry out, in the hope of being able to read at least some of it. We'd made out the date: one week ago. The television had stopped showing pictures two weeks ago. There was a week of history in there, if only we could save it.

"He was frozen stiff," I said. "We didn't get a good look . . . and anyway, who'd be coming here? And why? Maybe it was a good job—"

Ellie gasped. There was a tearing sound as she peeled apart more pages of the photo wallet and gasped again, this time struggling to draw in a breath afterward.

"Ellie?"

She did not answer. The others had turned to her, but she seemed not to notice. She saw nothing, other than the photographs in her hand. She stared at them for an endless few seconds, eyes moist yet unreadable in the glittering firelight. Then she scraped the chair back across the polished floor, crumpled the photo's into her back pocket and walked quickly from the room.

I followed, glancing at the others to indicate that they should stay where they were. None of them argued. Ellie was already halfway up the long staircase by the time I entered the hallway, but it was not until the final stair that she stopped, turned and answered my soft calling.

"My husband," she said, "Jack. I haven't seen him for two years." A tear ran icily down her cheek. "We never really made it, you know?" She looked at the wall beside her, as though she could stare straight through and discern logic and truth in the blanked-out landscape beyond. "He was coming here. For me. To find me."

There was nothing I could say. Ellie seemed to forget I was there and she mumbled the next few words to herself. Then she turned and disappeared from view along the upstairs corridor, shadow dancing in the light of disturbed candles.

Back in the living room I told the others that Ellie was all right, she had gone to bed, she was tired and cold and as human as the rest of us. I did not let on about her dead husband. I figured it was really none of their business. Charley glared at me with bloodshot eyes, and I was sure she'd figured it out. Brand flicked bits of carrot from his soup into the fire and watched them sizzle to nothing.

We went to bed soon after. Alone in my room I sat at the window for a long time, huddled in clothes and blankets, staring out at the moonlit brightness of the snow drifts and the fat flakes still falling. I tried to imagine Ellie's estranged husband struggling to steer the car through deepening snow, the radiator clogging in the drift the car had buried its nose in, splitting, gushing boiling water and steaming instantly into an icy trap. Sitting there, perhaps not knowing just how near he was, thinking of his wife and how much he needed to see her. And I tried to imagine what desperate events must have driven him to do such a thing, though I did not think too hard.

A door opened and closed quietly, footsteps, another door slipped open to allow a guest entry. I wondered who was sharing a bed tonight.

I saw Jayne, naked and beautiful in the snow, bearing no sign of the illness that had killed her. She beckoned me, drawing me nearer, and at last a door was opening for me as well, a shape coming into the room, white material floating around its hips, or perhaps they were limbs, membranous and thin. . . .

My eyes snapped open and I sat up on the bed. I was still dressed from the night before. Dawn streamed in the window and my candle had burnt down to nothing.

Ellie stood next to the bed. Her eyes were red-rimmed and swollen. I tried to pretend I had not noticed.

"Happy Christmas," she said. "Come on. Brand's dead."

Brand was lying just beyond the smashed conservatory doors behind the kitchen. There was a small courtyard area here, protected somewhat by an overhanging roof so that the snow was only about knee deep. Most of it was red. A drift had already edged its way into the conservatory, and the beer cans on the shelf had frozen and split. No more beer.

He had been punctured by countless holes, each the width of a thumb, all of them clogged with hardened blood. One eye stared hopefully out to the hidden horizon, the other was absent. His hair was also missing; it looked like he'd been scalped. There were bits of him all around—a finger here, a splash of brain there—but he was less mutilated than Boris had been. At least we could see that this smudge in the snow had once been Brand.

Hayden was standing next to him, posing daintily in an effort to avoid stepping in the blood. It was a lost cause. "What the hell was he doing out here?" he asked in disgust.

"I heard doors opening last night," I said. "Maybe he came for a walk. Or a smoke."

"The door was mine," Rosalie said softly. She had appeared behind us and nudged in between Ellie and me. She wore a long, creased shirt. Brand's shirt, I noticed. "Brand was with me until three o'clock this morning. Then he left to go back to his own room, said he was feeling ill. We thought perhaps you shouldn't know about us." Her eyes were wide in an effort not to cry. "We thought everyone would laugh."

Nobody answered. Nobody laughed. Rosalie looked at Brand with more shock than sadness, and I wondered just how often he'd opened her door in the night. The insane, unfair notion that she may even be relieved flashed across my mind, one of those awful thoughts you try to expunge but that hangs around like a guilty secret.

"Maybe we should go inside," I said to Rosalie, but she gave me such an icy glare that I turned away, looking at Brand's shattered body rather than her piercing eyes.

"I'm a big girl now," she said. I could hear her rapid breathing as she tried to contain the disgust and shock at what she saw. I wondered if she'd ever seen a dead body. Most people had, nowadays.

Charley was nowhere to be seen. "I didn't wake her," Ellie said when I queried. "She had enough to handle yesterday. I thought she shouldn't really see this. No need."

And you? I thought, noticing Ellie's puffy eyes, the gauntness of her face, her hands fisting open and closed at her sides. *Are you all right? Did you have enough to handle yesterday?*

"What the hell do we do with him?" Hayden asked. He was still standing closer to Brand than the rest of us, hugging himself to try to preserve some of the warmth from sleep. "I mean, Boris was all over the place, from what I hear. But Brand . . . we have to do something. Bury him, or something. It's Christmas, for God's sake."

"The ground's like iron," I protested.

"So we take it in turns digging," Rosalie said quietly.

"It'll take us—"

"Then I'll do it myself." She walked out into the bloodied snow and shattered glass in bare feet, bent over Brand's body and grabbed under each armpit as if to lift him. She was naked beneath the shirt. Hayden stared in frank fascination. I turned away, embarrassed for myself more than for Rosalie.

"Wait," Ellie sighed. "Rosalie, wait. Let's all dress properly, and then we'll come and bury him. Rosalie." The girl stood and smoothed Brand's shirt down over her thighs, perhaps realizing what she had put on display. She looked up at the sky and caught the morning's first snowflake on her nose.

"Snowing," she said. "Just for a fucking change."

We went inside. Hayden remained in the kitchen with the outside door shut and bolted while the rest of us went upstairs to dress, wake Charley and tell her the grim Yule tidings. Once Rosalie's door had closed I followed Ellie along to her room. She opened her door for me and invited me in, obviously knowing I needed to talk.

Her place was a mess. Perhaps, I thought, she was so busy being strong and mysterious that she had no time for tidying up. Clothes were strewn across the floor, a false covering like the snow outside. Used plates were piled next to her bed, those at the bottom already blurred with mold, the uppermost still showing the remains of the meal we'd had before Boris had been killed. Spaghetti bolognese, I recalled, to Hayden's own recipe, rich and tangy with tinned tomatoes, strong with garlic, the helpings massive. Somewhere out there Boris's last meal lay frozen in the snow, half digested, torn from his guts—

I snorted and closed my eyes. Another terrible thought that wouldn't go away.

"Brand really saw things in the snow, didn't he?" Ellie asked.

"Yes, he was pretty sure. At least, *a* thing. He said it was like a stag, except white. It was bounding along next to us, he said. We stopped a few times, but I'm certain I never saw anything. Don't think Charley did, either." I made space on Ellie's bed and sat down. "Why?"

Ellie walked to the window and opened the curtains. The snowstorm had started in earnest, and although her window faced the Atlantic, all we could see was a sea of white. She rested her forehead on the cold glass, her breath misting, fading, misting again. "I've seen something too," she said.

Ellie. Seeing things in the snow. Ellie was the nearest we had to a leader, though none of us had ever wanted one. She was strong, if distant. Intelligent, if a little straight with it. She'd never been much of a laugh, even before things had turned to shit, and her dogged conservatism in someone so young annoyed me no end.

Ellie, seeing things in the snow.

I could not bring myself to believe it. I did not want to. If I did accept it then there really were things out there, because Ellie did not lie, and she was not prone to fanciful journeys of the imagination.

"What something?" I asked at last, fearing it a question I would never wish to be answered. But I could not simply ignore it. I could not sit here and listen to Ellie opening up, then stand and walk away. Not with Boris frozen out there, not with Brand still cooling into the landscape.

She rocked her head against the glass. "Don't know. Something white. So how did I see it?" She turned from the window, stared at me, crossed her arms. "From this window," she said. "Two days ago. Just before Charley found Boris. Something flitting across the snow like a bird, except it left faint tracks. As big as a fox, perhaps, but it had more legs. Certainly not a deer."

"Or one of Boris's angels?"

She shook her head and smiled, but there was no humor there. There rarely was. "Don't tell anyone," she said. "I don't want anyone to know. We'll have to be careful. Take the guns when we try to bury Brand. A couple of us keep a lookout while the others dig. Though I doubt we'll even get through the snow."

"You and guns," I said perplexed. I didn't know how to word what I was trying to ask.

Ellie smiled wryly. "Me and guns. I hate guns."

I stared at her, saying nothing, using silence to pose the next question.

"I have a history," she said. And that was all.

Later, downstairs in the kitchen, Charley told us what she'd managed to read in the paper from the frozen car. In the week since we'd picked up the last TV signal and the paper was printed, things had gone from bad to worse. The illness that had killed my Jayne was claiming millions across the globe. The USA blamed Iraq. Russia blamed China. Blame continued to waste lives. There was civil unrest and shootings in the streets, mass burials at sea, martial law, air strikes, food shortages . . . the words melded into one another as Rosalie recited the reports.

Hayden was trying to cook mince pies without the mince. He was using stewed apples instead, and the kitchen stank sickeningly sweet. None of us felt particularly festive.

Outside, in the heavy snow that even now was attempting to drift in and cover Brand, we were all twitchy. Whoever or—now more likely—whatever had done this could still be around. Guns were held at the ready.

We wrapped him in an old sheet and enclosed this in torn black plastic bags until there was no white or red showing. Ellie and I dragged him around the corner of the house to where there were some old flower beds. We started to dig where we remembered them to be, but when we got through the snow the ground was too hard. In the end we left him on the surface of the frozen earth and covered the hole back in with snow, mumbling about burying him when the thaw came. The whole process had an unsettling sense of permanence.

As if the snow would never melt.

Later, staring from the dining room window as Hayden brought in a platter of old vegetables as our Christmas feast, I saw something big and white skimming across the surface of the snow. It moved too quickly for me to make it out properly, but I was certain I saw wings.

I turned away from the window, glanced at Ellie and said nothing.

two

the color of fear

During the final few days of Jayne's life I had felt completely hemmed in. Not only physically trapped within our home—and more often the bedroom where she lay—but also mentally hindered. It was a feeling I hated, felt guilty about and tried desperately to relieve, but it was always there.

I stayed, holding her hand for hour after terrible hour, our palms fused by sweat, her face pasty and contorted by agonies I could barely imagine. Sometimes she would be conscious and alert, sitting up in bed and listening as I read to her, smiling at the humorous parts, trying to ignore the sad ones. She would ask me questions about how things were in the outside world, and I would lie and tell her they were getting better. There was no need to add to her misery. Other times she would be a shadow of her old self, a gray stain on the bed with liquid limbs and weak bowels, a screaming thing with bloody growths sprouting across her skin and pumping their venom inward with uncontrollable, unstoppable tenacity. At these times I would talk truthfully and tell her the reality of things, that the world was going to shit and she would be much better off when she left it.

Even then I did not tell her the complete truth: that I wished I were going with her. Just in case she could still hear.

Wherever I went during those final few days I was under assault, besieged by images of Jayne, thoughts of her impending death, vague ideas of what would happen after she had gone. I tried to fill the landscape of time laid out before me, but Jayne never figured and so the landscape was bare. She was my whole world; without her I could picture nothing to live for. My mind was never free, although sometimes, when a doctor found time to visit our house and *tut* and sigh over Jayne's wasting body, I would go for a walk. Mostly she barely knew the doctor was there, for which I was grateful. There was nothing he could do. I would not be able to bear even the faintest glimmer of hope in her eyes.

I strolled through the park opposite our house, staying to the paths so that I did not risk stepping on discarded needles or stumbling across suicides decaying slowly back to nature. The trees were as beautiful as ever, huge emeralds against the grimly polluted sky. Somehow they bled the taint of humanity from their systems. They adapted, changed, and our arrival had really done little to halt their progress. A few years of poisons and disease, perhaps. A shaping of the landscape upon which we projected an idea of control.

But when we were all dead and gone, our industrial disease on the planet would be little more than a few twisted, corrupted rings in the lifetime of the oldest trees. I wished we could adapt so well.

When Jayne died there was no sense of release. My grief was as great as if she'd been killed at the height of health, her slow decline doing nothing to prepare me for the dread that enveloped me at the moment of her last strangled sigh. Still I was under siege, this time by death. The certainty of its black fingers rested on my shoulders day and night, long past the hour of Jayne's hurried burial in a local football ground alongside a thousand others. I would turn around sometimes and try to see past it, make out some ray of hope in a stranger's gaze. But there was always the blackness bearing down on me, clouding my vision and the gaze of others, promising doom soon.

It was ironic that it was not death that truly scared me, but living. Without Jayne the world was nothing but an empty, dying place.

Then I had come here, an old manor on the rugged South West coast. I'd thought that solitude—a distance between me and the terrible place the world was slowly becoming—would be a balm to my suffering. In reality it was little more than a placebo and realizing that negated it. I felt more trapped than ever.

The morning after Brand's death and botched burial—Boxing Day—I sat at my bedroom window and watched nature laying siege. The snow hugged the landscape like a funeral shroud in negative. The coast was hidden by the cliffs, but I could see the sea farther out. There was something that I thought at first to be an iceberg, and it took me a few minutes to figure out what it really was; the upturned hull of a big boat. A ferry, perhaps, or one of the huge cruise liners being used to ship people south, away from blighted Britain to the false promise of Australia. I was glad I could not see any more detail. I wondered what we would find washed up in the rock pools that morning, were Charley and I to venture down to the sea.

If I stared hard at the snowbanks, the fields of virgin white, the humped shadows that were our ruined and hidden cars, I could see no sign of movement. An occasional shadow passed across the snow, though it could have been from a bird flying in front of the sun. But if I relaxed my gaze, tried not to concentrate too hard, lowered my eyelids, then I could see them. Sometimes they skimmed low and fast over the snow, twisting like sea serpents or Chinese dragons and throwing up a fine mist of flakes behind them. At other times they lay still and watchful, fading into the background if I looked directly at them until one shadow looked much like the next, but could be so different.

I wanted to talk about them. I wanted to ask Ellie just what the hell they were, because I knew that she had seen them too. I wanted to know what was happening and why it was happening to us. But I had some mad idea that to mention them would make them real, like ghosts in the cupboard and slithering wet things beneath the bed. Best ignore them and they would go away.

I counted a dozen white shapes that morning.

* * *

"Anyone dead today?" Rosalie asked.

The statement shocked me, made me wonder just what sort of relationship she and Brand had had, but we all ignored her. No need to aggravate an argument.

Charley sat close to Rosalie, as if a sharing of grief would halve it. Hayden was cooking up bacon and bagels long past their sell-by date. Ellie had not yet come downstairs. She'd been stalking the manor all night, and now that we were up she was washing and changing.

"What do we do today?" Charley asked. "Are we going to try to get away again? Get to the village for help?"

I sighed and went to say something, but the thought of those things out in the snow kept me quiet. Nobody else spoke, and the silence was the only answer required.

We ate our stale breakfast, drank tea clotted with powdered milk, listened to the silence outside. It had snowed again in the night and our tracks from the day before had been obliterated. Standing at the sink to wash up I stared through the window, and it was like looking upon the same day as yesterday, the day before and the day before that; no signs of our presence existed. All footprints had vanished, all echoes of voices swallowed by the snow, shadows covered with another six inches and frozen like corpses in a glacier. I wondered what patterns and traces the snow would hold this evening, when darkness closed in to wipe us away once more.

"We have to tell someone," Charley said. "Something's happening. We should tell someone. We have to do something. We can't just . . ." She trailed off, staring into a cooling cup of tea, perhaps remembering a time before all this had begun, or imagining she could remember. "This is crazy."

"It's God," Rosalie said.

"Huh?" Hayden, already peeling wrinkled old vegetables, was ready for lunch, constantly busy, always doing something to keep his mind off everything else. I wondered how much really went on behind his fringed brow, how much theorizing he did while he was boiling, how much nostalgia he wallowed in as familiar cooking smells settled into his clothes.

"It's God, fucking us over one more time. Crazy, as Charley says. God and crazy are synonymous."

"Rosie," I said, knowing she hated the shortened name, "if it's not constructive, don't bother. None of this will bring—"

"Anything is more constructive than sod-all, which is what you lot have got to say this morning. We wake up one morning without one of us dead, and you're all tongue-tied. Bored? Is that it?"

"Rosalie, why—"

"Shut it, Charley. You more than anyone should be thinking about all this. Wondering why the hell we came here a few weeks ago to escape all the shit, and now we've landed right in the middle of it. Right up to our armpits. Drowning in it. Maybe one of us is a Jonah and it's followed—"

"And you think it's God?" I said. I knew that asking the question would give her open opportunity to rant, but in a way I felt she was right—we did need to talk. Sitting here stewing in our own thoughts could not help anyone.

"Oh yes, it's His Holiness," she nodded, "sitting on his pedestal of lost souls, playing around one day and deciding, hmm, maybe I'll have some fun today, been a year since a decent earthquake, a few months since the last big volcano eruption. Soooo, what can I do?"

Ellie appeared then, sat at the table and poured a cup of cold tea that looked like sewer water. Her appearance did nothing to interrupt Rosalie's flow.

"I know, he says, I'll nudge things to one side, turn them slightly askew, give the world a gasp before I've cleaned my teeth. Just a little, not so that anyone will notice for a while. Get them paranoid. Get them looking over their shoulders at each other. See how the wrinkly pink bastards deal with that one!"

"Why would He do that?" Hayden said.

Rosalie stood and put on a deep voice. "Forget me, will they? I'll show them. Turn over and open your legs, humanity, for I shall root you up the arse."

"Just shut up!" Charley screeched. The kitchen went ringingly quiet, even as Rosalie slowly sat down. "You're full of this sort of shit, Rosie. Always telling us how we're being controlled, manipulated. Who by? Ever seen anyone? There's a hidden agenda behind everything for you, isn't there? If there's no toilet paper after you've had a crap you'd blame it on the global dirty-arse conspiracy!"

Hysteria hung silently in the room. The urge to cry grabbed me, but also a yearning to laugh out loud. The air was heavy with held breaths and barely restrained comments, thick with the potential for violence.

"So," Ellie said at last, her voice little more than a whisper, "let's hear some truths."

"What?" Rosalie obviously expected an extension of her foolish monologue. Ellie, however, cut her down.

"Well, for starters has anyone else seen things in the snow?" Heads shook. My own shook as well. I wondered who else was lying with me. "Anyone seen anything strange out there at all?" she continued. "Maybe not the things Brand and Boris saw, but something else?" Again, shaken heads. An uncomfortable shuffling from Hayden as he stirred something on the gas cooker.

"I saw God looking down on us," Rosalie said quietly, "with blood in his eyes." She did not continue or elaborate, did not go off on one of her rants. I think that's why her strange comment stayed with me.

"Right," said Ellie, "then may I make a suggestion? Firstly, there's no point trying to get to the village. The snow's even deeper than it was yesterday, it's colder and freezing to death for the sake of it will achieve nothing. If we did manage to find help, Boris and Brand are long past it." She paused, waiting for assent.

"Fair enough," Charley said quietly. "Yeah, you're right."

"Secondly, we need to make sure the manor is secure. We need to protect ourselves from whatever got at Brand and Boris. There are a dozen rooms on the ground floor, we only use two or three of them. Check the others. Make sure windows are locked and storm shutters are bolted. Make sure French doors aren't loose or liable to break open at the slightest . . . breeze, or whatever."

"What do you think the things out there are?" Hayden asked. "Lock pickers?"

Ellie glanced at his back, looked at me, shrugged. "No," she said, "I don't think so. But there's no use being complacent. We can't try to make it out, so we should do the most we can here. The snow can't last forever, and when it finally melts we'll go to the village then. Agreed?"

Heads nodded.

"If the village is still there," Rosalie cut in. "If everyone isn't dead. If the disease hasn't wiped out most of the country. If a war doesn't start somewhere in the meantime."

"Yes," Ellie sighed impatiently, "if all those things don't happen." She nodded at me. "We'll do the two rooms at the back. The rest of you check the others. There are some tools in the big cupboard under the stairs, some nails and hammers if you need them, a crowbar too. And if you think you need timber to nail across windows . . . if it'll make you feel any better . . . tear up some floorboards in the dining room. They're hardwood, so they're strong."

"Oh, let the battle commence!" Rosalie cried. She stood quickly, her chair falling onto its back, and stalked from the room with a swish of her long skirts. Charley followed.

Ellie and I went to the rear of the manor. In the first of the large rooms the snow had drifted up against the windows to cut out any view or light from outside. For an instant it seemed as if nothing existed beyond the glass and I wondered if that was the case, then why were we trying to protect ourselves?

Against nothing.

"What do you think is out there?" I asked.

"Have you seen anything?"

I paused. There was something, but nothing I could easily identify or put a name to. What I had seen had been way beyond my ken, white shadows apparent against whiteness. "No," I said, "nothing."

Ellie turned from the window and looked at me in the half light, and it was obvious that she knew I was lying. "Well, if you do see something, don't tell."

"Why?"

"Boris and Brand told," she said. She did not say any more. They'd seen angels and stags in the snow and they'd talked about it, and now they were dead.

She pushed at one of the window frames. Although the damp timber fragmented at her touch, the snow drift behind it was as effective as a vault door. We moved on to the next window. The room was noisy with unspoken thoughts, and it was only a matter of time before they made themselves heard.

"You think someone in here has something to do with Brand and Boris," I said.

Ellie sat on one of the wide window sills and sighed deeply. She ran a hand through her spiky hair and rubbed at her neck. I wondered whether she'd had any sleep at all last night. I wondered whose door had been opening and closing; the prickle of jealousy was crazy under the circumstances. I realized all of a sudden how much Ellie reminded me of Jayne, and I swayed under the sudden barrage of memory.

"Who?" she said. "Rosie? Hayden? Don't be soft."

"But you do, don't you?" I said again.

She nodded. Then shook her head. Shrugged. "I don't bloody know. I'm not Sherlock Holmes. It's just strange that Brand and Boris . . ." She trailed off, avoiding my eyes.

"I have seen something out there," I said to break the awkward silence. "Something in the snow. Can't say what. Shadows. Fleeting glimpses. Like everything I see is from the corner of my eye."

Ellie stared at me for so long that I thought she'd died there on the window sill, a victim of my admission, another dead person to throw outside and let freeze until the thaw came and we could do our burying.

"You've seen what I've seen," she said eventually, verbalizing the trust between us. It felt good, but it also felt a little dangerous. A trust like that could alienate the others, not consciously but in our mind's eye. By working and thinking closer together, perhaps we would drive them further away.

We moved to the next window.

"I've known there was something since you found Jack in his car," Ellie said. "He'd never have just sat there and waited to die. He'd have tried to get out, to get here, no matter how dangerous. He wouldn't have sat watching the candle burn down, listening to the wind, feeling his eyes freeze over. It's just not like him to give in."

"So why did he? Why didn't he get out?"

"There was something waiting for him outside the car. Something he was trying to keep away from." She rattled a window, stared at the snow pressed up against the glass. "Something that would make him rather freeze to death than face it."

We moved on to the last window. Ellie reached out to touch the rusted clasp and there was a loud crash. Glass broke, wood struck wood, someone screamed, all from a distance.

We spun around and ran from the room, listening to the shrieks. Two voices now, a man and a woman, the woman's muffled. Somewhere in the manor, someone else was dying.

The reaction to death is sometimes as violent as death itself. Shock throws a cautious coolness over the senses, but your stomach still knots, your skin stings as if the Reaper is glaring at you as well. For a second you live that death, and then shameful relief floods in when you see it's someone else.

Such were my thoughts as we turned a corner into the main hallway of the manor. Hayden was hammering at the library door, crashing his fists into the wood hard enough to draw blood. "Charley!" he shouted, again and again. "Charley!" The door shook under his assault but it did not budge. Tears streaked his face, dribble strung from chin to chest. The dark old wood of the door sucked up the blood from his split knuckles. "Charley!"

Ellie and I arrived just ahead of Rosalie.

"Hayden!" Rosalie shouted.

"Charley! In there! She went in and locked the door, and there was a crash and she was screaming!"

"Why did she—" Rosalie began, but Ellie shushed us all with one wave of her hand.

Silence. "No screaming now," she said.

Then we heard other noises through the door, faint and tremulous as if picked up from a distance along a bad telephone line. They sounded like chewing; bone snapping; flesh ripping. I could not believe what I was hearing, but at the same time I remembered the bodies of Boris and Brand. Suddenly I did not want to open the door. I wanted to defy whatever it was laying siege to us here by ignoring the results of its actions. Forget Charley, continue checking the windows and doors, deny whomever or whatever it was the satisfaction—

"Charley," I said quietly. She was a small woman, fragile, strong but sensitive. She'd told me once, sitting at the base of the cliffs before it had begun to snow, how she loved to sit and watch the sea. It made her feel safe. It made her feel a part of nature. She'd never hurt anyone. "Charley."

Hayden kicked at the door again and I added my weight, shouldering into the tough old wood, jarring my body painfully with each impact. Ellie did the same and soon we were taking it in turns. The noises continued between each impact—increased in volume if anything—and our assault became more frantic to cover them up.

If the manor had not been so old and decrepit we would never have broken in. The door was probably as old as all of us put together, but its frame had been replaced some time in the past. Softwood painted as hardwood had slowly crumbled in the damp atmosphere and after a minute the door burst in, frame splintering into the coldness of the library.

One of the three big windows had been smashed. Shattered glass and snapped mullions hung crazily from the frame. The cold had already made the room its home, laying a fine sheen of frost across the thousands of books, hiding some of their titles from view as if to conceal whatever tumultuous history they contained. Snow flurried in, hung around for a while, then chose somewhere to settle. It did not melt. Once on the inside, this room was now a part of the outside.

As was Charley.

The area around the broken window was red and Charley had spread. Bits of her hung on the glass like hellish party streamers. Other parts had melted into the snow outside and turned it pink. Some of her was recognizable—her hair splayed out across the soft whiteness, a hand fisted around a melting clump of ice—other parts had never been seen before because they'd always been inside.

I leaned over and puked. My vomit cleared a space of frost on the floor so I did it again, moving into the room. My stomach was in agonized spasms, but I enjoyed seeing the white sheen vanish, as if I were claiming the room back for a time. Then I went to my knees and tried to forget what I'd seen, shake it from my head, pound it from my temples. I felt hands close around my wrists to stop me from punching myself, but I fell forward and struck my forehead on the cold timber floor. If I could forget, if I could drive the image away, perhaps it would no longer be true.

But there was the smell. And the steam, rising from the open body and misting what glass remained. Charley's last breath.

"Shut the door!" I shouted. "Nail it shut! Quickly!"

Ellie had helped me from the room, and now Hayden was pulling on the broken-in door to try to close it again. Rosalie came back from the dining room with a few splintered floorboards, her face pale, eyes staring somewhere no one else could see.

"Hurry!" I shouted. I felt a distance pressing in around me, the walls receding, the ceiling rising. Voices turned slow and deep, movement became stilted. My stomach heaved again, but there was nothing left to bring up. I was the center of everything, but it was all leaving me; all sight and sound and scent fleeing my faint. And then, clear and bright, Jayne's laugh broke through. Only once, but I knew it was her.

Something brushed my cheek and gave warmth to my face. My jaw clicked and my head turned to one side, slowly but inexorably. Something white blurred across my vision and my other cheek burst into warmth, and I was glad. The cold was the enemy; the cold brought the snow, which brought the fleeting things I had seen outside, things without a name or, perhaps, things with a million names. Or things with a name I already knew.

The warmth was good.

Ellie's mouth moved slowly and watery rumbles tumbled forth. Her words took shape in my mind, hauling themselves together just as events took on their own speed once more.

"Snap out of it," Ellie said, and slapped me across the face again.

Another sound dragged itself together. I could not identify it, but I knew where it was coming from. The

117

others were staring fearfully at the door, Hayden was still leaning back with both hands around the handle, straining to get as far away as possible without letting go.

Scratching. Sniffing. Something rifling through books, snuffling in long-forgotten corners at dust from long-dead people. A slow regular beat, which could have been footfalls or a heartbeat. I realized it was my own and another sound took its place.

"What . . . ?"

Ellie grabbed the tops of my arms and shook me harshly. "You with us? You back with us now?"

I nodded, closing my eyes at the swimming sensation in my head. Vertical fought with horizontal and won out this time. "Yeah."

"Rosalie," Ellie whispered. "Get more boards. Hayden, keep hold of that handle. Just keep hold." She looked at me. "Hand me the nails as I hold my hand out. Now listen. Once I start banging, it may attract—"

"What are you doing?" I said.

"Nailing the bastards in."

I thought of the shapes I had watched from my bedroom window, the shadows flowing through other shadows, the ease with which they moved, the strength and beauty they exuded as they passed from drift to drift without leaving any trace behind. I laughed. "You think you can keep them in?"

Rosalie turned a fearful face my way. Her eyes were wide, her mouth hanging open as if readying for a scream.

"You think a few nails will stop them—"

118

"Just shut up," Ellie hissed, and she slapped me across the face once more. This time I was all there, and the slap was a burning sting rather than a warm caress. My head whipped around and by the time I looked up again, Ellie was heaving a board against the doors, steadying it with one elbow and weighing a hammer in the other hand.

Only Rosalie looked at me. What I'd said was still plain on her face—the chance that whatever had done these foul things would find their way in, take us apart as it had done to Boris, to Brand and now to Charley. And I could say nothing to comfort her. I shook my head, though I had no idea what message I was trying to convey.

Ellie held out her hand and snapped her fingers. Rosalie passed her a nail.

I stepped forward and pressed the board across the door. We had to tilt it so that each end rested across the frame. There were still secretive sounds from inside, like a fox rummaging through a bin late at night. I tried to imagine the scene in the room now, but I could not. My mind would not place what I had seen outside into the library, could not stretch to that feat of imagination. I was glad.

For one terrible second I wanted to see. It would only take a kick at the door, a single heave and the whole room would be open to view, and then I would know whatever was in there for the second before it hit me. Jayne perhaps, a white Jayne from elsewhere, holding out her hands so that I could join her once more, just as she had promised on her deathbed. *I'll be with you again*, she had said, and the words had terrified me and comforted me and kept me going ever since. Sometimes I thought they were all that kept me alive. *I'll be with you again*.

"Jayne . . ."

Ellie brought the hammer down. The sound was explosive and I felt the impact transmitted through the wood and into my arms. I expected another impact a second later from the opposite way, but instead we heard the sound of something scampering through the already shattered window.

Ellie kept hammering until the board held firm. Then she started another, and another. She did not stop until most of the door was covered, nails protruding at crazy angles, splinters under her fingernails, sweat running across her face and staining her armpits.

"Has it gone?" Rosalie asked. "Is it still in there?"

"Is what still in there, precisely?" I muttered.

We all stood that way for a while, panting with exertion, adrenaline priming us for the chase.

"I think," Ellie said after a while, "we should make some plans."

"What about Charley?" I asked. They all knew what I meant: *We can't just leave her there; we have to do something; she'd do the same for us*.

"Charley's dead," Ellie said, without looking at anyone. "Come on." She headed for the kitchen.

"What happened?" Ellie asked.

Hayden was shaking. "I told you. We were checking the rooms, Charley ran in before me and locked the door, I heard glass breaking and . . ." He trailed off.

"And?"

"Screams. I heard her screaming. I heard her dying."

The kitchen fell silent as we all recalled the cries, as if they were still echoing around the manor. They meant different things to each of us. For me death always meant Jayne.

"Okay, this is how I see things," Ellie said. "There's a wild animal, or wild animals, out there now."

"What wild animals!" Rosalie scoffed. "Mutant badgers come to eat us up? Hedgehogs gone bad?"

"I don't know, but pray it is animals. If people have done all this, then they'll be able to get in to us. However fucking goofy crazy, they'll have the intelligence to get in. No way to stop them. Nothing we could do." She patted the shotgun resting across her thighs as if to reassure herself of its presence.

"But what animals—"

"Do you know what's happening everywhere?" Ellie shouted, not just at doubting Rosie but at us all. "Do you realize that the world's changing? Every day we wake up there's a new world facing us. And every day there're fewer of us left. I mean the big us, the worldwide us, us humans." Her voice became quieter. "How long before one morning, no one wakes up?"

"What has what's happening elsewhere got to do with all this?" I asked, although inside I already had an idea of what Ellie meant. I think maybe I'd known for a while, but now my mind was opening up, my beliefs stretching, levering fantastic truths into place. They fitted; that terrified me.

"I mean, it's all changing. A disease is wiping out millions and no one knows where it came from. Unrest everywhere, shootings, bombings. Nuclear bombs in the Med, for Christ's sake. You've heard what people have called it; it's the Ruin. Capital R, people. The world's gone bad. Maybe what's happening here is just not that unusual anymore."

"That doesn't tell us what they are," Rosalie said. "Doesn't explain why they're here, or where they come from. Doesn't tell us why Charley did what she did."

"Maybe she wanted to be with Boris again," Hayden said.

I simply stared at him. "I've seen them," I said, and Ellie sighed. "I saw them outside last night."

The others looked at me, Rosalie's eyes still full of the fear I had planted there and was even now propagating.

"So what were they?" Rosalie asked. "Ninja seabirds?"

"I don't know." I ignored her sarcasm. "They were white, but they hid in shadows. Animals, they must have been. There are no people like that. But they were canny. They moved only when I wasn't looking straight at them. Otherwise they stayed still and . . . blended in with the snow." Rosalie, I could see, was terrified. The sarcasm was a front. Everything I said scared her more.

"Camouflaged," Hayden said.

"No. They blended in. As if they melted in, but they didn't. I can't really . . ."

"In China," Rosalie said, "white is the color of death. It's the color of happiness and joy. They wear white at funerals."

Ellie spoke quickly, trying to grab back the conversation. "Right. Let's think of what we're going to do. First, no use trying to get out. Agreed? Good. Second, we limit ourselves to a couple of rooms downstairs, the hallway and staircase area and upstairs. Third, do what we can to block up, nail up, glue up the doors to the other rooms and corridors."

"And then?" Rosalie asked quietly. "Charades?"

Ellie shrugged and smiled. "Why not? It is Christmas time."

I'd never dreamt of a white Christmas. I was cursing Bing fucking Crosby with every gasped breath I could spare.

The air sang with echoing hammer blows, dropped boards and groans as hammers crunched fingernails. I was working with Ellie to board up the rest of the downstairs rooms while Hayden and Rosalie tried to lever up the remaining boards in the dining room. We did the windows first, Ellie standing to one side with the shotgun aiming out while I hammered. It was snowing again and I could see vague shapes hiding behind flakes, dipping in and out of the snow like larking dolphins. I think we all saw them, but none of us ventured to say for sure that they were there. Our imagination was pumped up on what had happened and it had started to paint its own pictures.

We finished one of the living rooms and locked the door behind us. There was an awful sense of finality in the heavy thunk of the tumblers clicking in, a feeling that perhaps we would never go into that room again. I'd lived the last few years telling myself that there was no such thing as never—Jayne was dead and I would certainly see her again, after all—but there was nothing in these rooms that I could ever imagine us needing again. They were mostly designed for luxury, and luxury was a conceit of the contented mind. Over the past few weeks, I had seen contentment vanish forever under the gray cloud of humankind's fall from grace.

None of this seemed to matter now as we closed it all in. I thought I should feel sad, for the symbolism of what we were doing if not for the loss itself. Jayne had told me we would be together again, and then she had died and I had felt trapped ever since by her death and the promise of her final words. If nailing up doors would take me closer to her, then so be it.

In the next room I looked out the window and saw Jayne striding naked toward me through the snow. Fat flakes landed on her shoulders and did not melt, and by the time she was near enough for me to see the look in her eyes she had collapsed down into a drift, leaving a memory there in her place. Something flitted past the window, sending flakes flying against the wind, bristly fur spiking dead white leaves.

I blinked hard and the snow was just snow once more. I turned and looked at Ellie, but she was concentrating too hard to return my stare. For the first time I could see how scared she was—how her hand clasped so tightly around the shotgun barrel that her knuckles were pearly white, her nails a shiny pink—and I wondered exactly what *she* was seeing out there in the white storm.

By midday we had done what we could. The kitchen, one of the living rooms and the hall and staircase were left open; every other room downstairs was boarded up from the outside in. We'd also covered the windows in those rooms left open, but we left thin viewing ports like horizontal arrow slits in the walls of an old castle. And like the weary defenders of those ancient citadels, we were under siege.

"So what did you all see?" I said as we sat in the kitchen. Nobody denied anything.

"Badgers," Rosalie said. "Big, white, fast. Sliding over the snow like they were on skis. Demon badgers from hell!" She joked, but it was obvious that she was terrified.

"Not badgers," Ellie cut in. "Deer. But wrong. Deer with scales. Or something. All wrong."

"Hayden, what did you see?"

He remained hunched over the cooker, stirring a weak stew of old vegetables and stringy beef. "I didn't see anything."

I went to argue with him but realized he was probably telling the truth. We had all seen something different, why not see nothing at all? Just as unlikely.

"You know," said Ellie, standing at a viewing slot with the snow reflecting sunlight in a band across her face, "we're all seeing white animals. White animals in the snow. So maybe we're seeing nothing at all. Maybe it's our imaginations. Perhaps Hayden is nearer the truth than all of us."

"Boris and the others had pretty strong imaginations, then," said Rosalie, bitter tears animating her eyes.

We were silent once again, stirring our weak milk-less tea, all thinking our own thoughts about what was out in the snow. Nobody had asked me what I had seen and I was glad. Last night they were fleeting white shadows, but today I had seen Jayne as well. A Jayne I had known was not really there, even as I watched her coming at me through the snow. *I'll be with you again.*

"The color of death . . ." Ellie said. She spoke at the boarded window, never for an instant glancing away. Her hands held on to the shotgun as if it had become one with her body. I wondered what she had been in the past: *I have a history,* she'd said. "White. Happiness and joy."

"It was also the color of mourning for the Victorians," I added.

"And we're in a Victorian manor." Hayden did not turn around as he spoke, but his words sent our imaginations scurrying.

"We're all seeing white animals," Ellie said quietly. "Like white noise. All tones, all frequencies. We're all seeing different things as one."

"Oh," Rosalie whispered, "well that explains a lot."

I thought I could see where Ellie was coming from; at least, I was looking in the right direction. "White noise is used to mask other sounds," I said.

Ellie only nodded.

"There's something else going on here." I sat back in my chair and stared up, trying to divine the truth in the patchwork mold on the kitchen ceiling. "We're not seeing it all."

Ellie glanced away from the window, just for a second. "I don't think we're seeing anything."

*   *   *

Later we found out some more of what was happening. We went to bed, doors opened in the night, footsteps creaked old floorboards. And through the dark the sound of lovemaking drew us all to another, more terrible death.

three

the color of mourning

I had not made love to anyone since Jayne's death. It was months before she died that we last indulged, a bitter, tearful experience when she held a sheet of polyethylene between our chests and stomachs to prevent her diseased skin from touching my own. It did not make for the most romantic of occasions, and afterward she cried herself to sleep as I sat holding her hand and staring into the dark.

After her death I came to the manor; the others came along to find something or escape from something else, and there were secretive noises in the night. The manor was large enough for us to have a room each, but in the darkness doors would open and close again, and every morning the atmosphere at breakfast was different.

My door had never opened and I had opened no doors. There was a lingering guilt over Jayne's death, a sense that I would be betraying her love if I went with someone else. A greater cause of my loneliness was my inherent lack of confidence, a certainty that no one here would be interested in me: I was quiet, introspective and uninteresting, a fledgling bird devoid of any hope of taking wing with any particular talent. No one would want me.

But none of this could prevent the sense of isolation, subtle jealousy and yearning I felt each time I heard footsteps in the dark. I never heard anything else—the walls were too thick for that, the building too solid— but my imagination filled in the missing parts. Usually, Ellie was the star. And there lay another problem— lusting after a woman I did not even like very much.

The night it all changed for us was the first time I heard someone making love in the manor. The voice was androgynous in its ecstasy, a high keening, dropping off into a prolonged sigh before rising again. I sat up in bed, trying to shake off the remnants of dreams that clung like seaweed to a drowned corpse. Jayne had been there, of course, and something in the snow, and another something that was Jayne and the snow combined. I recalled wallowing in the sharp whiteness and feeling my skin sliced by ice edges, watching the snow grow pink around me, then white again as Jayne came and spread her cleansing touch across the devastation.

The cry came once more, wanton and unhindered by any sense of decorum.

Who? I thought. *Obviously Hayden, but who was he with? Rosalie? Cynical, paranoid, terrified Rosalie?*

Or Ellie?

I hoped Rosalie.

I sat back against the headboard, unable to lie down and ignore the sound. The curtains hung open—I had no reason to close them—and the moonlight revealed that it was snowing once again. I wondered what was out there watching the sleeping manor, listening to the crazy sounds of lust emanating from a building still spattered with the blood and memory of those who had died so recently. I wondered whether the things out there had any understanding of human emotion— the highs, the lows, the tenacious spirit that could sometimes survive even the most downheartening, devastating events—and what they made of the sound they could hear now. Perhaps they thought they were screams of pain. Ecstasy and thoughtless agony often sounded the same.

The sound continued, rising and falling. Added to it now the noise of something thumping rhythmically against a wall.

I thought of the times before Jayne had been ill, before the great decline had really begun, when most of the population still thought humankind could clean up what it had dirtied and repair what it had torn asunder. We'd been married for several years, our love as deep as ever, our lust still refreshing and invigorating. Car seats, cinemas, woodland, even a telephone box, all had been visited by us at some stage, laughing like adolescents, moaning and sighing together, content in familiarity.

And as I sat there remembering my dead wife, something strange happened. I could not identify exactly when the realization hit me, but I was suddenly sure of one thing: The voice I was listening to was Jayne's. She was moaning as someone else in the house made love to her. She had come in from outside, that cold unreal Jayne I had seen so recently, and she had gone to Hayden's room, and now I was being betrayed by someone I had never betrayed, ever.

I shook my head, knowing it was nonsense but certain also that the voice was hers. I was so sure that I stood, dressed and opened my bedroom door without considering the impossibility of what was happening. Reality was controlled by the darkness, not by whatever light I could attempt to throw upon it. I may as well have had my eyes closed.

The landing was lit by several shaded candles in wall brackets, their soft light barely reaching the floor, flickering as breezes came from nowhere. Where the light did touch it showed old carpet, worn by time and faded by countless unknown footfalls. The walls hung with shredded paper, damp and torn like dead skin, the lath and plaster beneath pitted and crumbled. The air was thick with age, heavy with must, redolent with faint hints of hauntings. Where my feet fell I could sense the floor dipping slightly beneath me, though whether this was actuality or a runover from my dream I was unsure.

I could have been walking on snow.

I moved toward Hayden's room and the volume of the sighing and crying increased. I paused one door away, my heart thumping not with exertion but with the thought that Jayne was a dozen steps from me, making love with Hayden, a man I hardly really knew.

Jayne's dead, I told myself, and she cried out once, loud, as she came. Another voice then, sighing and straining, and this one was Jayne as well.

Someone touched my elbow. I gasped and spun around, too shocked to scream. Ellie was there in her nightshirt, bare legs hidden in shadow. She had a strange look in her eye. It may have been the subdued lighting. I went to ask her what she was doing here, but then I realized it was probably the same as me. She'd stayed downstairs last night, unwilling to share a watch duty, insistent that we should all sleep.

I went to tell her that Jayne was in there with Hayden, but then I realized how stupid this would sound, how foolish it actually *was.*

At least, I thought, *it's not Ellie in there. Rosalie it must be. At least not Ellie. Certainly not Jayne.*

And Jayne cried out again.

Goose bumps speckled my skin and brought it to life. The hairs on my neck stood to attention, my spine tingled.

"Hayden having a nice time?" someone whispered, and Rosalie stepped up behind Ellie.

I closed my eyes, listening to Jayne's cries. She had once screamed like that in a park, and the keeper had chased us out with his waving torch and throaty shout, the light splaying across our nakedness as we laughed and struggled to gather our clothes around us as we ran.

"Doesn't sound like Hayden to me," Ellie said.

The three of us stood outside Hayden's door for a while, listening to the sounds of lovemaking from within—the cries, the moving bed, the thud of wood against the wall. I felt like an intruder, however much I realized something was very wrong with all of this. Hayden was on his own in there. As we each tried to figure out what we were really hearing, the sounds from within changed. There was not one cry, not two, but many, overlying each other, increasing and expanding until the voice became that of a crowd. The light in the corridor seemed to dim as the crying increased, though it may have been my imagination.

I struggled to make out Jayne's voice and there was a hint of something familiar, a whisper in the cacophony that was so slight as to be little more than an echo of a memory. But still, to me, it was real.

Ellie knelt and peered through the keyhole, and I noticed for the first time that she was carrying her shotgun. She stood quickly and backed away from the door, her mouth opening, eyes widening. "It's Hayden," she said aghast, and then she fired at the door handle and lock.

The explosion tore through the sounds of ecstasy and left them in shreds. They echoed away like streamers in the wind, to be replaced by the lonely moan of a man's voice, pleading not to stop, it was so wonderful so pure so alive. . . .

The door swung open. None of us entered the room. We could not move.

Hayden was on his back on the bed, surrounded by the whites from outside. I had seen them as shadows against the snow, little more than pale phantoms, but here in the room they stood out bright and definite. There were several of them; I could not make out an exact number because they squirmed and twisted against each other, and against Hayden. Diaphanous limbs stretched out and wavered in the air, arms or wings or tentacles, tapping at the bed and the wall and the ceiling, leaving spots of ice like ink on blotting paper wherever they touched.

I could see no real faces, but I knew that the things were looking at me.

Their crying and sighing had ceased, but Hayden's continued. He moved quickly and violently, thrusting into the malleable shape that still straddled him, not yet noticing our intrusion even though the shotgun blast still rang in my ears. He continued his penetration, but slowly the white lifted itself away until Hayden's cock flopped back wetly onto his stomach.

He raised his head and looked straight at us between his knees, looked *through* one of the things where it flipped itself easily across the bed. The air stank of sex and something else, something cold and old and rotten, frozen forever and only now experiencing a hint of thaw.

"Oh please . . ." he said, though whether he spoke to us or the constantly shifting shapes I could not tell.

I tried to focus but the whites were minutely out of phase with my vision, shifting to and fro too quickly for me to concentrate. I thought I saw a face, but it may have been a false splay of shadows thrown as a shape turned and sprang to the floor. I searched for something I knew—an arm kinked slightly from an old break; a breast with a mole near the nipple; a smile turned wryly down at the edges—and I realized I was looking for Jayne. Even in all this mess, I thought she may be here. *I'll be with you again,* she had said.

I almost called her name, but Ellie lifted the shotgun and shattered the moment once more. It barked out once, loud, and everything happened so quickly. One instant the white things were there, smothering Hayden and touching him with their fluid limbs. The next, the room was empty of all but us humans, moth-eaten curtains fluttering slightly, window invitingly open. And Hayden's face had disappeared into a red mist.

After the shotgun blast there was only the wet sound of Hayden's brains and skull fragments pattering down onto the bedding. His hard-on still glinted in the weak candlelight. His hands each clasped a fistful of blanket. One leg tipped and rested on the sheets clumped around him. His skin was pale, almost white.

Almost.

Rosalie leaned against the wall, dry heaving. Her dress was wet and heavy with puke and the stink of it had found a home in my nostrils. Ellie was busy reloading the shotgun, mumbling and cursing, trying to look anywhere but at the carnage of Hayden's body.

I could not tear my eyes away. I'd never seen anything like this. Brand and Boris and Charley, yes, their torn and tattered corpses had been terrible to behold, but here . . . I had seen the instant a rounded, functional person had turned into a shattered lump of meat. I'd seen the red splash of Hayden's head as it came apart and hit the wall, big bits ricocheting, the smaller, wetter pieces sticking to the old wallpaper and drawing their dreadful art for all to see. Every detail stood out and demanded my attention, as if the shot had cleared the air and brought light. It seemed red tinged, the atmosphere itself stained with violence.

Hayden's right hand clasped the blanket, opening and closing very slightly, very slowly.

Doesn't feel so cold. Maybe there's a thaw on the way, I thought distractedly, perhaps trying to withdraw somewhere banal and comfortable and familiar. . . .

There was a splash of sperm across his stomach. Blood from his ruined head was running down his neck and chest and mixing with it, dribbling soft and pink onto the bed.

Ten seconds ago he was alive. Now he was dead. Extinguished, just like that.

Where is he? I thought. *Where has he gone?*

"Hayden?" I said.

"He's dead!" Ellie hissed, a little too harshly.

"I can see that." But his hand still moved. Slowly. Slightly.

Something was happening at the window. The curtains were still, but there was a definite sense of movement in the darkness beyond. I caught it from the corner of my eyes as I stared at Hayden.

"Rosalie, go get some boards," Ellie whispered.

"You killed Hayden!" Rosalie spat. She coughed up the remnants of her last meal, and they hung on her chin like wet boils. "You blew his head off! You shot him! What the hell, what's going on, what's happening here. I don't know, I don't know . . ."

"The things are coming back in," Ellie said. She

shouldered the gun, leaned through the door and fired at the window. Stray shot plucked at the curtains. There was a cessation of noise from outside, then a rustling, slipping, sliding. It sounded like something flopping around in snow. "Go and get the boards, you two."

Rosalie stumbled noisily along the corridor toward the staircase.

"You killed him," I said lamely.

"He was fucking them," Ellie shouted. Then, quieter: "I didn't mean to. . . ." She looked at the body on the bed, only briefly but long enough for me to see her eyes narrow and her lips squeeze tight. "He was fucking them. His fault."

"What were they? What the hell, I've never seen any animals like them."

Ellie grabbed my bicep and squeezed hard, eliciting an unconscious yelp. She had fingers like steel nails. "They aren't animals," she said. "They aren't people. Help me with the door."

Her tone invited no response. She aimed the gun at the open window for as long as she could while I pulled the door shut. The shotgun blast had blown the handle away, and I could not see how we would be able to keep it shut should the whites return. We stood that way for a while, me hunkered down with two fingers through a jagged hole in the door to try to keep it closed, Ellie standing slightly back, aiming the gun at the pocked wood. I wondered whether I'd end up getting shot if the whites chose this moment to climb back into the room and launch themselves at the door. . . .

Banging and cursing marked Rosalie's return. She carried several snapped floorboards, the hammer and nails. I held the boards up, Rosalie nailed, both of us now in Ellie's line of fire. Again I wondered about Ellie and guns, about her history. I was glad when the job was done.

We stepped back from the door and stood there silently, three relative strangers trying to understand and come to terms with what we had seen. But without understanding, coming to terms was impossible. I felt a tear run down my cheek, then another. A sense of breathless panic settled around me, clasping me in cool hands and sending my heart racing.

"What do we do?" I said. "How do we keep those things out?"

"They won't get through the boarded windows," Rosalie said confidently, doubt so evident in her voice.

I remembered how quickly they had moved, how lithe and alert they had been to virtually dodge the blast from Ellie's shotgun.

I held my breath; the others were doing the same.

Noises. Clambering and a soft whistling at first, then light thuds as something ran around the walls of the room, across the ceiling, bounding from the floor and the furniture. Then tearing, slurping, cracking, as the whites fed on what was left of Hayden.

"Let's go down," Ellie suggested. We were already backing away.

Jayne may be in danger, I thought, recalling her waving to me as she walked naked through the snow. If she was out there, and these things were out there as well, she would be at risk. She may not know, she may be too trusting, she may let them take advantage of her, abuse and molest her—

Hayden had been enjoying it. He was not being raped; if anything, he was doing the raping. Even as he died he'd been spurting ignorant bliss across his stomach.

And Jayne was dead. I repeated this over and over, whispering it, not caring if the others heard, certain that they would take no notice. Jayne was dead. Jayne was dead.

I suddenly knew for certain that the whites could smash in at any time, dodge Ellie's clumsy shooting and tear us to shreds in seconds. They could do it, but they did not. They scratched and tapped at windows, clambered around the house, but they did not break in. Not yet.

They were playing with us. Whether they needed us for food, fun or revenge, it was nothing but a game.

Ellie was smashing up the kitchen.

She kicked open cupboard doors, swept the contents of shelves onto the floor with the barrel of the shotgun, sifted through them with her feet, then did the same to the next cupboard. At first I thought it was blind rage, fear, dread; then I saw that she was searching for something.

"What?" I asked. "What are you doing?"

"Just a hunch."

"What sort of hunch? Ellie, we should be watching out—"

"There's something moving out there," Rosalie said.

She was looking through the slit in the boarded window. There was a band of moonlight across her eyes.

"Here!" Ellie said triumphantly. She knelt and rooted around in the mess on the floor, shoving jars and cans aside, delving into a splash of spilled rice to find a small bottle. "Bastard. The bastard. Oh God, the bastard's been doing it all along."

"There's something out there in the snow," Rosalie said again, louder this time. "It's coming to the manor. It's . . ." Her voice trailed off and I saw her stiffen, her mouth slightly open.

"Rosalie?" I moved toward her, but she glanced at me and waved me away.

"It's okay," she said. "It's nothing."

"Look." Ellie slammed a bottle down on the table and stood back for us to see.

"A bottle."

Ellie nodded. She looked at me and tilted her head. Waiting for me to see, expecting me to realize what she was trying to say.

"A bottle from Hayden's food cupboard," I said.

She nodded again.

I looked at Rosalie. She was still frozen at the window, hands pressed flat to her thighs, eyes wide and full of the moon. "Rosie?" She only shook her head. Nothing wrong, the gesture said, but it did not look like that. It looked like everything was wrong, but she was too afraid to tell us. I went to move her out of the way, look for myself, see what had stolen her tongue.

"Poison," Ellie revealed. I paused, glanced at the bottle on the table. Ellie picked it up and held it in front of a candle, shook it, turned it this way and that.

"Poison. Hayden's been cooking for us ever since we've been here. And he's always had this bottle. And a couple of times lately, he's added a little extra to certain meals."

"Brand," I nodded, aghast. "And Boris. But why? They were outside. They were killed by those things—"

"Torn up by those things," Ellie corrected. "Killed in here. Then dragged out."

"By Hayden?"

She shrugged. "Why not? He was fucking the whites."

"But why would he want to . . . Why did he have something against Boris and Brand? And Charley? An accident, like he said?"

"I guess he gave her a helping hand," Ellie mused, sitting at the table and rubbing her temples. "They both saw something outside. Boris and Brand, they'd both seen things in the snow. They made it known. They told us all about it, and Hayden heard as well. Maybe he felt threatened. Maybe he thought we'd steal his little sex mates." She stared down at the table, at the rings burnt there over the years by hot mugs, the scratches made by endless cutlery. "Maybe they told him to do it."

"Oh, come on!" I felt my eyes go wide like those of a rabbit caught in car headlights.

Ellie shrugged, stood and rested the gun on her shoulder. "Whatever, we've got to protect ourselves. They may be in soon, you saw them up there. They're intelligent. They're—"

"Animals!" I shouted. "They're animals! How could

they tell Hayden anything? How could they get in?"

Ellie looked at me, weighing her reply.

"They're white animals, like you said!"

Ellie shook her head. "They're new. They're unique. They're a part of the change."

New. Unique. The words instilled very little hope in me, and Ellie's next comment did more to scare me than anything that had happened up to now.

"They were using Hayden to get rid of us. Now he's gone . . . well, they've no reason not to do it themselves."

As if on cue, something started to brush up against the outside wall of the house.

"Rosalie!" I shouted. "Step back!"

"It's all right," she said dreamily. "It's only the wind. Nothing there. Nothing to worry about." The sound continued, like soap on sandpaper. It came from beyond the boarded windows, but it also seemed to filter through from elsewhere, surrounding us like an audio enemy.

"Ellie," I said, "what can we do?" She seemed to have taken charge so easily that I deferred to her without thinking, assuming she would have a plan with a certainty that was painfully cut down.

"I have no idea." She nursed the shotgun in the crook of her elbow like a baby substitute, and I realized I didn't know her half as well as I thought. Did she have children? I wondered. Where was her family? Where had this level of self-control come from?

"Rosalie," I said carefully, "what are you looking at?" Rosalie was staring through the slit at a moonlit scene none of us could see. Her expression had dropped from scared to melancholy, and I saw a tear trickle down her cheek. She was no longer her old cynical, bitter self. It was as if all her fears had come true and she was content with the fact. "Rosie!" I called again, quietly but firmly.

Rosalie turned to look at us. Reality hit her, but it could not hide the tears. "But he's dead," she said, half question, half statement. Before I could ask whom she was talking about, something hit the house.

The sound of smashing glass came from everywhere: behind the boards across the kitchen windows; out in the corridor; muffled crashes from elsewhere in the dark manor. Rosalie stepped back from the slit just as a long, shimmering white limb came in, glassy nails scratching for her face but ripping the air instead.

Ellie stepped forward, thrust the shotgun through the slit and pulled the trigger. There was no cry of pain, no scream, but the limb withdrew.

Something began to batter against the ruined kitchen window, the vibration traveling through the hastily nailed boards, nail heads emerging slowly from the gouged wood after each impact. Ellie fired again, though I could not see what she was shooting at. As she turned to reload she avoided my questioning glance.

"They're coming in!" I shouted.

"Can it!" Ellie said bitterly. She stepped back as a sliver of timber broke away from the edge of one of the boards, clattering to the floor stained with frost. She shouldered the gun and fired twice through the widening gap. White things began to worm their way between the boards, fingers perhaps, but long and thin and more flexible than any I had ever seen. They twisted and felt blindly across the wood . . . and then wrapped themselves around the exposed nails.

They began to pull.

The nails squealed as they were withdrawn from the wood, one by one.

I hefted the hammer and went at the nails, hitting each of them only once, aiming for those surrounded by cool white digits. As each nail went back in, the things around them drew back and squirmed out of sight behind the boards, only to reappear elsewhere. I hammered until my arm ached, resting my left hand against the vibrating timber. Not once did I catch a white digit beneath the hammer, even when I aimed for them specifically. I began to giggle and the sound frightened me. It was the voice of a madman, the utterance of someone looking for his lost mind, and I found that funnier than ever. Every time I hit another nail it reminded me more and more of an old fairground game. Pop the gophers on the head. I wondered what the prize would be tonight.

"What the hell do we do?" I shouted.

Rosalie had stepped away from the windows and now leaned against the kitchen counter, eyes wide, mouth working slowly in some unknown mantra. I glanced at her between hammer blows and saw her chest rising and falling at an almost impossible speed. She was slipping into shock.

"Where?" I shouted to Ellie over my shoulder.

"The hallway."

"Why?"

"Why not?"

I had no real answer, so I nodded and indicated with a jerk of my head that the other two should go first. Ellie shoved Rosalie ahead of her and stood waiting for me.

I continued bashing with the hammer, but now I had fresh targets. Not only were the slim white limbs nudging aside the boards and working at the nails, but they were also coming through the ventilation bricks at skirting level in the kitchen. They would gain no hold there, I knew; they could never pull their whole body through there. But still I found their presence abhorrent and terrifying, and every third hammer strike was directed at these white monstrosities trying to twist around my ankles.

And at the third missed strike, I knew what they were doing. It was then, also, that I had some true inkling of their intelligence and wiliness. Two digits trapped my leg between them—they were cold and hard, even through my jeans—and they jerked so hard that I felt my skin tearing in their grasp.

I went down and the hammer skittered across the kitchen floor. At the same instant a twisting forest of the things appeared between the boards above me, and in seconds the timber had started to snap and splinter as the onslaught intensified, the attackers now seemingly aware of my predicament. Shards of wood and glass and ice showered down on me, all of them sharp and cutting. And then, looking up, I saw one of the whites appear in the gap above me, framed by broken wood, its own limbs joined by others in their efforts to widen the gap and come in to tear me apart.

145

Jayne stared down at me. Her face was there, but the thing was not her; it was as if her image were projected there, cast onto the pure whiteness of my attacker by memory or circumstance, put there because it knew what the sight would do to me.

I went weak, not because I thought Jayne was there—I knew I was being fooled—but because her false visage inspired a flood of warm memories through my stunned bones, hitting cold muscles and sending me into a white-hot agony of paused circulation, blood pooling at my extremities, consciousness retreating into the warmer parts of my brain, all thought of escape and salvation and the other two survivors erased by the plain whiteness that invaded from outside, sweeping in through the rent in the wall and promising me a quick, painful death, but only if I no longer struggled, only if I submitted—

The explosion blew away everything but the pain. The thing above me had been so intent upon its imminent kill that it must have missed Ellie, leaning in the kitchen door and shouldering the shotgun.

The thing blew apart. I closed my eyes as I saw it fold up before me, and when I opened them again there was nothing there, not even a shower of dust in the air, no sprinkle of blood, no splash of insides. Whatever it had been, it left nothing behind in death.

"Come on!" Ellie hissed, grabbing me under one arm and hauling me across the kitchen floor. I kicked with my feet to help her, then finally managed to stand, albeit shakily.

There was now a gaping hole in the boards across the kitchen windows. Weak candlelight bled out and illuminated the falling snow and the shadows behind it. I expected the hole to be filled again in seconds and this time they would pour in, each of them a mimic of Jayne in some terrifying fashion.

"Shut the door," Ellie said calmly. I did so and Rosalie was there with a hammer and nails. We'd run out of broken floor boards, so we simply nailed the door into the frame. It was clumsy and would no doubt prove ineffectual, but maybe it would give us a few more seconds.

But for what? What good would time do us now, other than to extend our agony?

"Now where?" I asked hopelessly. "Now what?" There were sounds all around us; soft thuds from behind the kitchen door, and louder noises from farther away. Breaking glass; cracking wood; a gentle rustling, more horrible because they could not be identified. As far as I could see, we really had nowhere to go.

"Upstairs," Ellie said. "The attic. The hatch is outside my room, and it's got a loft ladder. As far as I know it's the only way up. Maybe we could hold them off until . . ."

"Until they go home for tea," Rosalie whispered. I said nothing. There was no use in verbalizing the hopelessness we felt at the moment because we could see it in each other's eyes. The snow had been here for weeks and maybe now it would be here forever. Along with whatever strangeness it contained.

Ellie checked the bag of cartridges and handed them to me. "Hand these to me," she said. "Six shots left. Then we have to beat them up."

It was dark inside the manor, even though dawn must now be breaking outside. I thanked God that at least we had some candles left . . . but that got me thinking about God and how He would let this happen, launch these things against us, torture us with the promise of certain death and yet give us these false splashes of hope. I'd spent most of my life thinking that God was indifferent, a passive force holding the big picture together while we acted out our own foolish little plays within it. Now, if He did exist, He could only be a cruel God indeed. And I'd rather there be nothing than a God who found pleasure or entertainment in the discomfort of His creations.

Maybe Rosalie had been right. She had seen God staring down with blood in his eyes.

As we stumbled out into the main hallway I began to cry, gasping out my fears and my grief, and Ellie held me up and whispered into my ear. "Prove Him wrong if you have to. Prove Him wrong. Help me to survive, and prove Him wrong."

I heard Jayne beyond the main front doors, calling my name into the snowbanks, her voice muffled and bland. I paused, confused, and then I even smelled her; apple-blossom shampoo, the sweet scent of her breath. For a few seconds Jayne was there with me and I could all but hold her hand. None of the last few weeks had happened. We were here on a holiday, but there was something wrong and she was in danger outside. I went to open the doors to her, ask her in and help her, assuage whatever fears she had.

I would have reached the doors and opened them

if it were not for Ellie striking me on the shoulder with the stock of the shotgun.

"There's nothing out there but those things!" she shouted. I blinked rapidly as reality settled down around me, but it was like wrapping paper, only disguising the truth I thought I knew, not dismissing it completely.

The onslaught increased.

Ellie ran up the stairs, shotgun held out before her. I glanced around once, listening to the sounds coming from near and far, all of them noises of siege, each of them promising pain at any second. Rosalie stood at the foot of the stairs doing likewise. Her face was pale and drawn and corpse-like.

"I can't believe Hayden," she said. "He was doing it with them. I can't believe . . . does Ellie really think he . . . ?"

"I can't believe a second of any of this," I said. "I hear my dead wife." As if ashamed of the admission, I lowered my eyes as I walked by Rosalie. "Come on," I said. "We can hold out in the attic."

"I don't think so." Her voice was so sure, so full of conviction, that I thought she was all right. Ironic that a statement of doom should inspire such a feeling, but it was as close to the truth as anything.

I thought Rosalie was all right.

It was only as I reached the top of the stairs that I realized she had not followed me.

I looked out over the ornate old banister, down into the hallway where shadows played and cast false impressions on eyes I could barely trust anyway. At first I thought I was seeing things because Rosalie was not stupid; Rosalie was cynical and bitter, but never stupid. She would not do such a thing.

She stood by the open front doors. How I had not heard her unbolting and opening them I do not know, but there she was, a stark shadow against white fluttering snow, dim daylight parting around her and pouring in. Other things came in too, the whites, slinking across the floor and leaving paw prints of frost wherever they came. Rosalie stood with arms held wide in a welcoming embrace.

She said something as the whites launched at her. I could not hear the individual words, but I sensed the tone; she was happy. As if she were greeting someone she had not seen for a very long time.

And then they hit her and took her apart in seconds.

"Run!" I shouted, sprinting along the corridor, chasing Ellie's shadow. In seconds I was right behind her, pushing at her shoulders as if this would make her move faster. "Run! Run! Run!"

She glanced back as she ran. "Where's Rosalie?"

"She opened the door." It was all I needed to say. Ellie turned away and concentrated on negotiating a corner in the corridor.

From behind me I heard the things bursting in all around. Those that had slunk past Rosalie must have broken into rooms from the inside even as others came in from outside, helping each other, crashing through our pathetic barricades by force of cooperation.

I noticed how cold it had become. Frost clung

to the walls and the old carpet beneath our feet crunched with each footfall. Candles threw erratic shadows at icicle-encrusted ceilings. I felt ice under my fingernails.

Jayne's voice called out behind me and I slowed, but then I ran on once more, desperate to fight what I so wanted to believe. She'd said we would be together again and now she was calling me . . . but she was dead, she was dead. Still she called. Still I ran. And then she started to cry because I was not going to her, and I imagined her naked out there in the snow with white things everywhere. I stopped and turned around.

Ellie grabbed my shoulder, spun me and slapped me across the face. It brought tears to my eyes, but it also brought me back to shady reality. "We're here," she said. "Stay with me." Then she looked over my shoulder. Her eyes widened. She brought the gun up so quickly that it smacked into my ribs, and the explosion in the confined corridor felt like a hammer pummeling my ears.

I turned and saw what she had seen. It was like a drift of snow moving down the corridor toward us, rolling across the walls and ceiling, pouring along the floor. Ellie's shot had blown a hole through it, but the whites quickly regrouped and moved forward once more. Long, fine tendrils felt out before them, freezing the corridor seconds before the things passed by. There were no faces or eyes or mouths, but if I looked long enough I could see Jayne rolling naked in there with them, her mouth wide, arms holding whites to her, into her. If I really listened I was sure I would hear her sighs as she fucked them. They had passed from luring to mocking now that we were trapped, but still . . .

They stopped. The silence was a withheld chuckle.

"Why don't they rush us?" I whispered. Ellie had already pulled down the loft ladder and was waiting to climb up. She reached out and pulled me back, indicating with a nod of her head that I should go first. I reached out for the gun, wanting to give her a chance, but she elbowed me away without taking her eyes off the advancing white mass. "Why don't they . . . ?"

She fired again. The shot tore a hole, but another thing soon filled that hole and stretched out toward us. "I'll shoot you if you stand in my way anymore," she said.

I believed her. I handed her two cartridges and scurried up the ladder, trying not to see Jayne where she rolled and writhed, trying not to hear her sighs of ecstasy as the whites did things to her that only I knew she liked.

The instant I made it through the hatch the sounds changed. I heard Ellie squeal as the things rushed, the metallic clack as she slammed the gun shut again, two explosions in quick succession, a wet sound as whites ripped apart. Their charge sounded like a steam train: wood cracked and split, the floorboards were smashed up beneath icy feet, ceilings collapsed. I could not see, but I felt the corridor shattering as they came at Ellie, as if it were suddenly too small to house them all and they were plowing their own way through the manor.

Ellie came up the ladder fast, throwing the shotgun through before hauling herself up after it. I saw a flash of white before she slammed the hatch down and locked it behind her.

"There's no way they can't get up here," I said. "They'll be here in seconds."

Ellie struck a match and lit a pathetic stub of candle. "Last one." She was panting. In the weak light she looked pale and worn out. "Let's see what they decide," she said.

We were in one of four attics in the manor roof. This one was boarded but bare, empty of everything except spiders and dust. Ellie shivered and cried, mumbling about her dead husband Jack frozen in the car. Maybe she heard him. Maybe she'd seen him down there. I found with a twinge of guilt that I could not care less.

"They herded us, didn't they?" I said. I was breathless and aching, but it was similar to the feeling after a good workout; energized, not exhausted.

Ellie shrugged, then nodded. She moved over to me and took the last couple of cartridges from the bag on my belt. As she broke the gun and removed the spent shells her shoulders hitched. She gasped and dropped the gun.

"What? Ellie?" But she was not hearing me. She stared into old shadows that had not been bathed in light for years, seeing some unknown truths there, her mouth falling open into an expression so unfamiliar on her face that it took me some seconds to place it—

a smile. Whatever she saw, whatever she heard, it was something she was happy with.

I almost let her go. In the space of a second, all possibilities flashed across my mind. We were going to die, there was no escape, they would take us singly or all in one go, they would starve us out, the snow would never melt, the whites would change and grow and evolve beneath us, we could do nothing, whatever they were they had won already, they had won when humankind brought the ruin down upon itself. . . .

Then I leaned over and slapped Ellie across the face. Her head snapped around and she lost her balance, falling onto all fours over the gun.

I heard Jayne's footsteps as she prowled the corridors searching for me, calling my name with increasing exasperation. Her voice was changing from sing-song, to monotone, to panicked. The whites were down there with her, the white animals, all animals, searching and stalking her tender naked body through the freezing manor. I had to help her. I knew what it would mean, but at least then we would be together, at least then her last promise to me would have been fulfilled.

Ellie's moan brought me back and for a second I hated her for that. I had been with Jayne and now I was here in some dark, filthy attic with a hundred creatures below trying to find a way to tear me apart. I hated her and I could not help it one little bit.

I moved to one of the sloping roof lights and stared out. I looked for Jayne across the snowscape, but the whites now had other things on their mind. Fooling me was not a priority.

"What do we do?" I asked Ellie, sure even now that she would have an idea, a plan. "How many shots have you got left?"

She looked at me. The candle was too weak to light up her eyes. "Enough." Before I even realized what she was doing she had flipped the shotgun over, wrapped her mouth around the twin barrels, reached down, curved her thumb through the trigger guard and blasted her brains into the air.

It's been over an hour since Ellie killed herself and left me on my own.

In that time snow has been blown into the attic to cover her body from view. Elsewhere it's merely a sprinkling, but Ellie is little more than a white hump on the floor now, the mess of her head a pink splash across the ever-whitening boards.

At first the noise from downstairs was terrific. The whites raged and ran and screamed, and I curled into a ball and tried to prepare myself for them to smash through the hatch and take me apart. I even considered the shotgun . . . there's one shot left . . . but Ellie was brave; Ellie was strong. I don't have that strength.

Besides, there's Jayne to think of. She's down there now, I know, because I have not heard a sound for ten minutes. Outside it is snowing heavier than I've ever seen, it must be ten feet deep, and there is no movement whatsoever. Inside, below the hatch and throughout the manor, in rooms sealed and broken open, the whites must be waiting. Here and there, Jayne will be waiting with them. For me. So that I can be with her again.

Soon I will open the hatch, make my way downstairs and out through the front doors. I hope, Jayne, that you will meet me there.

The Unfortunate

"Oh, look," said Adam, "a four-leaf clover." He stroked the little plant and sighed, pushing himself to his feet, stretching his arms and legs and back. He had been laying on the grass for a long time.

He walked across the lawn and onto the gravel driveway, past the Mercedes parked mock-casual, through the front door of the eight-bedroom house and into the study.

Two walls were lined with books. Portraits of the people he loved stared down at him and he should have felt at peace, should have felt comforted . . . but he did not. There was a large map on one wall, a thousand intended destinations marked in red, half a dozen places he had already visited pinned green. Travel was no longer on his agenda, neither was reading, because his family had gone. He was still about to make a journey, however, somewhere even stranger than the places he had seen so recently. Stranger than anyone had ever seen to tell of, more terrifying, more final. After the past year he was keener than ever to find his own way there.

And he had a map. It was in the bureau drawer. A

.44 magnum, gleaming snakelike silver, slick to the touch, cold, impersonal. He warmed it between his legs before using it. May as well feel comfortable when he put it in his mouth.

Outside, the fourth leaf on the clover glowed brightly and disappeared into a pinprick of light. Then, nothing.

"Well," Adam said to the house full of memories, "it wasn't bad to begin with . . . but it could have been better."

He heard footsteps approaching along the driveway, frantic footsteps crunching quickly toward the house.

"Adam!" someone shouted, panic giving the voice an androgynous lilt.

He looked around the room to make sure he was not being observed. He checked his watch and smiled. Then he calmly placed the barrel of the gun inside his mouth, angled it upward and pulled the trigger.

He had found them in the water.

At least he liked to think he found them, but later, in the few dark and furtive moments left to him when his mind was truly his own, he would realize that this was not the case. *They* had found *him*. Gods or fairies or angels or demons—mostly just one or another, but sometimes all four—they appeared weak and delicate.

It was not long, however, before Adam knew that looks counted for nothing.

Put on your life jackets, the cabin crew had said. *Only inflate them when you're outside the aircraft. Use the whistle to attract attention, and make for one of the life rafts.* As if disaster had any ruling factor, as if control could be gained over something so powerful, devastating and final.

As soon as the 747 hit the water, any semblance of control vanished. This was no smooth crash landing; it was a catastrophe, the shell splitting and the wings slicing through the fuselage and a fire—brief but terrible—taking out first class and the cockpit. There was no time even to draw away from the flames before everything fell apart, and Adam was pitched into a cool, dark, watery grave. *Alison,* he thought, and although she was not on the flight—she was back at home with Jamie—he felt that she was dead already. Strange, considering it was he who was dying.

Because in the chaos, he *knew* that he was about to die. The sounds of rending metal and splitting flesh had been dampened by their instant submersion into the North Atlantic, but a new form of blind panic had taken over. Bubbles exploded around him, some of them coming from inside torn bodies, and sharp, broken metal struck out at him from all around. The cold water masked the pain for a while, but he could still feel the numbness where his leg had been, the ghostly echo of a lost limb. He wondered whether his leg was floating above or below him. Then he realized that he could not discern up or down, left or right, and so the idea was moot. He was blinded too, and he did not know why. Pain? Blood? Perhaps his eyes were elsewhere, floating around in this deathly soup of waste and suffering, sinking to the sea-bed where unknown bottom-crawlers would snap them up and steal everything he had ever seen with one dismissive *clack* of their claws.

He had read accounts of how young children could live for up to an hour submerged in freezing water. They still retained a drowning reflex from being in the womb, their vocal cords contracted and drew their throats shut, and as long as they expelled the first rush of water from their lungs they could survive. Body temperature would drift down to match their surroundings, heart rate would halve, oxygen to the brain would be dramatically lessened, brain activity drawn in under a cowl of unconsciousness. So why, then, was he thinking all this now? Why panic? He should be withdrawing into himself, creating his own mini-existence where the tragedies happening all around him, here and now, could not break through.

Why not just let everything happen as it would?

Adam opened his eyes and finally saw through the shock. A torn body floated past him, heading down, trailing something pale and fleshy behind it. It had on a pair of shorts and Bart Simpson socks. No shoes. Most people kicked off their shoes on a long-haul flight.

The roaring sound around him increased as everything began to sink. Great bursts of bubbles stirred the terrible brew of the sea, and Adam felt a rush of something warm brushing his back. *A coffeepot crushed and is spewing its contents,* he thought. That was all. Not the stewardess holding it being opened up by the thousands of sharp edges, gushing her own warm insides across his body as they floated apart like lost lovers in the night . . .

And then he *really* opened his eyes, although he was so far down now that everything was pitch black. He opened them not only to what was happening around him, but to what was happening *to* him. He was still strapped in his seat. One of his legs appeared to be missing . . . but maybe not, maybe in the confusion he had only dreamed that he had lost a leg. Perhaps he had been dreaming it when the aircraft took its final plunge, and the nightmares—real and imagined—had merely blended together. He thought he felt a ghost ache there, but perhaps ghosts can be more real than imagination allows, and he held out his hands and felt both knees intact.

Other hands moved up his body from his feet, squeezing the flesh so that he knew it was still there, pinching, lifting . . . dragging him up through the maelstrom and back toward the surface. He gasped in water and felt himself catch on fire, every nerve end screaming at the agony in his chest. His mind began to shut down—

yes, yes, that is the way, go to sleep, be that child again.

—and then he broke surface.

The extraordinary dragged his sight from the merely terrifying. He was aware of the scenes around him— the bodies and parts of bodies floating by, the aircraft wreckage bobbing and sinking and still smoldering in places, the broken-spined books sucking up water, suitcases spilling their insides in memory of their shattered owners—but the shapes that rose out of the water with him were all that he really registered, all that he really comprehended. Although true comprehension . . . that was impossible.

They were fairies.

Or demons.

Or angels.

Or gods.

There were four of them, solid yet transparent, strong yet unbelievably delicate. Their skin was clear, but mottled in places with a darker light, striped like a glass tiger. They barely seemed to touch him, yet he could feel the pinch of their fingers on his legs and arms where they held him upright. The pain seemed at odds with their appearance. He closed his eyes and opened them again. The pain was still there, and so were the things.

They were saving him. He was terrified of them. For one crazy moment he looked around at the carnage and wished himself back in the water, struggling against his seat restraint as it dragged him down, feeling his ears crunch in and his eyeballs implode as awful pressures took their toll, sucking out the last of his air and flooding him and filling him. Perhaps he would see Alison again—

she's dead!

—love her as he had always loved her, feel every moment they had shared. He thought it was a fallacy that a drowning man's life flashes before him. But it was a romantic view of death, and if he had to die then a hint of romance . . .

"You are not going to die," a voice said. None of the things seemed to have spoken and the voice appeared in his head, unaccented, pure, like a playback of every voice ever saying the same thing.

He looked around at them. He could see no expressions because their faces were ambiguous, stains on the air at best. He reached out and touched one, and it was warm. It was *alive*. He laid his palm flat against its chest.

"That is all right," the same voice intoned. "Feel what you must. You have to trust us. If you have to believe that we are here in order to trust us, then make sure you do. Because we have a gift for you. We can save you, but . . . you must never forget us or deny us."

Adam held out his other hand. "You're there," he whispered as he felt a second heartbeat beneath his palm. For some reason, it felt disgusting.

"So pledge."

He was balanced on a fine line between life and death. He was in no condition to make such a decision. That is why all that happened later was so unfair.

He nodded. And then he realized the truth.

"I'm dead." It was obvious. He had been drifting down, down, following the other bodies deep down, perhaps watched by some of them as he too had watched. He had known his leg had gone, he had felt the water enter him and freeze him and suck out his soul. He was dead.

"No," the voice said, "you are very much alive." And then one of the things scraped its nails across his face.

Adam screamed. The pain was intense. The scratches burned like acid streaks, and he touched his cheek and felt blood there. He took his hand away and saw a red smear. He looked down at his legs; still whole. He looked back up at the four things that were holding him and his wrecked seat just out of reach of the water. Their attitude had not changed, their unclear faces were still just that.

163

He saw a body floating past, a person merged some- how with a piece of electrical paneling, metallic and biological guts both exposed.

"We have something to show you," the voice said.

And then he was somewhere else.

He actually felt the seat crumple and vanish beneath him, and he was suddenly standing on a long, wide street. His clothes were dry and whole, not ripped by the crash and soaked with sea water and blood. His limbs felt strong, he was warm, he was invigorated. His face still hurt. . . .

The four things—the demons, the angels, whatever they were—stood around him, holding out their hands as if to draw his attention to this, to that. They gave the impression that they lived there, but to Adam they did not seem to feel at home.

"Where is this place?" Adam said. "Heaven?"

"How is your face?"

"It still hurts." Adam touched the scratches on his cheek, but the blood had almost ceased flowing now, and already he could feel the wounds scabbing over. They were itching more than burning. He wondered just how long ago the crash had been.

"You are alive, you see," the voice said, "but we brought you here for a while to show you some things. And to give you a gift. Come with us."

"But who are you? *What* are you?"

The things all turned to look at him. They were still transparent but solid, shapes made of flowing glass. Try as he might, he could not discern any features with which to distinguish one from another, yet they all acted in slightly different ways. The one on his far left tilted its head slightly as it watched him; the one to his right leaned forward with unashamed curiosity whenever he spoke.

"Call us Amaranth," the voice said, "for we are eternal."

Adam thought about running. He would turn and sprint along the street, shout for help if the things pursued him, slap off their hands if they chose to grasp at him. He would escape them. He *wanted* to escape them . . . even though, as yet, they had done him only good.

Am I really here, he thought, *or am I floating at the bottom of the sea? Fishes darting into my mouth. Crustaceans plucking at my brain as these final insane thoughts seek their escape.*

"For the last time," Amaranth said, and this time two of them attacked him. One held him down, while the other reached into his mouth and grasped his tongue. Its hand was sickly warm, the skin—or whatever surface sheen it possessed—slick to the touch. It brought his tongue forward and then pricked at it with an extended finger.

The pain was bright, explosive, exquisite. Blood gushed into Adam's throat as he struggled to stand. The things moved aside to let him up and he spat out a gob of blood, shaking with shock and a strange, subdued fury.

"You are alive," Amaranth said, "and well, and living here for now. We shall not keep you long because we know you wish to return to your world . . . to your Alison and Jamie . . . but the price of our saving you is for you to see some things. Follow us. And do not be afraid. You are one of the lucky ones."

Adam wanted nothing more than to see his family. His conviction that Alison was dead had gone, had surely been a result of his own impending death. And Jamie—sweet little Jamie, eighteen months old and just discovering himself—how cruel for him to suddenly be without a father. How pointless. Yes, he needed to see them soon.

"Thank you," Adam said. "Thank you for saving me."

Amaranth did not reply. Adam was truly alive, the pain in his tongue told him that. This was unreal and impossible, yet he felt completely, undeniably alive. As to whether he really had been saved . . . time would tell.

One of the things gently took his hand and guided him along the street.

At first Adam thought he could have been in London. The buildings on either side presented tall, grubby façades, with their shop fronts all glazing and posters and flashing neon. A bar spewed music and patrons into the street on one corner, some of them sitting at rickety wooden tables, others standing around, mingling, chatting, laughing. They were all laughing. As he watched, a tall man—hair dyed a bright red, body and legs clad in leather, and sporting a monstrous tattoo of a dragon across his forehead, down the side of his neck and onto his collarbone—bumped into a table and spilled several drinks. Glass smashed. Beer flowed and gurgled between brick paviors. The couple at the table stood, stared at the leather-clad man and smiled. He set his own drinks down on their table, sat and started chatting to them. Adam heard them introducing themselves, and as he and Amaranth passed the bar, the three were laughing and slapping each other's shoulders as if they had been friends forever.

The tall man looked up and nodded at Adam, then again at each of the things with him. His eyes were wide and bright, his face tanned and strong, and it shone. Not literally, not physically, but his good humor showed through. He was a walking ad for never judging people by their appearances.

Within a few paces the street changed, so quickly that Adam felt as though it were actually shifting around him. He could see nothing strange, but suddenly the buildings were lower, the masonry lighter, eaves adorned with ancient gargoyles growling grotesquely at the buildings opposite, old wooden windows rotting in their frames, pigeons huddling along sills. He could have moved from London to Italy in the space of a second. And if anything the street felt more real, more meant-to-be than he had ever experienced. It was as if nature itself had built this place specifically for these people to inhabit, carving it out of the landscape as perfectly as possible, and even though the windows were rotting and the buildings had cracks scarring their surfaces like old battle wounds, these things made it even more perfect.

"It's like a painting," Adam said.

"It is art, true." The thing holding his hand let go and another took its place, this one warmer, its flesh silkier. "This way."

The sudden music of smashing glass filled the street,

followed by a scream and a sickening thud as something hit the road behind them. Adam spun around, heart racing, scalp stretching as he tried not to imagine what he was about to see.

What he did see was certainly not what he expected.

A woman was laying stretched over the high gutter, half on the pavement, half on the road. As he watched, she stood and brushed diamond-shards of broken glass from her clothes. She picked them from her face too, but they had not torn the skin. Her limbs had not suffered in her tumble from the second-story window, her suit trousers and jacket were undamaged, her skull was whole. In fact, as she ruffled up her hair, stretched her back with a groan and glanced up at where she had fallen from, she looked positively radiant. An extreme sports fan perhaps? Maybe this was just a stunt she was used to doing day-in, day-out?

She saw Adam watching her and threw him a disarmingly calm smile. "That was lucky," she said.

"What the hell's lucky about falling from a window?"

She shrugged. Looked around. Waved at someone farther along the street. "I didn't die," she said, not even looking at Adam anymore. And without saying another word she walked past him and Amaranth to a small Italian café.

Amaranth steered Adam past the café and into a side alley. Again, scenery changed without actually shifting, as if flickering from place to place in the instant that it took him to blink. This new setting was straight out of all the American cops-and-robbers television shows he had ever seen. There was a gutter running down the center of the alley overflowing with

rubbish and excrement, boxes piled high against one wall just begging a speeding car to send them flying, pull-down fire escapes hanging above head height, promising disaster. Doorways were hidden back under the shadows of walls, and in some of those shadows darker shadows shifted.

Someone rolled from a doorway into their path. Adam stopped, caught his breath, ready for the gleam of metal and the demand for money.

Amaranth paused as well. Were they scared?

And then he realized something else. People had seen him and Amaranth; he had noticed them looking—looking and smiling—and they were not out of place.

"This isn't real," he said, and a shape stood before him.

The man wore a long coat. His hair was an explosion of dirt and fleas and other insects, his shoes had burst and his toes stuck out, as if seeking escape from the wretched body they belonged to.

He looked up.

"My friend!" he said, although Adam had never seen him before. "My friend, how are you? Welcome here, welcome everywhere, I'm sure. Oh, so I see they've found you too?" He nodded at the shapes around Adam and they shifted slightly, as if embarrassed at being noticed. "They're angels, you know," the man said quietly. "Look at me. Down-and-out, you'd guess? Ready to blow you or stab you for the money to buy a bottle of paint stripper."

"The thought had crossed my mind," Adam said, but only because he knew, already, that he was wrong.

169

There was something far stranger, far more wonderful at work here.

"Maybe years ago." The man nodded. "But not anymore. See, I'm one of the lucky ones. Take a look!" He opened his coat to display a glimmering, golden suit. It looked ridiculous but comfortable. The man *himself* looked comfortable. In fact, Adam had rarely seen anyone looking so contented with his lot, so at home with where and what he was.

"It's . . . nice," Adam said.

"It's fucking awful! Garish and grotesque, but if that's what I want to be sometimes, hey, who's to deny me that? Nobody, right? In the perfect world, nobody. In the perfect world, I can do and be what I want to do and be, whenever I want. Yesterday I was making love with a princess. Tomorrow I may decide to crash a car. Today . . . today I'm just reliving how I used to be. I hated it, of course; who wouldn't? Today, here . . . in the perfect world, it's not so bad."

"But just where are we?" Adam asked, hoping—realizing—that perhaps this man could tell him what Amaranth would not. "I was in a plane crash, I was sinking, I was dying—"

"Right," the man said, nodding and blinking slowly. "And then you were rescued. And they brought you here for a look around. Well . . . you're one of the lucky ones. We're all lucky ones here."

There was the sound of something moving quickly down the alley, still hidden by shadows but approaching rapidly. For an instant Adam thought it could be gun-fire and he prepared to dive for cover, but then he saw the magnificent shape emerge into the sunlight.

"Hold up!" the man said with a distinctly Cockney accent. " 'Ere comes my ride."

Adam and Amaranth stood aside, and Adam watched aghast as the unicorn galloped along the alley. It did not slow down—did not even seem to notice the man—but he grabbed on to its mane as it ran, swung himself easily up onto its back and rode it out into the street. It paused for a moment and reared up, and Adam was certain it was a show just for him. The man in the golden suit waved an imaginary hat back at Adam, then nudged the unicorn with his knees and they disappeared along the street.

He heard the staccato beat of hooves for a long time.

For the first time he wondered whether it was *all* a display put on for him, and him alone. The red-haired man . . . the jumper . . . the down-and-out. They had all looked at him. Somehow, it was all too perfect.

He pressed his sore tongue against the roof of his mouth.

"Do you get the idea?" Amaranth asked.

"What idea?"

The things milled around him, touching him, and now their touch was more pleasant than repulsive. His skin jumped wherever they made contact. He found himself aroused and he went with the feeling. It did not feel shameful or inappropriate. It felt just right. While he was here, why not enjoy it?

"The idea that good luck is a gift," Amaranth said.

A talent or a present? Adam wanted to ask, but already they were pulling him farther along the alley toward whatever lay beyond its far end.

He smelled the water before he saw it, rich and cloying, heavy with effluent and rubbish. As they emerged from the mouth of the alley and turned a corner, the lake came into view. It was huge, not just a city lake, more like a sea. Adam was reminded briefly of Venice, but there were no gondoliers here, and the waters were rougher and more violent than Venice ever experienced. And there were things among the waves, far out from the shore, shiny gray things breaking the surface and screeching before heading back down to whatever depths they came from.

A woman walked past them whistling, nodded a hello, indicated the lake with a nod and looked skyward, as if to say: *oh dear, that lake, huh?* She wore so much jewelery on her fingers and wrists that Adam was sure she would sink, were she to enter the waters. But she never would, no one in their right mind would, because to go in there would be to die.

Things are in there, Adam thought. *Shattered aircraft, perhaps? Bodies of passengers I chatted with being ripped and torn and eaten? Where am I now? Where, really, am I?*

"We stand on the shore of bad luck," Amaranth said. "Out there . . . the island, do you see? . . . there live the unlucky ones."

Now that it had been pointed out to him, Adam could see the island, although he was sure it had not been there before. *You never notice a damn thing until it's pointed out to you,* Alison would say to him, and she was right, he was not very observant. But this island was huge—growing larger—and eventually, even though nothing seemed to have actually changed, the lake was a moat and the island filled most of his field of vision.

Sounds reached him then, although they were dulled and weary with distance. Screams, shouts, cries, the rending crunch of buildings collapsing, an explosion, the roar of flames taking hold somewhere out of sight. Adam edged closer to the shore of the moat, straining to see through the hazy air, struggling to make out what was happening on the island. There were signs erected all along its shore. Some of them seemed to be moving. Some of them . . .

They were not signs. They were crucifixes, and most of them were occupied. Heads lolled on shoulders, knees moved weakly as the victims tried to shift their weight, move the pain around their bodies so that it did not burn its way through their flesh.

Beneath some of the crosses, fires had been set.

"It's Hell!" Adam gasped, turning around to glare at the four things with him.

"No," Amaranth said, "we have explained. Those over there are the unlucky ones, but they are not dead. Not yet. Many of them will be soon . . . unlucky ones always die . . . but first, there is pain and suffering."

Adam felt tears burning behind his eyes. He did not understand any of this. Sinking into the Atlantic, dying, being a nameless statistic on an airline's list of victims, that he understood. Losing Alison and Jamie, even— never seeing them again—that he could understand.

But not this.

"I want my family," he said. "If you've saved me like

173

you say, I want my family. I don't want to be here. I don't know where here is."

"Do you ever, truly?"

"Oh, Jesus," Adam gasped in despair, dropping to his knees and noticing as he did so that the shore was scattered with pale white bones. Washed up from the island of the unlucky ones, no doubt.

He closed his eyes.

And tumbled into the moat.

He had been expecting fresh water—polluted by refuse perhaps, rancid with death—but inland water nonetheless. His first mouthful was brine.

Beneath him, the aircraft seat. Around his waist the seatbelt, which would ensure that he sank to his death. Above him, the wide blue sky he had fallen from.

Under his arms and around his legs, hands lifting him to safety.

"Here's a live one!" a voice shouted, and it was gruff and excited, not like Amaranth or the people he had heard back there in the land of the lucky. This one held a whole range of experience.

"Unlucky," Adam muttered, spitting out sea water and feeling a dozen pains bite into him at the same instant. "Bad luck . . ."

"No, mate," said a voice with an Irish lilt from somewhere far away. "You're as lucky as fuck. Everyone else is dead."

Adam tried to speak, to ask for Alison and Jamie because he knew he was about to die. He had already visited Heaven and slipped back again for his final breath. But the bright sunlight faded to black and the voices receded. Already, he was leaving once more. . . .

As he passed out he fisted his hands so that nothing could hold on to them.

The next time he awakened, Alison was staring down at him. There had been no dreams, no feelings, no sensations. It felt as if a second had passed since he had been in the sea, but he knew instantly that it was much longer. There was a ceiling and fluorescent lights, and the cloying stench of antiseptic, and the metallic grumble of trolley wheels on vinyl flooring.

And there was Alison leaning over him, hair haloed by a bright light.

"Honey," she said. She began to cry.

Adam reached up to her and tried to talk, but his throat was dry and rough. He rasped instead, just making a noise, happy that he could do anything to let her know he was still alive.

"Alive," he croaked eventually. "You're alive."

She looked down at him and frowned, but the tears were too powerful and her face took on the shine of relief once more. "Yes, you're alive. Oh honey, I was so terrified, I saw the news and I knew you were dead, I just *knew* . . . and I came here. Mum didn't want me to, but I just had to be here when they started . . . when they started bringing in the bodies. And the worst thing," she whispered, touching his cheek, ". . . I *wanted* them to find your body. I couldn't live knowing you were still out there somewhere. In the sea." She buried her face in the sheets covering him and swung her arm across his stomach, hugging him tight, a hug *so* tight that he would never forget it.

This is what love is, he thought to himself. *Never wanting to let go.* He put his hand behind her head and revelled in the feel of her hair between his fingers.

"Come on," he said, "it's all right now. We're both all right now." A terrible thought came out of nowhere. In seconds, it became a certainty. *My leg!*

"I am all right, aren't I? Alison, am I hurt? Am I damaged?"

She looked up and grinned at him, red-rimmed eyes and snotty nose giving her a strange childlike quality. "You're fine! They said it was a miracle, you're hardly touched. Bruises here and there, a few scratches on your face and you bit your tongue quite badly. But you escaped . . . well, you're on the front page of the papers. I kept them! Jamie, he's got a scrapbook!"

"Scrapbook? How long have I been here?"

"Only two days," Alison said. She sat down on the bed, never relinquishing contact with him, eye or hand. He wondered whether she'd ever let go again.

"Two days." He thought of where he had been and the things that had taken him there. As in all particularly vivid dreams, he retained some of the more unusual sensory data from the experience—he could smell the old back alley, the piss and the refuse . . . he could hear the woman hitting the street, feel the jump in his chest as he realized what had happened. He could taste the strange fear he had experienced every second of that waking dream, even though Amaranth had professed benevolence.

A nightmare, surely? A sleeping, verge-of-death nightmare.

"Where's Jamie?"

Alison started crying again because they were talking about their son, their son who still had his father after all. "He's at home with Mum, waiting for you. Mum's told him you fell out of the sky but were caught by angels. Bless him, he—"

"What does she mean by that?" Adam whispered. His throat was burning and he craved a drink. He felt as if someone were slowly strangling him. *Angels, demons, who can tell?*

Alison shrugged. "Well, you know Mum, she's just telling Jamie stories. Trying to imbue him with her religion without us noticing."

"But she actually said angels?"

His wife frowned and shrugged and nodded at the same time. This was obviously not how she had expected him to react after surviving a crash into the sea in a passenger jet. "Why, hon? You really see some?"

What would you think if I said yes, he thought.

Alison brought him some ice water. Then she kissed him.

Three days later they let him go home.

In the time he had been in hospital, several major newspapers and magazines had contacted Alison and offered her five-figure payments for Adam's exclusive story. He was a star, a survivor among so much death, a miracle man who had lived through a thirty-nine thousand feet plunge into the North Atlantic and come out of it with hardly a scratch.

Hardly. The three parallel lines on his cheek had

scarred. *You were lucky,* the doctors had said. *Very lucky.*

Lucky to be scarred for life? Adam had almost asked, but thankfully he had refrained. At least he hadn't died.

On his first full day back at home the telephone rang twice before breakfast. Alison answered and calmly but firmly told whomever was on the other end to go away and spend his time more productively. On the third ring she turned the telephone off altogether.

"If anyone wants us badly enough, they can come to see us. And if it's family, they have my mobile number."

"Maybe I should do it," Adam said, sipping from a cup of tea. Jamie was playing at his feet, building complex Lego constructions and then gleefully smashing them down again. A child's appetite for creation and destruction never ceased to amaze Adam. His son had refused to move from his feet since they had risen from bed, even when tempted to the breakfast table with the promise of a yogurt. He loved that. He loved that his wife wanted to hold him all the time; he loved that Jamie wanted to be close in his personal space. Even though his son barely looked up at him—he was busy with blocks and cars and imaginary lands—Adam felt himself at the center of Jamie's attention.

"You sure you want to do that?" Alison asked. She sat down and leaned against him, snuggling her head onto his shoulder. He felt her breath on his neck as she spoke. "I mean, they're after sensation, you know. They're after miracle escapes and white lights at the end of tunnels. They don't want to hear . . . well, what happened to you. The plane fell. You passed out. You woke up in the fishing boat."

Adam shrugged. "Well, I could tell them . . . I could tell them more."

"What more is there?"

He did not elaborate. How could he? *I dreamed of angels. I dreamed of demons scratching my face when I did not believe in them, of a place where good luck and bad luck were distilled into very refined, pure qualities. I dreamed that I gave a pledge.*

"You need time at home. Here with us. Time to get over it."

"To be honest, honey, I don't feel too bad about it all." And that was shockingly true. He was the sole survivor of a disaster that had killed over three hundred people, but all the guilt and anger and frustration he thought he should feel was thankfully absent. Perhaps in time . . . but he thought not. After all, he was one of the lucky ones. "Besides," he said quietly, "think of the money. Think what we could do with twenty grand."

Alison did not respond.

He could hear her thinking about it all.

They sat that way for half an hour, relishing the contact and loving every sound or motion Jamie made. He joined them on the settee several times, hugging them and pointing at Adam's ears and eyes, as if he knew what secrets lay within. Then he was back on the floor, back in make believe. They both loved him dearly and he loved them too, and what more could a family ask? Really, Adam thought, what more?

There *was* more. The ability to pay the mortgage

each month without worrying about going overdrawn. The occasional holiday, here and there. Adam's job as a publishing representative paid reasonably well, and he did get to travel, but Alison's previous marriage had damaged her financially, and they were both still paying for her mistakes. Money was not God, but there really was so much more they could ask for.

After lunch, Adam took a look at the numbers and names Alison had been noting down over the past week. He chose a newspaper that he judged to be more serious than most, selling merely glorified news, not outright lies. He rang them, told them who he was, and arranged for a reporter to visit the house.

That afternoon they decided to visit the park. It was only a short stroll from their home, so they held Jamie's hands and let him walk. The stroller was easier, but Adam liked his son walking alongside him, glancing up every now and then to make sure his father was still there. Their neighbors said a friendly hello and greeted Adam with honest joy. Other people they did not know smiled and stared with frank fascination. On that first trip out, Adam truly came to realize just how much he had been the subject of news over the past week. The last time these people had seen him he had been on a television screen, a pixellated victim of a distant disaster, bloodied face stark against the white hospital pillows. Now that he was flesh and blood once more, they did not quite know how to react.

Just before reaching the park, an old stone bridge crossed a stream. Adam loved to sit on the parapet and listen to the water gurgling underneath. Sometimes Alison and Jamie would go on to the park and leave Adam to catch up, but not today. Today Alison refused to leave his side, and she held their son in her arms as they both sat on the cold stone.

"We'll get moss on our arses," she said, glancing over her shoulder.

"I'll lick it off when Jamie's in bed."

"You! Saucy sod."

"You don't know what surviving a fatal air crash does for one's libido," Adam said, and he realized it was true. He could feel the heat of Alison's arm through his shirt sleeve, feel her hip nudging against his. He felt himself growing hard, so he turned away and looked at the opposite parapet. There was a date block set in there, testifying that the bridge had been built over a hundred years ago. He tried to imagine the men who had built it, what they had talked about as they were pointing between the stones, whether they considered who would cross the bridge in the future. Probably not. Most people rarely thought that far ahead.

Something glittered in the compressed leaves at the base of the wall. He frowned, squinted, and leaned forward for a closer look. Something metallic, perhaps, but glass as well. He crossed the quiet road and bent down to see what it was.

"Adam? What have you found, honey?"

Adam could only shake his head.

"Honey, we should go. Young rascal's getting restless. He needs his slide and swing fix."

"I'll be damned," Adam gasped.

"What is it?"

He took the watch back to Alison, gently wiping dirt

181

from its face and picking shredded leaves from the expanding metal strap. He showed it to her and watched her face.

"Does it work?"

He looked, tapped it against his palm, looked again. The second hand wavered and then began to move, ticking on from whatever old time it had been stuck in. Strangely, the time was now exactly right.

"Looks quite nice," she said, cringing as Jamie twisted in her arms.

"Nice? It's priceless. It's Dad's. You remember Dad's old watch, the one he left me, the one we lost in the move?"

Alison nodded and stared at him strangely. "We moved here six years ago."

Adam nodded, too excited to talk.

It told the right time!

"Six years, Adam. It's not your dad's watch, just one that looks a bit—"

"Look." He flipped the strap inside out and showed his wife the back of the watch casing. *For Dear Jack, love from June,* it said. Jack, his father. June, his mother.

"Holy shit."

"Shit, shit, shit," Jamie gurgled, and they looked at each other and laughed because their swearing son took their attention for a moment, stole it away from this near-impossibility.

They walked in silence, Adam studiously cleaning dirt from the watch, checking its face for cracks, winding it, running his fingers over the faded inscription.

At the entrance to the park Alison let Jamie run to

the playground and took the timepiece from Adam. "What a stroke of luck," she said. "Oh, you've put it right."

Adam did not say anything. He accepted the watch back and slipped it into his pocket. Maybe this was something that would make a nice end to his interview with the newspaper, but straight away he knew he would never tell them.

With Jamie frolicking on the climbing frame and Alison hugging him, Adam silently began to get his story straight.

Nobody is news forever, even to the ones they love. Stories die down, a newer tragedy or celebrity gossip takes first place, family problems beg attention. It's something to do with time, and how it heals and destroys simultaneously. And luck, perhaps. It has a lot to do with luck.

Three weeks after leaving the hospital, Adam's name disappeared from the papers and television news, and he was glad. Those three weeks had exhausted him, not only because he was still aching and sore and emotionally unhinged by the accident—although he did not feel quite as bad as everyone seemed to think he should—but because of the constant, unstinting attention. He had sat through that painful first interview, the paper had run it, he and Alison had been paid. Days later a magazine called and requested one interview per month for the next six months. The airline wrote to ask him to become involved with the accident investigation, and to perhaps be a patron of the charity hastily being set up to help the victims' families. A local church requested that he make a speech at its next service, discussing how God has been involved in his survival and what it felt like to be cradled in the Lord's hand, while all those around him were filtering through His divine fingers. The suggestion was that Adam was pure and good, and those who had died were tainted in some way. The request disgusted him. He told them so. When they persisted he told them to fuck off, and he did not hear from them again.

His reaction was a little extreme, he knew. But perhaps it was because he did not know exactly what *had* saved him.

He turned down every offer. He had been paid twenty thousand pounds by the newspaper, and nobody else was offering anywhere near as much. Besides, he no longer wanted to be a sideshow freak: *Meet the miracle survivor!*

The telephone rang several times each night—family, friends, well-wishers, people he had not spoken to for so long that he could not truly even call them friends anymore—and eventually he stopped answering. Alison became his buffer, and he gave her carte blanche to vet the calls however she considered appropriate.

This was how he came to speak to Philip Howards.

Jamie was in bed. Adam had his feet up on the settee, a beer in his hand and a book propped face-down on his lap. He was staring at the ceiling through almost-closed eyes, remembering the crash, his thoughts dipping in and out of dream as he catnapped. On the waking side, there was water and the nudge of dead bodies; when he just edged over into sleep, transparent shapes flitted behind his eyes and showed him miracles. Sometimes the two images mixed and merged. He had been drinking too much that evening.

Alison went straight to the telephone when it rang, sighing, and Adam opened one eye fully to follow her across the room. They had been having a lot of sex since he came home from the hospital.

"Hello?" she answered, and then she simply stood there for a full minute, listening.

Adam closed his eyes again and thought of the money. Twenty thousand. And the airline would certainly pay some amount in compensation as well, something to make them appear benevolent in the public eye. He could take a couple of years off work. Finish paying the mortgage. Start on those paintings he had wanted to do for so long.

He opened his eyes again and appraised his artist's fingers where they were curved around the bottle. He was stronger there, more creative. He felt more of an emotional input to what he was doing. The painting he had started two weeks ago was the best he had ever done.

All in all, facing death in the eye had done wonders for his life.

"Honey, there's a guy on the phone. He says he really has to talk to you."

"Who is it?" The thought of having to stand, to walk, to actually talk to someone almost drove him back to sleep.

"Philip Howards."

Adam shrugged. He didn't know him.

"He says it's urgent. Says it's about the angels." Alison's voice was neutral, but its timbre told Adam that she was both intrigued and angry. She did not like things she could not understand. And she hated secrets.

The angels! Adam's near-death hallucination flooded back to him. He reached up to touch the scars on his cheek and Alison saw him do it. He stood quickly to prevent her asking him about it, covering up the movement with motion.

She looked at him strangely as he took the receiver from her. He knew that expression: *We'll talk about it later.* He also knew that she would not forget.

"Can I help you?"

There was nothing to begin with, only a gentle static and the sound of breathing down the line.

"Hello?"

"You're one of the lucky ones," the voice said. "I can tell. I can hear it in your voice. The unlucky ones—poor souls, poor bastards—whatever they're saying, they always sound like they're begging for death. Sometimes they do. One of them asked me to kill her once, but I couldn't do it. Life's too precious for me, you see."

Adam reeled. He recalled his dream again, the island of unlucky souls surrounded by the stinking moat. He even sniffed at the receiver to see whether this caller's voice stank of death.

"Has something happened?" the man continued. "Since you came back, has something happened that you can't explain? Something wonderful?"

"No," Adam spoke at last, but then he thought: *the watch, I found Dad's watch!*

"I'm not here to cause trouble, really. It's just that when this happens to others, I always like to watch. Always like to get in touch, ask about the angels, talk about them. It's my way of making sure I'm not mad."

The conversation dried for a moment, and Adam stood there breathing into the mouthpiece, not knowing what to say, hearing Philip Howards doing the same. They were like two duelling lovers who had lost the words to fight, but who were unwilling to relinquish the argument.

"What do you know about them?" Adam said at last. Alison sat up straight in her chair and stared at him. He averted his eyes. He could not talk to this man and face her accusing gaze, not at the same time. *What haven't you told me,* her stare said.

The man held his breath. Then, very quietly: "I was right."

"What do you know?"

"Can we meet? Somewhere close to where you live, soon?"

Adam turned to Alison and smiled, trying to reassure her that everything was all right. "Tomorrow," he said.

Howards agreed, they arranged where and when, and the strangest phone call of Adam's life ended.

"What was that?" Alison asked.

He did not know what to say. What could he say? Could he honestly try to explain? Tell Alison that her mother had been right in what she'd told Jamie, that angels really had caught and saved him?

Angels, demons, fairies . . . gods.

187

"Someone who wants to talk to me," he said.

"About angels?"

Adam nodded.

Alison stared at him. He could see that she was brimming with questions, but her lips pressed together and she narrowed her eyes. She was desperately trying not to ask any more, because she could tell Adam had nothing to say. He loved her for that. He felt a lump in his throat as he stooped down, put his arms around her shoulders and nuzzled her neck.

"It's all right," he said. Whether she agreed or not, she loved him enough to stay silent. "And besides," he continued, "you and Jamie are coming too."

He never could keep a secret from Alison.

Later that night, after they had made love and his wife drifted into a comfortable slumber with her head resting on his shoulder, Adam had the sudden urge to paint. This had happened to him before but many years ago, an undeniable compulsion to get up in the middle of the night and apply brush to canvas. Then, it had resulted in his best work. Now, it just felt right.

He eased his arm out from beneath Alison, dressed quickly and quietly and left the room. On the way along the landing he looked in on Jamie for inspiration, and then he carried on downstairs and set up his equipment. They had a small house—certainly no room for a dedicated studio, even if he was as serious about his art now as he had been years ago—so the dining room doubled as his work room when the urge took him.

He began to paint without even knowing what he was going to do.

By morning, he knew that they had lost their dining room for a long, long time.

"You're a very lucky man," Philip Howards said. He was sitting opposite Adam, staring over his shoulder at where Alison was perusing the menu board, Jamie wriggling in her arms.

Adam nodded. "I know."

Howards look at him intently, staring until Adam had to avert his gaze. Shit, the old guy was a spook and a half! Fine clothes, gold weighing down his fingers, a healthy tan, the look of a traveled man about him. His manner also gave this impression, a sort of weary calmness that came with wide and long experience, and displayed a wealth of knowledge. He said he was seventy, but he looked fifty.

"You really are. The angels, they told you that didn't they?"

Adam could not look at him.

"The angels. Maybe you thought they were fairies or demons. But with them, it's all the same thing really. How did you get those scars on your cheek?"

Adam glanced up at him. "You know how or you wouldn't have asked."

Howards raised his head to look through the glasses balanced on the tip of his nose. He was inspecting Adam's face. "You doubted them for a while."

Adam did not nod, did not reply. To answer this man's queries—however calmly they were being put to him—would be to admit to something unreal. They were dreams, that was all, he was sure. Two men could share the same dreams, couldn't they?

"Well, I did the same. I got this for my troubles." He pulled his collar aside to display a knotted lump of scar tissue below his left ear. "One of them bit me."

Adam looked down at his hands in his lap. Alison came back with Jamie, put her hands on his shoulders and whispered into his ear. "Jamie would prefer a burger. We're not used to jazzy places like this. I'll take him to McDonald's—"

"No, stay here with me."

She kissed his ear. "No arguing. I think you want to be alone anyway, yes? I can tell. And later, *you* can tell. Tell me what all this is about."

Adam stood and hugged his wife, ruffled Jamie's hair. "I will," he said. He squatted down and gave his son a bear hug. "You be a good boy for Mummy."

"Gut boy."

"That's right. You look after her. Make sure she doesn't spend too much money!"

"Goodbye, Mr. Howards," Alison said.

Howards stood and shook her hand. "Charmed." He looked sadly at Jamie and sat back down.

Alison and Jamie left. Adam ordered a glass of wine. Howards, he knew, was not taking his eyes from him for a second.

"You'll lose them," he said.

"What?"

Howards nodded at the door, where Alison and Jamie had just disappeared past the front window. "You'll lose them. It's part of the curse. You do well, everyone and everything else goes."

"Don't you talk about my family like that! I don't even know you. Are you threatening me?" He shook his head when the old man did not answer. "I should have fucking known. You're a crank. All this bullshit about angels, you're trying to confuse me. I'm still not totally settled, I was in a disaster, you're trying to confuse me, get money out of me—"

"I have eight million pounds in several bank accounts," Howards said. "More than I can ever spend . . . and the angels call themselves Amaranth."

Adam could only stare open-mouthed. Crank or no crank, there was no way Howards could know that. He had told no one, he had never mentioned it. He had not even hinted at the strange visions he experienced as he waited to die in the sea.

"I'll make it brief," Howards said, stirring his glass of red wine with a finely manicured finger. "And then, when you believe me, I want you to do something for me."

"I don't know—"

"I was on holiday in Cairo with my wife and two children. This was back in '59. Alex was seven. Sarah was nine. There was a fire in the hotel and our room was engulfed. Alex . . . Alex died. Sarah and my wife fled. I could not leave Alex's body, not in the flames, not in all the heat. It just wasn't right. So I stayed there with him, fully expecting rescue. It was only as I was blinded by heat and the smoke filled my lungs that I knew no rescue was going to come.

"Then something fell across me—something clear and solid, heavy and warm—and protected me from the flames. It took the smoke from inside me . . . I can't

191

explain, I've never been able to, not even to myself. It just sucked it out, but without touching me.

"Then I was somewhere else, and Amaranth was there, and they told me what a lucky man I was."

Adam shook his head. "No, I'm not hearing this. You know about me, I've talked in my sleep or . . . or . . ."

"Believe me, I've never been to bed with you." There was no humor in Howards's comment.

How could he know? He could not. Unless . . .

"Amaranth saved you?"

Howards nodded.

"From the fire?"

"Yes."

"And they took you . . . they took you to their place?"

"The streets of Paris and then a small Cornish fishing village. Both filled with people of good fortune."

Adam shook his head again, glad at last that there was something he could deny in this old man's story. "No, no, it was London and Italy and then America somewhere, New York I've always thought."

Howards nodded. "Different places for different people. Never knew why, but I suppose that's just logical really. So where were the damned when you were there?"

"The damned . . ." Adam said quietly. He knew exactly what Howards meant, but he did not even want to think about it. If the old man had seen the same thing as he, then it was real, and people truly did suffer like that.

"The unlucky, the place . . . You know what I mean. Please, Adam, be honest with me. You really must if you ever want to understand any of this or help yourself through it. Remember, I've been like this for over forty years."

Adam swirled his wine and stared into its depths, wondering what he could see in there if he concentrated hard. "It was an island," he said, "in a big lake. Or a sea, I'm not sure, it all seemed to change without moving."

Howards nodded.

"And they were crucified. And they were burning them." Adam swallowed his wine in one gulp. "It was horrible."

"For me it was an old prison," Howards said, "on the cliffs above the village. They were throwing them from the high walls. There were hundreds of bodies broken on the rocks, and seagulls and seals and crabs were tearing them apart. Some of them were still alive."

"What does this mean?" Adam said. "I don't know what to do with this. I don't know what to tell Alison."

Howards looked down at his hands where they rested on the table. He twirled his wedding band as he spoke. "I've had no family or friends for thirty years," he said. "I'm unused to dealing with such . . . intimacies."

"But you're one of the lucky ones, like me? Amaranth said so. What happened to your family? What happened to your wife and your daughter Sarah?"

Howards looked up, and for an instant he appeared much older than he had claimed, ancient. It was his eyes, Adam thought. His eyes had seen everything.

"They're all dead," Howards said. "And still those things follow me everywhere."

Adam was stunned into silence. There was chatter around them, the sound of Howards's rings tapping against his glass as he stirred his wine, the sizzle of hot plates bearing steaks and chicken. He looked at Howards's down-turned face, trying to see if he was crying. "They follow you?" he gasped.

Howards nodded and took a deep breath, steeling himself. "Always. I see them from time to time, but I've known they're always there for years now. I can feel them . . . watching me. From the shadows. From hidden corners. From places just out of sight." His demeanor had changed suddenly, from calm and self-assured to nervous and frightened. His eyes darted left and right like a bird's, his hands closed around his wine glass and his fingers twisted against each other. Someone opened the kitchen door quickly and he sat up, a dreadful look already on his face.

"Are they here now?" Adam asked. He could not help himself.

Howards shrugged. "I can't see them. But they're always somewhere."

"I've not seen them. Not since I dreamed them."

The old man looked up sharply when Adam said *dreamed.* "We're their sport. Their game. I can't think why else they would continue to spy . . ."

"And your family? Sport?"

Howards smiled slightly, calming down. It was as if casting his mind back decades helped him escape the curse he said he lived under in the present. "You ever heard Newton's third law of motion? To every action, there is an equal and opposite reaction."

Adam thought of Alison and Jamie, and without any

warning he began to cry. He sobbed out loud and buried his face in his napkin, screwing his fingers into it, pressing it hard against his eyes and nose and mouth. He could sense a lessening in the restaurant's commotion as people turned to look and, soon after, a gradual increase in embarrassed conversation.

"And that's why I have to ask you something," Howards said. "I've been asking people this for many years now, those few I meet by chance or happen to track down. Amaranth doesn't disturb me; they must know that no one will agree to what I ask. My asking increases their sport, I suppose. But I continue to try."

"What?" Adam asked. He remembered the certainty, as he floated in the sea, that Alison was dead. It brought a fresh flow of tears, but these were silent, more heartfelt and considered. He could truly imagine nothing worse—except for Jamie.

"Deny them. Take away their sport. They've made you a lucky man, but you can reject that. If you don't . . . your family will be gone."

"Don't you fucking threaten me!" Adam shouted, standing and throwing down his napkin, confused, terrified. The restaurant fell completely silent this time, and people stared. Some had a look in their eyes—a hungry look—as if they knew they were about to witness violence. Adam looked straight at Howards, never losing eye contact, trying to see the madness in his face. But there was none. There was sorrow mixed with contentment, a deep and weary sadness underlying healthy good fortune. "Why don't you do it yourself! Why, if it's such a good idea, don't *you* deny them!"

"It's too late for me," Howards said quietly, glancing around at the other patrons watching him. "They were dead before I knew."

"Fuck you!" Adam shouted. "You freak!" He turned and stormed out of the restaurant, a hundred sets of eyes scoring his skin. He wondered if any of the diners recognized him from his fifteen minutes of fame.

As the restaurant door slammed behind him and he stepped out into the street, the sun struck his tearful eyes, blinding him for a moment. Across the pedestrian area, sandwiched between a travel agent's and a baker's shop, a green door liquefied for a second and then reformed. Its color changed to deep-sea blue.

Before his sight adjusted, Adam saw something clear and solid pass through the door.

"So?" Alison asked.

"Fruitcake." He slid across the plastic seat and hugged his son to him. Then he leaned over the food-strewn table and planted a kiss squarely on his wife's mouth. She was unresponsive.

"The angels, then?" She was injecting good cheer into her voice, but she was angry. She wanted answers, and he knew that. He had never been able to lie to his wife. Even white lies turned his face bloodred.

Adam shook his head and sighed, stealing a chip from Jamie's tray and fending off his son's tomato-sauce retribution. He looked up, scanned the burger bar, searching for strange faces that he could not explain.

"Adam," Alison said, voice wavering, "I want to know what's going on. I saw the look on your face when you were on the phone with him yesterday. It's like you were suddenly somewhere else, seeing something different, feeling something horrible. You turned white. Remember that time you tried some pot and couldn't move for two hours and felt sick? You looked worse than you did then."

"Honey, it's just that what he said reminded me of the crash."

Alison nodded and her face softened. She wanted to keep on quizzing, he could tell, but she was also a wonderful wife. She did not want to hurt him, or to inspire thoughts or memories that might hurt him.

"And what your mum said to Jamie about the angels saving me. When Howards mentioned angels, it brought it all back. I was sinking, you know? Sinking into the sea. Bodies around me. Then I floated back up, I saw the sunlight getting closer. And . . . he just reminded me of when I broke the surface." He was lying! He was creating untruths, but he was doing it well. Even so he felt wretched, almost as if he were betraying Alison, using her supportive nature against her. He looked outside and wondered whether those things were enjoying his lies. He felt sick.

"Park!" Jamie shouted suddenly. "Go to park! Swing, swing!"

"All right tiger, here we go!" Adam said, pleased to be able to change the subject. Tears threatened once more as he wrestled with Jamie and stole his chips and heard his son squeal with delight as he tickled him.

Deny them, Howards had said. *If you don't . . . your family will be gone.*

He thought of the watch, and the interview money, and his painting, and the new-found closeness that surrounded him and Alison and Jamie like a sphere of solid crystal, fending off negative influences from outside, reflecting all the badness that bubbled in the world around them.

How could he give any of this up? Even if it were possible—even if Howards was not the madman Adam knew him to be—how could he possibly turn his back on this?

In the park, he and Alison sat on a bench and hugged each other. Jamie played on a toddler's climbing frame, occasional tumbles making him giggle, not cry. He was an adventurous lad and he wore his grazed knees and bruised elbows as proud testaments to this. Adam kissed Alison. It turned from a peck on the lips to a long, lingering kiss, tongues meeting, warmth flooding through him as love made itself so beautifully known.

Then the inevitable shout from Jamie as he saw his parents involved in each other for a moment, instead of him.

"I could have lost you both," Adam said, realizing as he spoke how strange it sounded.

"We could have lost you."

He nodded. "That's what I meant." He looked across to the trees bordering the park, but there were no flitting shadows beneath them. Nobody was spying on them from the gate. The hairs on the back of his neck stayed down.

They watched Jamie for a while, taking simple but

heartfelt enjoyment in every step he climbed, each little victory he won for himself.

"I started a painting this morning," Adam said.

"I know. I saw you leave the room and heard you setting up."

"It's . . . incredible. It's already painted in here," he said, tapping his head, "and it's coming out exactly how I envisoned it. No imperfections. You know the quote from that Welsh writer, 'I dream in fire—' "

" '—and work in clay.' Of course I know it. You've spat it out every month since I've known you."

Adam smiled. "Well, this morning I was working in fire. Dreaming and working in fire. I'm alight . . . my fingers and hands are doing the exact work I want of them. I can't explain it, but . . . maybe the crash has given me new insight. New vigor."

"Made you realize how precious life is," Alison mused, watching Jamie slip giggling down the slide.

Adam looked at her and nodded. He kissed her temple. He worshipped her, he realized. She was his bedrock.

He could smell the rich scent of flowers, hear birds chirping in the trees bordering the park, feel the warmth of the wooden bench beneath him, taste the sweetness of summer in the air. He truly was alight.

He finished the painting the following morning. That afternoon he called Maggie, his former art agent, and asked her to come up from London, take a look. Two days later he had placed it in a major exhibition in a London gallery.

The painting was entitled "Dreaming in Fire and Ice." Only Alison saw it for what it really was: an affir-

mation of his love, and a determination that nothing—
nothing—would ever rip their family apart. He was a
good man. He would never let that happen.

On the first day of the exhibition he sold the painting
for seven thousand pounds. That same evening, Alison's elderly mother, Molly, slipped and fell downstairs, breaking her leg in five places.

"How is she?"

Alison looked up from the magazine she was not
reading and Adam's heart sank. Her eyes were dark,
her skin pale, nose red from crying. "Not too good.
There's a compound fracture, and they're sure her
hip's gone as well. She's unconscious. Shock. In someone so old, they said . . . well, I told them she was
strong."

He went to his wife and hugged her, wondering
whether he was being watched by Amaranth even
now. He had seen one of them on the way to the hospital, he was certain, hunkered down on the back of
a flatbed truck, raising its liquid head as he motored
the other way. He had glanced in the rearview mirror
and seen something, but he could not be sure. The car
was vibrating, the road surface uneven. It could have
been anything. Maybe it was light dancing in his eyes
from the panic he felt.

"Oh, honey," he said, "I'm so sorry. I'm sure she'll
be all right. She'll pull through. Stubborn old duck
wouldn't dream of doing anything otherwise, you
know that."

"I just don't want her to meet her god that quickly,"
Alison said, and she cried into his neck. He felt her

warm tears growing cold against his skin, the shuddering as she tried to stop but failed, and he started to cry as well.

"The angels will save her," Adam said without thinking, for something to say more than anything, and because it was what Molly would have said. He didn't mean it. He felt Alison stiffen and held his breath.

They won't, he thought. *They won't save her. They've got their sport in me.*

Something ran a finger down his spine, and he knew that there were eyes fixed upon him. He turned as best he could to look around, but the corridor was empty in both directions. There were two doors half open, a hose reel coiled behind a glass panel, a junction two dozen steps away, a tile missing from the suspended ceiling grid. Plenty of places to hide.

"I wonder if she's scared," Alison said. "If she's still thinking in there, if she's dreaming. I wonder if she's scared? I mean, if she dies she goes to Heaven. That's what she believes."

"Of course she will, but it doesn't matter. She'll come around. She will." Adam breathed into his wife's hair and kissed her scalp. A door snicked shut behind him. He did not even bother turning around to look.

He knew that Howards was right, purely because his senses told him so.

He was being watched.

Maggie's call came three days later. An influential London gallery wanted to display his paintings. And more than that, they were keen to commission some work for the vestibule of their new wing. They had offered twenty-five thousand for the commission. Maggie had already accepted. They wanted to meet Adam immediately to talk the projects through.

Alison's mother had not woken up, other than for a few brief moments during the second night. No one had been there with her, but a nurse had heard her calling in the dark, shouting what appeared to be a plea: *Don't do it again, don't, please don't!* By the time the nurse reached the room Molly was unconscious once more.

"You have to go," Alison said. "You simply have to. No two ways about it." She was washing a salad while Adam carved some ham. Jamie was playing in their living room, building empires in Lego and then cheerfully aiding their descent.

Adam felt awful. There was nothing he wanted more than to travel to London, meet with the gallery, smile and shake hands—and to see himself living the rest of his life as what he had always dreamed of becoming: an artist. It was so far-fetched, so outlandish. But he was a lucky man now. The faces at distant windows told him so. He was lucky, and he was being watched.

Deny them, Howards had said. *If you don't . . . your family will be gone.*

He could still say no. Maggie had accepted, but there was no contract, and she really should have consulted him before even commencing a deal of such magnitude. He could say no thank you, I'm staying here with my family because they need me, and besides, I'm scared of saying yes, I'm scared of all the good luck. Every action has an equal and opposite reaction, you know.

There was still money left from the interview. They didn't really *need* the cash.

And he could always go back to work—they'd been asking for him, after all.

"I'm doing some of the best work of my life," he said, not sure even as he spoke whether he had intended to say it at all. "It's a golden opportunity. I really can't turn it down."

"I know," Alison replied. She was slicing a cucumber into very precise, very regular slices. It was something her mother always did. "I don't *want* you to turn it down. You have to go, there's no argument."

Adam popped a chunk of ham into his mouth and chewed. "Yes, there is," he said around the succulent mouthful. "The argument is, your mum is ill. She's doing very poorly. You're upset and you need me here. And there's no one else who baby-sits Jamie for us on such a regular schedule. I could ask my parents down from Scotland . . . but, well, you know."

"Not baby types."

"Exactly."

Alison came to him and wrapped her arms around his waist. She nuzzled his ear. When she did that, it made him so glad he had married someone the same height as him. "I know how much you've been aching for this for years," she said. "You remember that time on holiday in Cornwall . . . the time we think we conceived Jamie in the sauna . . . remember what you said to me? *We'll have a big posh car, a huge house with a garden all the way around and a long gravel driveway, a study full of books; you can be my muse and I'll work by day in the rooftop studio, and in the evenings I'll play with my children."*

"What a memory for words you have," Adam said. He could remember. It used to be the only thing he ever thought of.

"Go," his beautiful wife said. "I'll be fine. Really. Go and make our fortune. Or if you don't, bring a cuddly toy for Jamie and a bottle of something strong for me."

Good fortune, he thought. *That's what I have. Good fortune.*

Deny them, Howards had said. But Howards was a crank. Surely he was.

"Fuck it," he whispered.

"What?"

"I'll go. And I promise I'll be back within two days. And thanks, honey."

Later that night they tried to make love, but Alison began to cry, and then the tears worsened because she could not forget about her mother, not even for a moment. Adam held her instead, turning away so that his erection did not nudge against her, thinking she may find it horrible that he was still turned on when she was crying, talking about her injured mother, using his shoulder as a pain-sink.

When she eventually fell asleep he went to look in on Jamie. His son was snoring quietly in the corner of his bed, blankets thrown off, curled into a ball of cuteness. Adam bent over and kissed his forehead. Then he went to visit the bathroom.

Something moved back from the frosted glass window as he turned on the light. It may have been nothing—as substantial as a puff of smoke, there for less than a blink of an eye—but he closed the curtains anyway. And held his breath as he used the toilet. Listening.

In the morning Alison felt better, and Jamie performed so as to draw her attention to him. He threw his breakfast to the floor, chose a time when he was diaper-less to take a leak and caused general mayhem throughout the house. And all this before nine o'clock.

Adam took a stroll outside for a cigarette and looked up at the bathroom window. There was no way up there, very little to climb, nothing to hold on to even if someone could reach the window. But then, Amaranth did not consist of someones, but *somethings*. He shivered, took a drag on the cigarette, looked at the garden through a haze of smoke.

He was being watched. Through the conifers bordering the garden and a small public park peered two faces, pale against the evergreens.

Adam caught his breath and let it out slowly from his nose in a puff of smoke. He narrowed his eyes. No, they did not seem to be watching him—seemed not to have even noticed him, in fact—but rather they were looking at the house. They were discussing something, one of them leaning sideways to whisper to the other. A man and a woman, Adam saw now, truly flesh and blood, nothing transparent about them, nothing demonic.

Maybe they were staking the place out? Wondering when and how to break in, waiting for him to leave so that they could come inside and strip the house, not realizing that Alison and Jamie—

But I'm a lucky man.

Surely Amaranth would never permit that to happen to him.

Adam threw the cigarette away and sprinted across the garden. The grass was still damp with dew—he heard the hiss of the cigarette being extinguished—and it threw up fine pearls of water as he ran. Each footfall matched a heartbeat. He emerged from shadow into sunlight and realized just how hot it already was.

It may have been that their vision was obscured by the trees, but the couple did not see him until he was almost upon them. They wanted to flee, he could see that, but knowing he had noticed them rooted them to the spot. That was surely not the way of thieves.

"What do you want?" Adam shouted as he reached the screen of trees. He stood well back from the fence and spoke to them between the trunks, a hot sense of being family protector flooding his veins. He felt pumped up, ready for anything. He felt strong.

"Oh, I'm so sorry," the woman said, hands raised to her face as if holding in her embarrassment.

"Well, what are you doing? Why are you staring at my house? I should call the police, perhaps?"

"Oh Christ, no," the man said, "don't do that! We're sorry, it's just that . . . well, we love your house. We've been walking through the park on our way to work . . . we've moved into the new estate down the road . . . and we can't help having a look now and then. Just to see . . . well, whether you've put it on the market."

"You love my house. It's just a two-bed semi."

The woman nodded. "But it's so perfect. The garden, the trees, the location. We've got a child on the way,

206

we need a garden. We'd buy it the minute you decided to sell!"

"Not a good way to present ourselves as potential house-buyers, I suppose," the man said, mock-grim faced.

Adam shook his head. "Especially so keen. I could double the price," he smiled. They seemed genuine. They *were* genuine, he could tell that, and wherever the certainty came from he trusted it. In fact, far from being angry or suspicious, he suddenly felt sorry for them.

"Boy or girl?" he asked.

"I'm sorry?"

"Are you having a boy or a girl?"

"Oh," the woman said, still holding her face, "we haven't a clue. We want it to be a surprise. We just think ourselves lucky we can have children."

"Yes, they're precious," Adam said. He could hear Jamie faintly, giggling as Alison wiped breakfast from his mouth, hands and face.

"Sorry to have troubled you," the man said. "Really, this is very embarrassing. I hope we haven't upset you, scared you? Here," he fished in his pocket for his wallet and brought out a business card. He offered it through the fence.

Adam stepped forward and took the card. He looked at both of them—just long enough to make them avert their eyes—and thought of his looming trip to London, what it might bring if things went well. He pictured his fantasized country house with the rooftop art studio and the big car and the gym.

"It just so happens," he said, "your dream may come sooner than you think."

"Really?" the woman asked. She was cute. She had big eyes and a trim, athletic figure. Adam suddenly knew, beyond a shadow of a doubt, that she would screw him if he asked. Not because she wanted his house, or thought it may help her in the future. Just because he was who he was.

He shrugged, pocketed the card and bid them farewell. As he turned and walked across the lawn to the back door, he could sense them simmering behind him. They wanted to ask more. They wanted to find out what he had meant by his last comment.

Let them stew. That way, perhaps they would be even more eager if and when the time came.

Saying goodbye at the train station was harder than he had imagined. It was the first trip he had been on without his family since the disastrous plane journey several weeks ago, and that final hug on the platform felt laden with dread. For Adam it was a distant fear, however, as if experienced for someone else in another life, not a disquiet he could truly attribute to himself. However hard he tried, he could not worry. Things were going too well for that.

Amaranth would look after him.

On the way to the station he had seen the things three times: once, a face staring from the back of a bus several cars in front; once, a shape hurrying across the road behind them, seen briefly and fleetingly in the rearview mirror; and finally in the station itself, a misplaced shadow hiding behind the high-level TV monitors that displayed departure and arrival times. Each time he had thought to show Alison, tell her why everything would be all right, that these beings were here to watch over him and bless him—

demon, angel, fairy, god

—but then he thought of her mother lying in a coma. How could he tell her that now? How could he tell her that everything was fine?

So the final hug, the final sweet kiss, and he could hardly look at her face without crying.

"I'll be fine," he said.

"Last time you told me that, ten hours later you were bobbing about in the Atlantic."

"The train's fully equipped with life-jackets and non-flammables."

"Fool." She hugged him again and Jamie snickered from his stroller.

Adam bent down and gave his son a kiss on the nose. He giggled, twisting Adam's heart around his childish finger one more time.

"And you, you little rascal. When your daddy comes home, he's going to be a living, breathing, working artist."

"Don't get too optimistic and you won't be disappointed," Alison whispered in his ear.

"I won't be disappointed," he whispered back. "I know it."

He boarded the train and waved as it drifted from the station. His wife and son waved back.

The journey was quiet but exciting, not because anything happened, but because Adam felt as though he was approaching some fantastic junction in his life.

209

One road led the way he had been heading for years, and it was littered with stalled dreams and burned-out ambition. The other road—the new road, offered to him since the plane crash and all the strangeness that had followed it—was alight with exciting possibilities and new vistas. He had been given a chance at another life, a newer, better life. It was something most people never had.

He would take that road. This trip was simply the first step to get there.

Howards had been offered the same chance, had taken it, and look at him now! Rich, well-traveled, mad perhaps, but harmless with it. Lonely. No family or friends. Look at him now. . . .

But he would not think of that.

The train arrived at Paddington and Adam stepped out onto the platform.

Someone screamed: "Look out!"

He turned and his eyes widened, hands raised as if they would hold back the luggage cart careening toward him. It would break his legs at the very least, cast him aside and crumple him between the train and the concrete platform—

Something shimmered in the air beside the panic-stricken driver, like heat haze but more defined, more solid.

A second and the cart would hit him. He was frozen there, not only by the impending impact and the pain that would instantly follow, but also by what he saw.

The driver, yanked to the side.

The ambiguous shape thrusting its hand through the

metallic chassis and straight into the vehicle's electric engine.

The cart, jerking suddenly at an impossible right angle to crunch into the side of the train carriage mere inches from Adam's hip.

He gasped, finding it difficult to draw a breath, winded by shock.

The driver had been flung from the cart and now rolled on the platform, clutching his arm and leaving dark, glistening spots of blood on the concrete. People ran to his aid, some of them diverting to Adam to check whether he had been caught in the impact.

"No, no, I'm fine," he told them, waving them away. "The driver . . . he's bleeding, he'll need help. I'm fine, really."

The thing had vanished from the cart. High overhead pigeons took flight, their wings sounding like a pack of cards being thumbed. *Game of luck,* Adam thought, but he did not look up. He did not want to see the shapes hanging from the girders above him.

He walked quickly away, unwilling to become involved in any discussion or dispute about the accident. He was fine. That was all that mattered. He just wanted to forget about it.

"I saw," a voice croaked behind him as he descended the escalator to the tube station. And then the smell hit him. A grotesque merging of all bad stenches, a white-smell of desperation and decay and hopelessness. There was alcohol mixed in with urine, bad food blended with shit, fresh blood almost driven under by the rancid tang of rot. Adam gagged and bile rose into his mouth, but he grimaced and swallowed it back down.

Then he turned around.

He had seen people like her many times before, but mostly on television. He did not truly believe that a person like this existed because she was so different from the norm, so unkempt, so wild, so *unreal*. Had she been a dog she would have been caught and put to sleep ages ago. And she knew it. In her eyes, the street person displayed a full knowledge of what had happened to her. And worse than that—they foretold of what *would* happen. There was no hope in her future. No rescue. No stroke of luck to save her.

"I saw," she said again, breathing sickness at his face. "I saw you when you were meant to be run over. I saw your eyes when it didn't happen. I saw that you were looking at one of . . . *them.*" She spat the final word, as if expelling a lump of dog turd from her mouth.

Adam reached the foot of the escalator and strode away. His legs felt weak, his vision wavered, his skin tingled with goose bumps. Howards talking about the things he had seen could have been fluke or coincidence. Now, here was someone else saying the same things. Here, for Adam, was confirmation.

He knew the street person was following him; he could hear the shuffle of her disintegrating shoes. A hand fell on his shoulder. The sleeve of her old coat ended frayed and torn and bloodied, as if something had bitten it and dragged her by the arm.

"I said, I saw. You want to talk about it? You want me to tell you what you're doing? You lucky fuck."

Adam turned around and tried to stare the woman down, but he could not. She had nothing to lose, and so she held no fear. "Just leave me alone," he said instead. "I don't know what you're on about. I'll call the police if you don't leave me alone."

The woman smiled, a black-toothed grimace that split her face in two and squeezed a vile, pinkish pus from cracks in her lips. "You know what they did to me? Huh? You want to hear? I'll tell you that first, and then I'll let you know what they'll do to you."

Adam turned and fled. There was nothing else to do. People moved out of his way, but none of them seemed willing to help. As confused and doubtful as he was about Amaranth, he still thought: *Where are you now?* But maybe they were still watching. Maybe this was all part of their sport.

"They took me from my family," the woman continued. "I was fucking my husband when they came, we were conceiving, it was the time my son was conceived. They said they saved me, but I never knew what from. And they took me away, showed me what was to become of me. And you know what?"

"Leave me alone!" Adam did not mean to shout, but he was unable to prevent the note of panic in his voice. Still, none of his fellow travelers came to his aid. Most looked away. Some watched, fascinated. But none of them intervened.

"They crucified me!" the street person screamed. She grunted with each footstep, punctuating her speech with regular exclamations of pain. "They nailed me up and cut me open, fed my insides to the birds and the rats. Then they left me there for a while.

And they let me see over the desert, across to the golden city where pricks like you were eating and screwing and being oh-so-bloody wonderful."

Adam put on a spurt of speed and sensed the woman falling behind.

"In the end, they took me from my family for good!" she shouted after him. "They're happy now, my family. They're rich and content, and my husband's fucked by an actress every night, and my son's in private school. Happy!"

He turned around; he could not help it. The woman was standing in the center of the wide access tunnel, people flowing by on both sides, giving her a wide berth. She had her hands held out as if feigning the crucifixion she claimed to have suffered. Her dark hair was speckled gray with bird shit. The string holding her skirt up was coming loose. Adam was sure he could see things crawling on the floor around her, tiny black shapes that could have been beetles or wood lice or large ants. They all moved away, spreading outward like living ripples from her death-stinking body.

"It'll happen to you, too!" the bug lady screamed. "This will happen to you! The result is always the same, it's just the route that's different!"

Adam turned a corner and gasped in relief. Straight ahead a tube train stood at a platform. He did not know which line it was on, which way it was going, where it would eventually take him. He slipped between the doors nevertheless, watched them slide shut, fell into a seat and rested his head back against the glass. He read the poem facing straight down at him.

Wise is he who heeds his foe,
For what will come? You never know.

The bug lady made it onto the platform just as the train pulled away, waving her hands, screaming, fisting the air as if to fight existence itself.

"Bloody Bible bashers," said a woman sitting across from Adam. And he began to laugh.

He was still giggling three stations later. Nerves and fear and an overwhelming sense of unreality brought the laughter from him. His shoulders shook and people began to stare at him, and by the fourth station the laughter was more like sobbing.

It was not the near-accident that had shaken him, or the continuing sightings of Amaranth, not even the bug lady and what she had been saying. It was her eyes. Such black, hopeless pits of despondency, lacking even the wish to save herself, let alone the ability to try. He had never seen eyes like it before. Or if he had, they had been too distant to make out. Far across a polluted lake. Heat from fires obscuring any characteristics from view.

In the tunnels faces flashed by, pressing out from the century-old brickwork, lit only by borrowed light from the tube train. They strained forward to look in at Adam, catching only the briefest glimpse of him but seeing all. They were Amaranth. Still watching him— still watching *over* him.

And if Howards had been right—and Adam could no longer find any reason to doubt him—still viewing him as sport.

*   *   *

The hotel was a smart four-star within a stone's throw of Leicester Square. His room was spacious and tastefully decorated, with a direct outside telephone, a TV, a luxurious *en-suite* and a mini-bar charging exorbitant prices for mere dribbles of alcohol. Adam opened three miniatures of whiskey, added some ice he had fetched from the dispenser in the corridor and sat back on the bed, trying not to see those transparent faces in his mind's eye. Surely they couldn't be in there as well? On the backs of his eyelids, invading his self as they'd invaded his life? He'd never seen them there, at least. . . .

And really, even if he had, he could feel no anger toward them.

After he had finished the whiskey and his nerves had settled, he picked up the phone and dialed home. His own voice shocked him for a moment, and then he left a message for Alison on the machine telling her he had arrived safely, glancing at his watch as he did so. They were usually giving Jamie his dinner around this time. Maybe she was at the hospital with her mother.

He opened a ridiculously priced can of beer from the fridge and went out to stand on the small balcony. Catching sight of the busy streets seemed to draw their noise to him, and he spent the next few minutes taking in the scenery, watching people go about their business unaware that they were being observed; cars snaking along the road as if bad driving could avoid congestion, paper bags floating on the breeze above all this, pigeons huddled on sills and rooftops, an aircraft passing silently high overhead. He wondered

who was on the plane, and whether they had any inkling that they were being watched from the ground at
that instant. He looked directly across the street into a
third-story office window. A woman was kneeling in
front of a photocopier, hands buried in its mechanical
guts as she tried unsuccessfully to clear a paper jam.
Did she know she was being watched, he wondered?
Did the hairs on the nape of her neck prickle, her back
tingle? She smacked the machine with the palm of her
hand, stood and started to delve into her left nostril
with one toner-blackened finger. No, she didn't know.
None of these people knew, not really. A few of them
saw him standing up here and walked on, a little more
self-consciously than before, but many were in their
own small world.

Most of them did not even know that there was a
bigger world out there at all. Much bigger. Way beyond the solid confines of earth, wind, fire and water.

He took another swig of beer and tried to change
the way he was looking. He switched viewpoints from
observer to observed, seeking to spy out whoever or
whatever was watching him. Down in the street the
pedestrians all had destinations in mind, and like most
city-dwellers they rarely looked higher than their own
eye level. Nothing above that height was of interest to
them. In the hive of the buildings opposite the hotel,
office workers sat tapping at computers, stood by coffee machines, huddled around desks or tables, flirted,
never imagining that there was anything worth looking
at beyond the air-conditioned confines of their do-
mains.

He was being watched. He knew it. He could feel

217

it. It was a feeling he had become more than used to since Howards had forced him, eventually, to entertain the truth of what was happening to him.

The rooftops were populated by pigeons; no strange faces up there. The street below was a battlefield of business, and if Amaranth were down there, Adam certainly could not pick them out. The small balconies to each side of him were unoccupied. He even turned around and stared back into his own room, fully expecting to find a face pressed through the wall like a wax corpse, or the wardrobe door hanging ajar. But he saw nothing. Wherever they were, they were keeping themselves well hidden for now.

A car tooted angrily and he looked back down over the railing—straight into the eyes of the bug lady. She was standing on the pavement outside the building opposite the hotel, staring up at Adam, her gaze unwavering. Even from this distance, Adam could see the hopelessness therein.

There was little he could do. He went back inside and closed and locked the doors behind him, pulled the curtains, grabbed a miniature of gin from the fridge because the whiskey had run out.

He tried calling Alison again, but his own voice greeted him from the past. He had recorded that message before the flight, before the crash, before Amaranth. He was a different person now. He dialed and listened again, knowing how foolish it was: yes, a different person. He had known so little back then.

"Just sign on the dotted line," Maggie said. "Then the deal's done and you'll have to sleep with me for what I've done for you."

"Mags, I'd sleep with you even if you hadn't just closed the biggest deal of my life, you know that." Maggie was close to seventy years old, glamorous in her own way, and Adam was sure she'd never had enough sex in her earlier years. Sometimes, when he really thought about it, he wondered just how serious she was when she joked and flirted.

He picked up the contract and scanned it one more time. Sixth reading now, at least. He hated committing to anything, and there was little as final and binding as signing a contract. True, the gallery had yet to countersign, but once he'd scrawled his name along the bottom there was little chance to change anything.

And besides, this was too good to be true.

He wondered how Alison and Jamie were. And then he wondered *where* they were as well.

It'll happen to you, too, the bug lady had screamed at him, pus dripping from her lips, insects fleeing her body as if they already thought she was dead.

You'll lose them, Howards had stated plainly.

"Mags . . ." he muttered, uncertain of exactly what he was about to say. The alcohol had gone to his head, especially after the celebratory champagne Maggie had brought to his room. His aim had been good. The cork had gone flying through the door and out over the street, and he'd used that as an excuse to take another look. The bug lady had gone, but Adam had been left feeling uncomfortable, unsettled.

That, and his missing wife and son.

The contract wavered on the bed in front of him, uncertain, unreal. He held the pen above the line and imagined signing his name, tried to see what effect it would have. Surely this was his own good fortune, not something thrown his way by Amaranth? But he had only been working in fire since the accident. . . .

"Mags, I just need to call Alison." He put the pen down. "I haven't told her I've arrived safely yet."

Maggie nodded, eyebrows raised.

Adam dialed and fully expected to hear his own voice once more, but Alison snapped up the line. "Yes?"

"Honey?"

"Oh Adam, you're there. I got your messages, but I was hoping you'd ring. . . ."

"Anything the matter?"

"No, no . . . well, Mum's taken a turn for the worse. They think . . . she arrested this afternoon."

"Oh, no."

"Look, how's it going? Maggie there with you? Tell her to keep her hands off my husband."

"Honey, I'll come home."

Alison sighed down the phone. "No, you won't. Just call me, okay? Often? Make it feel like you're really here and I'll be fine. But you do what you've got to do to make our damn fortune."

He held the phone between his cheek and shoulder and made small talk with his wife, asked how Jamie was, spoke to his son. And at the same time he signed the three copies of the contract and slid them across the bed to Maggie.

"Love you," he said at last. Alison loved him too. They left it at that.

"Shall we go out to celebrate?" Maggie asked.

Adam shook his head. "Do you mind if we just stay

in the hotel? Have a meal in the restaurant, perhaps? I'm tired and a bit drunk, and . . ." *And I don't want to go outside in case the bug lady's there,* he thought. *I don't want to hear what she's telling me.*

In the restaurant an ice sculpture was melting slowly beneath the lights, shedding shards of glittering movement as pearls of water slid down its sides. As they sat down Adam thought he saw it twitch, its face twist to watch him, limbs flex. He glanced away and looked again. Still he could not be sure. Well, if Amaranth chose to sit and watch him eat—celebrate his success, his good luck—what could he do about it?

What could he do?

The alcohol and the buzz of signing the deal and the experience of meeting the bug lady, all combined to drive Adam into a sort of dislocated stupor. He heard what Maggie said, he smelled the food, he tasted the wine, but they were all vicarious experiences, as if he were really residing elsewhere for the evening, not inside his own body. Later, he recalled only snippets of conversation, brief glimpses of events. The rest vanished into blankness.

"This will lead to a lot more work," Maggie said, her words somehow winging their way between the frantic chords of the piano player. "And the gallery says that they normally sell at least half the paintings at any exhibition."

A man coughed and spat his false teeth onto his table. The restaurant bustled with restrained laughter. The shadows of movement seemed to follow seconds behind.

A waiter kept filling his glass with wine, however much he objected.

The ice sculpture reduced, but the shape within it stayed the same size. Over the course of the evening, one of the Amaranth things was revealed to him. Nobody else seemed to notice.

The ice cream tasted rancid.

Maggie touched his knee beneath the table and suggested they go to his room.

Next, he was alone in his bed. He must have said something to her, something definite and final about the way their relationship should work. He hoped he had not been cruel.

Something floated above his bed, a shadow within shadows. "Do not deny us," it said inside his head, a cautionary note in its voice. "Believe in us. Do not deny us."

Then it was morning, and his head thumped with a killer hangover, and although he remembered the words and the sights of last night, he was sure it had all been a dream.

Adam managed to flag down a taxi as soon as he stepped from the hotel. He was dropped off outside the gallery, and as he crossed the pavement he bumped into an old man hurrying along with his head down. They exchanged apologies and turned to continue on their way, but then stopped. They stared at each other for a moment, frowning, all the points of recognition slotting into place almost visibly as their faces relaxed and the tentative smiles came.

"You were on the horse," Adam said. "The unicorn."

"You were the disbeliever. You believe now?" The man's smile was fixed, like a painting overlying his true feelings. There was something in his eyes . . . something about giving in.

"I do," Adam said, "but I've met some people . . . a lucky one, and an unlucky one . . . and I'm beginning to feel scared." Verbalizing it actually brought it home to him; he *was* scared.

The man leaned forward and Adam could smell expensive cologne on his skin. "Don't deny Amaranth," he said. "You can't anyway, nobody ever has. But don't even think about it."

Adam stepped back as if the man had spat at him. He remembered Howards telling him that he would lose his family, and the bug lady spewing promises darker than that.

He wondered how coincidental his meeting these three people was. "How is your family?" he asked.

The unicorn man averted his gaze. "Not as lucky as me."

Adam looked up at the imposing façade of the gallery, the artistically wrought modern gargoyles that were never meant for anything other than ornamentation. Maybe they should have been imbued with a power, he thought. Because there really were demons. . . .

He wondered how Molly was, whether she had woken yet. He should telephone Alison to find out, but if he hesitated here any longer he may just turn around and flee back home. Leave all this behind— all this success, this promise, this hope for a comfortable and long sought-after future . . .

When he looked back down, the man had vanished along the street, disappearing into the crowds. *Don't deny Amaranth*, he had said. Adam shook his head. How could anyone?

He stepped through the circular doors and into the air-conditioned vestibule of the gallery building. Marble solidified the area, with only occasional soft oases of comfortable seating breaking it up here and there. Maggie rose from one of these seats, two men standing behind her. The gallery owners, Adam knew. The men who had signed checks ready to give him.

"Adam!" Maggie called across to him.

His mobile phone rang. He flipped it open and answered. "Alison?"

"Adam, your lateness just manages to fall into the league of fashionable," Maggie cooed.

"Honey. Adam, Mum's died. She went a few minutes ago. Oh . . ." Alison broke into tears and Adam wanted to reach through the phone, hug her to him, kiss and squeeze and love her until all of this went away. He glanced up at the men looking expectantly at him, at Maggie chattering away, and he could hear nothing but his wife crying down the phone to him.

"I'll be home soon," Adam said. "Alison?"

"Yes." Very quietly. A plea as well as a confirmation.

"I'll be home soon. Is Jamie all right?"

A wet laugh. "Watching *Teletubbies*. Bless him."

"Three hours. Give me three hours and I'll be home."

"Adam?" Maggie stood before him now. It had taken her this long to see that something was wrong. "What is it?"

"Alison's mother just died."

224

"Oh . . . oh shit."

"You got those contracts, Mags?"

She nodded and handed him a paper file.

He looked up at the two men, at their fixed smiles, their money-maker's suits, the calculating worry lines around their eyes. "This isn't art," he said, and he tore the contracts in half.

As he left the building, he reflected that it was probably the most artistic thing he had ever done.

There was a train due to leave five minutes after he arrived at the station, as he knew there would be. He was lucky like that. Not so his family, of course, his wife, or his wife's mother. But *he* was lucky.

He should not have taken the train—he should have denied Amaranth and the conditional luck they had bestowed upon him—but he needed to be with Alison. *One more time,* he thought. *Just this one last time.*

They made themselves known in the station. He had been aware of them following him since the gallery, curving in and out of the ground like sea serpents, wending their way through buildings, flying high above him and merging with clouds of pigeons. Sometimes he caught sight of one reflected in a shop window, but whenever he turned around, it was gone.

At the station, the four of them were standing together at the far end of the platform. People passed them by. People walked *through* them, shuddering and glancing around with startled expressions as if someone had just stepped on their graves. Nobody else seemed to see them.

Adam boarded the train at the nearest end. As he

stepped up, he saw Amaranth doing the same several carriages along.

He sat in the first seat he found and they were there within seconds.

"Go away," he whispered. "Leave me alone." He hoped nobody could hear or see him mumbling to himself.

"You cannot deny us," their voice said. "Think of what you will lose."

Adam was thinking of what he would gain. His family, safe and sound.

"Not necessarily."

Was that humor there? Was Amaranth laughing at him, enjoying this? And Adam suddenly realized that an emotionless, indifferent Amaranth was not the most frightening thing he could think of. No, an Amaranth possessed of humor—irony—was far more terrifying.

They were sitting at his table. He had a window seat, two sat opposite, a third in the seat beside him. The fourth rested on the table, sometimes halfway through the window glass. The acceleration did not seem to concern the thing, which leaned back with one knee raised and its face pointing at the ceiling, for all the world looking as if it were sunbathing.

So far, thankfully, nobody else had taken the seats.

"Leave me alone," he said again, "and leave my family alone as well." His voice was rising, he could not help it. Anger and fear combined to make a heady brew.

"We are not touching your family," Amaranth soothed. "Whatever happens there simply . . . happens. Our interest is in you."

"But why?"

"That is our business, not yours. But you are in danger . . . in danger of denying us, refuting our existence."

"You're nothing but nightmares." He stared down at the table so that he did not have to look at them, but from the corner of his eye he could see the hand belonging to the one on the table, see it flexing and flowing as it moved.

"Since when did a dream give a man the power to survive?"

He glared up at them then, hating the smug superiority in their voice. "Power of the mind!" he could not help shouting. "Now leave me! I can't see you anymore."

Surprisingly, Amaranth vanished.

Pale faces turned away from him as he scanned along the carriage. Everyone must have heard him—he had been very loud—but this was London, he thought. Strange things happened in London all the time. Strange people. The blessed and the cursed mixed within feet of each other, each cocooned in their own blanket of fate. Maybe he had simply seen beyond his, for a time.

He had been unfaithful to Alison only once. It had been a foolish thing, a one-hour stand, not even bearing the importance to last a night. A woman in a bar—he was drunk with his friends—an instant attraction, a few whiskeys too many, a damp screw against the moldy wall behind the pub. Unsatisfying, dirty more than erotic, frantic rather than tender. He had felt forlorn, but it had taken only days for him to drive it down in his mind, believe it was a fantasy rather than something that had truly happened.

On the surface, at least.

Deep down, in places he only visited in the darkest, most melancholy times, he knew that it was real. He had done it. And there was no escape from that.

Now, he tried to imagine that Amaranth was a product of his imagination, and those people he had met—Howards, the bug lady, the man who had ridden the unicorn—were all coincidental players in a fantasy of his own creation. . . .

And all the while, he knew deep down that this was bullshit. He could camouflage the truth with whatever colors he desired, but it was all still there, plain as day in the end.

They left him alone until halfway through the journey. He had been watching, trying to see them between the trees rushing by the window, looking for their faces in clouds, behind hedges, in the eyes of the other passengers on the train. Nothing. With no hidden faces to see, he realized just how under siege he had been feeling.

He began to believe they had gone for good. He began to believe his own lies.

And then the woman sat opposite him.

She was beautiful, voluptuous, raven-haired, well-dressed, clothes accentuating rather than revealing her curves. Adam averted his eyes and looked out the window, but he could not help glancing back at her, again and again. Yes. She was truly gorgeous.

"I hate trains," she said. "So boring." Then her unshod foot dug into his crotch.

He gasped, unable to move, all senses focusing on his groin as her toes kneaded, stroked and pressed him to erection. He closed his eyes and thought of Alison, crying while Jamie caused chaos around her. Her father was long dead and there was no close family nearby, so unless she had called one of her friends around to sit with her, she would be there on her own, weeping. . . .

And then he imagined himself guiding this woman into the cramped confines of a train toilet, sitting on the seat and letting her impale herself upon him, using the movements of the train to match their rhythms.

He opened his eyes and knew that she was thinking the same thing. Her foot began to work faster. He stared out the window and saw a plane trail being born high above.

Realized how tentative the other passengers' grips on life were.

Saw just how fortunate he was to still be here.

He reached down, grasped the woman's ankle and forced her foot away from him. *This isn't luck,* he thought, *not for my family, not even for me. It's fantasy, maybe, but not luck. What's lucky about betraying my wife when she needs me the most?*

They're desperate. Amaranth is desperate to keep me as they want me.

No, he thought.

"No."

"What?" the woman said, frowning, looking around, staring back at him. Her eyes went wide. "Oh Jesus . . . oh, I'm . . ." She stood quickly, hurried along the carriage and disappeared from sight.

Amaranth returned. "Do not deny us," the voice said, deeper than he had ever heard it, stronger.

He closed his eyes. The vision he had was so powerful, quick and sharp that he almost felt as if he were physically experiencing it then and there. He smelled the vol-au-vents and the caviar and the champagne at the exhibition, he saw Maggie's cheerful face and the gallery owners nodding to him that he had just sold another painting, he tasted the tang of nerves as one of the viewers raved about the painting of his they had just bought, minutes ago, for six thousand pounds.

He forced his eyes open against a stinging tiredness, rubbed his face and pinched his skin to wake himself up. "No," he said. "My wife needs me."

"You will regret it!" Amaranth screeched, and Adam thought he was hearing it for the first time as it really was. The hairs stood on the back of his neck, his balls tingled, his stomach dropped. The things came from out of the table and the seats and reached for him, swiping out with clear, sharp nails, driving their hands into his flesh and grabbing his bones, plucking at him, swirling and screaming and cursing in ways he could never know.

None of them touched him.

They could *not*.

They could not *touch* him.

Adam smiled. "There's a bit of luck," he whispered.

And with one final roar, they disappeared.

Half an hour from the station he called Alison and arranged for her to come and collect him. He knew it was false, but she sounded virtually back to normal, more in control. She said she had already ordered some Chinese takeaway and bought a bottle of wine. He could barely imagine sitting at home, eating and drinking and chatting—one of their favorite times together—with Molly lying dead less than two miles away. He would see her passing in every movement of Alison's head, every twitch of her eyelids. She would be there with them more than ever. He was heading for strange times.

As the train pulled into the station, his mobile phone rang. It was Maggie.

"Adam, when are you coming back? Come on, artistic tempers are well and good when you're not getting anywhere, but that was plain rude. These guys really have no time for prima donnas, you know. Are you at your hotel?"

"I'm back home," Adam said, hardly believing her tone of voice. "Didn't you hear what I said, Mags? Alison's mum is dead."

"Yes, yes . . ." she said, trailing off. "Adam. The guys at the gallery have made another offer. They'll commission the artwork for the same amount, but they'll also—"

"Mags, I'm not interested. This is not . . . me. It'll change me too much."

"One hundred thousand."

Adam did not reply. He could not. His imagination, kicked into some sort of overdrive for the past few weeks, was picturing what that sort of money could do for his family.

He stood from his seat and followed the other passengers toward the exit. "No, Mags," he said, shaking his head. He saw the woman who had sat opposite him, it was obvious that she had already spotted him because her head was down, frantically searching for some unknown item in her handbag. "No. That's not me. I didn't do any of it."

"You didn't do those paintings?"

Adam thought about it for a moment as he shuffled along the aisle: the midnight awakenings when he knew he had to work; the smell of oils and coffee as time went away, and it was just him and the painting; his burning finger and hand and arm muscles after several hours work, the feeling that he truly was creating in fire.

"No, Mags," he said, "I didn't." He turned the phone off and stepped onto the platform.

Alison and Jamie were there to meet him. Alison was the one who had lost her mother, but on seeing them it was Adam who burst into tears. He hugged his wife and son, she crying into his neck in great wracking sobs, Jamie mumbling, "Daddy, Daddy," as he struggled to work his way back into his parents' world.

Adam picked Jamie up, kissing his forehead and unable to stop crying. *You'll lose them,* Howards had said. How dare he? How dare he talk about someone else's family like that?

"I'm so sorry," he said to Alison.

She smiled grimly, a strange sight in combination with her tears and puffy eyes and gray complexion. "Such a bloody stupid way to go," she managed to gasp before her own tears came again.

Adam touched her cheek. "I'll drive us home."

As they walked along the platform toward the bridge

to the car park, Adam looked around. Faces stared at him from the train—one of them familiar, the woman who had been rubbing him with her foot—but none of them were Amaranth. Some were pale and distant, others almost transparent in their dissatisfaction with their lot, but all were human.

The open girders of the roof above were lined only with pigeons.

The waste-ground behind the station was home to wild cats and rooks and rusted shopping carts. Nothing else.

Around them, humanity went about its toils. Businessmen and travelers and students dodged each other across the platform. None of them looked at Adam and his family, or if they did they glanced quickly away. Everyone knew grief when they saw it, and most people respected its fierce privacy.

In the car park Alison sat in the passenger seat and Adam strapped Jamie into his seat in the back. "You a good boy?" he asked. "You been a good boy for your mummy?"

"Tiger, tiger!" Jamie hissed. "Daddy, Daddy, tiger." He smiled, showing the gap-toothed grin that never failed to melt Adam's heart. Then he giggled.

He was not looking directly at Adam. His gaze was directed slightly to the left, over Adam's shoulder.

Adam spun around.

Nothing.

He scanned the car park. A hundred cars, and Amaranth could be hiding inside any one of them, watching, waiting, until they could touch him once more.

He climbed into the car and locked the doors.

"Why did you do that?" Alison asked.

"Don't know." He shook his head. She was right. Locked doors would be no protection.

They headed away from the station and into town. They lived on the outskirts on the other side. A couple of streets away lay the small restaurant where Adam had talked with Howards. He wondered where the old man was now. Whether he was still here. Whether he remained concerned for Adam's safety, his life, his luck, since Adam had stormed out and told him to mind his own business.

Approaching the traffic lights at the foot of the river bridge, Adam began to slow down.

A hand reached out of the seat between his legs and clasped the wheel. He could feel it, icy-cool where it touched his balls, a burning cold where it actually passed through the meat of his inner thighs.

"No!" he screamed. Jamie screeched and began to cry. Alison looked up in shock.

"What? Adam?"

"Oh no, don't you fucking—" He was already stamping hard on the brakes, but it did no good.

"Come see us again," Amaranth said between his ears, and the hand twisted the wheel violently to the left.

Adam fought. A van loomed ahead of them, scaffold poles protruding from its tied-open rear doors. Terrible images of impalement and bloodied, rusted metal leaped into his mind and he pulled harder, muscles burning with the strain of fighting the hand. The windscreen flowed into the face of one of the things, still expressionless but exuding malice all the same. Adam looked straight through its eyes at the van.

The brakes were not working.

"Tiger!" Jamie shouted.

At the last second the wheel turned a fraction to the right and they skimmed the van, metal screeching on metal, the car shuddering with the impact.

Thank God, Adam thought.

And then the old woman stepped from the pavement directly in front of them.

This time, Amaranth did not need to turn the wheel. Adam did it himself. And he heard the sickening *crump* as the car hit the woman sideways on, and he felt the vehicle tilting as it mounted the pavement, and he saw a lamppost splitting the windscreen in two. His family screamed.

There was a terrible coldness as eight unseen hands closed around his limbs.

The car gave the lamppost a welcoming embrace.

"I'm dead," Adam said. "I've been dead for a long time. I'm floating in the Atlantic. I know this because nothing that has happened is possible. I've been dreaming. Maybe the dead can dream." He moved his left hand and felt his father's lost watch chafe his wrist.

A hand grasped his throat and quicksilver nails dug in. "Do the dead hurt?" the familiar voice intoned.

Adam tried to scream, but he could not draw a breath.

Around him, the world burned.

"Keep still and you will not die . . . yet."

"Alison!" Adam began to struggle against the hands holding him down. The sky was smudged with greasy black smoke, and the stench reminded him of rotten roadkill he had found in a ditch when he was a boy, a dead creature too decayed to identify. Something wet was dripping on him, wet and warm. One of the things was leaning over him. Its mouth was open and the liquid forming on its lips was transparent, and of the same consistency as its body. It was shedding pieces of itself onto him.

"You will listen to us," Amaranth said.

"Jamie! Alison!"

"You will see them again soon enough. First, listen. You pledged to believe in us and to never deny us. You have reneged. Reaffirm your pledge. We gave you a gift, but without faith we are—"

"I don't want your gift," Adam said, still struggling to stand. He could see more now, as if this world were opening up to him as he came to. Above the heads of the things standing around him, the ragged walls and roofs of shattered buildings stood out against the hazy sky. Flames licked here and there, smoke rolled along the ground, firestorms did their work in some unseen middle distance. Ash floated down and stuck to his skin like warm snow. He thought of furnaces and ovens, concentration camps, lime pits. . . .

"But you have it already. You have the good luck we bestowed upon you. And you have used it . . . we have seen . . . we have observed."

"Good luck? Was that crash good luck?"

"You avoided the van that would have killed you. You survived. We held you back from death."

"You *steered* me!"

Amaranth said nothing.

"What of Alison? Jamie?"

Once more, the things displayed a loathsome hint of emotion. "Who knows?" the voice said slowly, drawing out the last word with relish.

At last Adam managed to stand, but only because the things had moved back and freed him. "Leave me be," he said, wondering if begging would help, or perhaps flattery. "Thank you for saving me, that first time . . . I know you did, and I'm grateful because my wife has a husband, my son has a father. But please leave me be." All he wished for was to see his family again.

Amaranth picked him up slowly, the things using one hand each, lifting and lifting, until he was suspended several feet above the ground. From up there he could see all around, view the devastated landscape surrounding him—and he realized at last where he was.

Through a gap in the buildings to his left, the glint of violent waters. Silhouetted against this, dancing in the flickering flames that were eating at it even now, a small figure hung crucified.

"Oh, no."

"Be honored," Amaranth said, "you are the first to visit both places." They dropped him to the ground and stood back. "Run."

"What? Where?" He was winded, certain he had cracked a rib. It felt like a hot coal in his side.

"Run."

"Why?"

And then he saw why.

Around the corner, where this shattered street met the next, capered a horde of burning people. Some

237

of them had only just caught aflame, beating at clothes and hair as they ran. Others were engulfed, arms waving, flaming pieces of them falling as they made an impossible dash away from the agony. There were smaller shapes among them—children— just as doomed as the rest. Some of them screamed, those who still had vocal cords left to make any sound. Others, those too far gone, sizzled and spat.

Adam staggered, wincing with the pain in his side, and turned to run. Amaranth had moved down the street behind him and stood staring, all their eyes upon him. He sprinted toward them. They receded back along the rubble-strewn street without seeming to walk. Every step he took moved them farther away.

He felt heat behind him and a hand closed over his shoulder, the same shoulder the bug lady had grasped. Someone screaming, pleading, a high-pitched sound as the acrid stink of burning clothes scratched at his nostrils. The flames crept across his shoulder and down onto his chest, but they were extinguished almost immediately by something wet splashing across him.

He looked down. There were no burns on his clothing and his chest was dry.

Adam shook the hand from him and ran. He passed a shop where someone lay half in, half out of the doorway, a dog chewing on the weeping stump of one of her legs. She was still alive. Her eyes followed him as he dashed by, as if coveting his ability to run. He recognized those eyes. He even knew that face, although when he had first seen her, the bug lady had seemed more alive.

"Let me back!" he shouted at the figures receding along the decimated street ahead of him. From behind, he heard thumps as burning people hit the ground to melt into pools of fat and charred bone. He risked a look over his shoulder and saw even more of them, new victims spewing from dilapidated doorways and side alleys to join in the flaming throng.

Someone walked out into the street ahead of him, limping on crutches, staring at the ground. The figure looked up and the expression that passed across her face was one of relief. Adam passed her by—he only saw it was a woman when he drew level—and heard the feet of the burning horde trample her into the dirt.

"Let me back, you bastards!" The last time he was here—although he had been on the other side of the lake, of course, staring across and pitying those poor unfortunates on this side—he had not known what was happening to him. Now he did. Now he knew that there was a way back, if only it was granted to him.

"You are really a very interesting one," the voice said as loud as ever, even though Amaranth stood in the distance. "You will be . . . fun."

As Adam tripped over a half-full skull, the burning people fell across him and a voice started shouting again. "Tiger! Tiger!" It went from a shout to a scream, an unconscious, childish exhalation of terror and panic.

The world was on its side, and the legs of the burning people milled beyond the shattered windscreen. One of them was squatting down, reaching in, grasping at his arms even as he tried to push them away.

Something still dripped onto him. He looked up. Alison was suspended above him in the passenger seat, the seatbelt holding her there, holding in the pieces that were still intact. The lamppost had done something to her. She was no longer whole. She had changed. Adam snapped his eyes shut as something else parted from her and hit his shoulder.

Heat gushed and caressed his face, but then there was a gentle ripping sound above him, and coppery blood washed the flames away from his skin like his wife brushing crumbs from his stubble. The flames could never take him. Not when he was such a lucky man.

You are the first to visit both places, Amaranth's voice echoed like the vague memory of pain. *You will be . . . fun.*

"Tiger!"

Jamie?

"Jamie!"

Flames danced around him once more. Fingers snagged his jacket. A hand reached in bearing a knife and he crunched down into shattered glass as his seatbelt was sliced. Something else fell from above him as he was dragged out, a final present, a last, lasting gift from his Alison. As he was hauled through the windscreen, hands beating at the burning parts of him, his doomed son screaming for him from the doomed car, he wondered whether it was a part of her that he had ever seen before.

He was laying out on the lawn. It had not been cut for a long time because his riding lawnmower had broken down. Besides, he liked the wild appearance it gave the garden. Alison had liked wild. She had loved the countryside; she had been agnostic, but she had said the smells and sounds and sights made her feel closer to God.

Adam felt close to no one, certainly not God. Not with Amaranth peering at him from the woods sometimes, following him on his trips into town, watching as good fortune and bad luck juggled with his life and health.

No, certainly not God.

Alison had been buried alongside her mother over a year ago. He had not been to the cemetery since. He remembered her in his own way—he was still painting—and he did not wish to be reminded of what her ruined body had become beneath the ground. But he was reminded every day. Every morning, on his bus trip into town to visit Jamie in the hospital, he was reminded. Because he so wanted his son to join her.

That was guilt. That was suffering. That was the sickest irony about the whole thing. *He's a lucky lad,* the doctors would still tell him, even after a year. *He's a fighter. He'll wake up soon, you'll see. He'll have scars, yes* . . . And then Adam would ask about infection and the doctors would nod, yes, there has been something over the last week or two, inevitable with burns, but we've got it under control, it's just bad luck that . . .

And so on.

His wife, dead. His son in a coma from which he had only awakened three times, and each time some minor complication had driven him back under. He was growing up dead. And still Adam went to him every day to talk to him, to whisper in his ear, to try and bring him around with his favorite nursery rhymes and the secret dad-voices he had used on him when things were good, when life was normal. When chance was still a factor in his existence, and fate was uncertain.

He looked across at the house. It was big, bought with Alison's life insurance, their old home sold for a good profit to the couple who had wanted it so much. This new property had an acre of land, a glazed rooftop studio with many panes already cracked or missing, a Mercedes in the driveway—a prison. A Hell. His own manufactured Hell, perhaps to deny the idea that such a grand home could be seen as fortunate, lucky to come by. The place was a constant reminder of his lost family because he had made it so. No new start for him.

The walls of the house were lined with his own portraits of Alison and Jamie. Some of them were bright and full of sunshine and light and positive memories. Others contained thoughts that only he could read— bad memories of the crash—and what he had seen of Alison and heard of Jamie before being dragged out from the car. The reddest of these paintings hung near the front door for all visitors to see.

Not that he had many visitors. Until yesterday.

Howards had tracked him down. Adam had let him in, knowing it was useless to fight, and knowing also that he truly wanted to hear what the old man had to say.

"I've found a way out," he had whispered. "I tried it last week . . . I injected myself with poison, then used the antidote at the last minute. But I could have done it. I could have gone on. They weren't watching me at the time."

"Why didn't you?"

"Well . . . I've come to terms with it. Life. As it is. I just wanted to test the idea. Prove that I was still in control of myself."

Adam had nodded, but he did not understand.

"I thought it only fair to offer you the chance," Howards had said.

Now, Adam knew that he had to take that chance. Whether Jamie ever returned or not—and his final screams, his shouts of *Tiger! Tiger!*, had convinced Adam that his son had been the twitching shape on the burning cross—he could never be a good father to him. Not with Amaranth following him, watching him. Not when he knew what they had done.

Killed his wife.

Given his son bad luck.

Yesterday afternoon he had been lucky enough to find someone willing to sell him a gun, the weapon with which he would blow his own brains out. And that, he thought, perfectly summed up what his life had become.

"Oh, look," Adam muttered, "a four-leaf clover." He flicked the little plant and sighed, pushing himself to his feet, stretching. He had been laying on the grass for a long time.

He walked across the lawn and onto the gravel driveway, past the Mercedes parked mock-casual. Its tires were flat and the engine rusted through, although it was only a year old. One of a bad batch, he had thought, and he still tried to convince himself of that, even after all this time.

He entered the house and passed into the study.

Two walls were lined with moldy books he had never read, and never would read. The portraits of the people he loved stared down at him and he should have felt at peace, should have felt comforted, but he did not. There was a large map on one wall, a thousand intended destinations marked in red, the half dozen places he had visited pinned green. Travel was no longer on his agenda, neither was reading. He could go anywhere on his own because he had the means to do so, but he no longer felt the desire. Not now that his family was lost to him.

He was about to take a journey of a different kind. Somewhere even stranger than the places he had already seen. Stranger than anyone had seen, more terrifying, more—final. After the past year he was keener than ever to find his way there.

And he had a map. It was in the bureau drawer. A .44 Magnum, gleaming snakelike silver, slick to the touch, cold, impersonal. He hugged it between his legs to warm it. May as well feel comfortable for his final seconds.

Outside, the fourth leaf on the clover glowed brightly and then disappeared into a pinprick of light. A transparent finger rose from the ground to scoop it up. Then it was gone.

"Well," Adam said to the house, empty but alive with the memories he had brought here, planted and allowed to grow. "It wasn't bad to begin with . . . but it could have been better."

He heard footsteps approaching along the gravel driveway, frantic footsteps pounding toward the house.

"Adam!" someone shouted, emotion giving the voice an androgynous lilt.

It may have been Howards, regretting the news he had brought.

Or perhaps it was Amaranth? Realizing that he had slipped their attention for just too long. Knowing, finally, that he would defeat them.

Whoever. It was the last sound he would hear.

He placed the barrel of the gun inside his mouth, angled it upward and pulled the trigger.

The first thing he heard was Howards.

". . . bounced off your skull and shattered your knee. They took your leg off too. But I suppose that won't really bother you much. The doctors say you were so lucky to survive. But then, they would."

The shuffle of feet, the creak of someone standing from a plastic chair.

"I wish you could hear me. I wish you knew how sorry I am, Adam. I thought perhaps you could defeat them. . . ."

He could not turn to see Howards. He saw nothing but the cracked ceiling. A polystyrene tile had shifted in its grid, and a triangle of darkness stared down at him. Perhaps there were eyes hidden within its gloom even now.

"I'm sorry."

Footsteps as Howards left.

With a great effort, one that burned into his muscles

and set them aflame, Adam lifted his hands. And he felt what was left of his head.

A face pressed down at him from the ceiling, lifeless, emotionless, transparent but for darker stripes across its chin and cheeks. Another joined it, then two more.

They watched him for quite some time.

For all the world, Adam wished he could look away.

Naming of Parts

"A child grows up when he realizes that he will die."
                                   —proverb

That night, something tried to break into the house.
Jack heard the noises as he lay awake staring at the
ceiling, attempting to see sense in the shadowy cracks
that scarred the paintwork. The sounds were insistent
and intelligent, and before long they were fingering
not only at window latches and handles, but also at
the doorways of his mind.

He liked listening to the night before he went to
sleep, and out here in the country there was much to
hear. Sometimes he was afraid, but then he would
name all the different parts that went to make up that
fear and it would go away. *A sound I cannot identify.*
A shape I cannot see. Footsteps that may be human, but
which are most likely animal. There's nothing to be
afraid of; there are no monsters. Dad and Mum both say
so; there are no such things as monsters.

So he would lie there and listen to the hoots and
rustles and groans and cries, content in the knowledge
that there was nothing to fear. All the while the blan-

kets would be his shield, the bedside light his protector and the gentle grumble of the television from downstairs his guarantee.

But that night—the night all guarantees were voided—there were few noises beyond his bedroom window, and with less to hear, there was more to be afraid of. Against the silence every snapped twig sounded louder, each rustle of fur across masonry was singled out for particular attention by his galloping imagination. It meant that there was something out there to frighten everything else into muteness.

And then the careful caress of fingertips across cold glass.

Jack sat up in bed and held his breath. Weak moonlight filtered through the curtains, but other than that his room was filled with darkness. He clutched at his blankets to retain the heat. Something hooted in the distance, but the call was cut off sharply, leaving the following moments painfully empty.

Click click click. Fingernails picking at old, dried glazing putty, perhaps? It sounded like it was coming from outside and below, but it could just as easily have originated within his room, behind the flowing curtains, something frantically trying to get out rather than break in.

He tried naming his fears, this time unsuccessfully; he was not entirely sure what was scaring him.

A floorboard creaked on the landing, the one just outside the bathroom door. Three creaks down, three back up. Jack's heart beat faster and louder and he let out a gasp, waiting for more movement, listening for the subtle scratch of fingernails at his bedroom door.

He could not see the handle, it was too dark, it may even be turning now—

Another creak from outside, and then he heard his mother's voice and his father hissing back at her.

"Dad!" Jack croaked. There were other sounds now: the soft thud of something tapping at windows; a whispering sound, like a breeze flowing through the ivy on the side of the house, though the air was dead calm tonight.

"Dad!" He called louder this time, fear giving his voice a sharp edge to cut through the dark.

The door opened and a shadow entered, silhouetted against the landing light. It moved toward him, unseen feet creaking more boards. "It's okay, son," his father whispered. "Just stay in bed. Mum will be in with you now. Won't you, Janey?"

Jack's mother edged into the room and crossed to the bed, cursing as she stumbled on something he'd left on the floor. There was always stuff on the floor in Jack's room. His dad called it Jack debris.

"What's going on, Dad?" he asked. "What's outside?"

"There's nothing outside," his father said. His voice was a monotone that Jack recognized, the one he used to tell fatherly untruths. And then Jack noticed, for the first time, that he was carrying his shotgun.

"Dad?" Jack said uncertainly. Cool fingers seemed to touch his neck, and they were not his mother's.

She hugged him to her. "Gray, you're scaring him."

"Janey—"

"Whatever . . . just be careful. Be calm."

Jack did not understand any of this. His mother hugged him and in her warmth he found the familiar comfort, though tonight it felt like a lie. He did not want this comfort, this warmth, not when there was something outside trying to get in, not when his father stood in his pajamas, shotgun closed and aimed at the wall, not broken open over his elbow as he carried it in the woods.

The woods. Thinking of them focused Jack's attention, and he finally noticed just how utterly silent it was out there. No voices or night calls, true, but no trees swishing and swaying in sleep, no sounds of life, no hint of anything existing beyond the house at all.

His father moved to the window and reached out for the curtains. Jack knew what he would find when he pulled them back—nothing. Blankness, void or infinity . . . and infinity scared Jack more than anything. How could something go on forever? What was there after it ended? Occasionally he thought he had some bright idea, but then sleep would come and steal it away by morning.

"Dad, don't, there's nothing out there!" he said, his voice betraying barely controlled panic.

"Shhh, shhh," his mother said, rocking him.

"I know," his father said without turning to offer him a smile. He grabbed a curtain and drew it aside.

Moonlight. The smell of night, a spicy dampness that seemed always to hide from the sun. And the noises again, tapping and scraping, tapping and scraping.

"Mum, don't let Dad open the window," Jack said, but his mother ignored him because she was hugging him, and that was usually enough. He would forget his bad dreams and go back to sleep. Mum would smile at the foolishness he'd spouted, but didn't she know?

Didn't she see that they were all awake, and that what he was thinking was not foolishness because his dad really was standing in his room with a shotgun, opening the window, leaning out now, aiming the weapon before him like a torch—

There was an explosion. Like an unexpected scream in the depths of night it tore through Jack's nerves, shred his childish sense of valor and set him screaming and squirming in his mother's lap. Her arms tightened around him and she screamed too. He could smell the sudden tang of her fear, could feel the dampness between her breasts as he pressed his face to her chest.

"Gray, what the fuck—"

Her words shocked Jack, but he could not lift his face to see.

"What the hell? What are you doing? What are you shooting at?"

Somewhere in the blind confusion his father came across and offered soothing words, but they were edged with his own brand of fear. Jack could not see him, but he could imagine him standing there in silence, staring at a wall and avoiding his mother's eyes. It was his way of thinking about what to say next.

He said nothing. Instead, Jack felt his dad's strong hands under his arms, lifting him up out of the warmth of his mother's fear and letting the dark kiss his sweaty skin cool.

"Dad," Jack sobbed, "I'm scared!"

His dad rocked him back and forth and whispered into his ear, but Jack could barely hear what he was saying. Instead he tried to do what he had once been told, name the parts of his fear in an attempt to identify them and set them open to view, to consideration, to understanding.

Something, outside in the dark. Dad, he saw it and shot it. The sounds, they've gone, no more picking, no more prodding at our house. Monsters, there are none of course. But if there are . . . Dad scared them off.

"Gray," his mother said, and Jack looked up sharply.

"They weren't monsters, were they, Dad?" His father did not say a word. He was shaking.

"Gray," his mum said again, standing and wrapping them both in her arms. "We should try the police again."

"You know the phone's dodgy, Janey."

"You shot at someone. We should try the police."

"*Someone?* But you saw, you—"

"Someone," Jack's mum whispered softly. "Robbers, I expect, come to steal our Jackie's things." She ruffled his hair, but Jack could not find a smile to give her.

"I heard them picking at the putty," he said. "Robbers would just smash the window. Least, they do in *The Bill.* And there's nothing else making a noise, like the fox in the woods. I always hear the fox before I go to sleep, but I haven't heard it tonight. Dad!"

His father turned and stared at him, his face unreadable.

"Did you shoot someone, Dad?"

His father shook his head. He began to smile as he pulled Jack's face into his neck, but the expression was grotesque, like one of those old gargoyles Jack had seen on churches when they were in France last year. "Of course not, Jack. I fired into the air."

But he had not fired into the air, Jack knew. He had

leaned out and aimed down. Jack could not help imagining something squirming on the ground even now, its blood running into the gravel alongside the house, screams of pain impossible because it had no jaw left to open—

"Come on," his dad said, "our room for now, son."

"Didn't you try the mobile?" Jack asked suddenly, but the look on his mother's face made him wish he hadn't.

"That's not working at all."

"I expect the batteries have run out," he said wisely.

"I expect."

His father carried him across the creaking landing and into their bedroom, a place of comfort. He dropped him gently onto the bed, and as he stood the telephone on the bedside table rang.

"I'll get it!" Jack shouted, leaping across the bed.

"Son—"

He answered in the polite manner he had been taught: "Hello, Jack Haines, how may I help you?" *It's the middle of the night,* he thought. *Who rings in the middle of the night? What am I going to hear? Do I really want to hear it, whatever it is?*

"Hey, Jackie," a voice said, masked with crackles and pauses and strange, electronic groans. "Jackie . . . the town . . . dangerous . . . get to Tewton . . . Jackie? Jackie? Ja . . . ?"

"Mandy," he said, talking both to her and his parents. "It's Mandy!"

His mother took the receiver from his hand. "Mandy? You there?" She held it to her ear for a few seconds, then glanced at Jack. "No one there," she said. "Line's dead. It did that earlier." She turned to his dad and offered the receiver, but he moved to the window and shaded his eyes so he could see out.

"She said we should go to Tewton," Jack said, trying to recall her exact words, afraid that if he did he would also remember the strange way she had spoken. Mandy never called him Jackie. "She said it was safe there."

"It's safe here," his dad said without turning around. He was holding the shotgun again and Jack wanted to believe him, wanted to feel secure.

His mum stood and moved to the window. "What's that?" Jack heard her mutter.

"Fire."

"A fire?"

His father turned and tried to smile, but it seemed to hurt. "A bonfire," he said, "over on the other side of the valley."

"At night? A bonfire in the middle of the night?" Jack asked.

His parents said nothing. His mother came back to the bed and held him, and his father remained at the window.

"It *was* Mandy," Jack said.

His mother shrugged. "I didn't hear anyone."

He tried to move away from her, but she held him tight, and he thought it was for her own comfort as much as his. He didn't like how his mum and dad sometimes talked about Mandy. He liked even less the way they often seemed to forget about her. He was old enough to know some stuff had happened—he could remember the shouting, the screaming on the last day

Mandy had been with them—but he was not really old enough to realize exactly what.

It was so quiet that Jack could hear his father's throat clicking as he breathed.

They stayed that way until morning.

"There are secrets in the night," Mandy once told him. She was sitting next to his bed, looking after him because he'd been lost in the woods. He usually liked it when Mandy talked to him, told him things, but today even she could not cheer him up. She and his parents were hardly speaking, and when they did it was to exchange nothing but nastiness.

"What do you mean?"

She smiled. "You know, Jack. Secrets. You lie awake sometimes, listening for them. Don't you? I know I do."

"I just like listening," he said, but he guessed she was right. He guessed there was more going on than most people knew, and he wanted to find out what.

"If you find a secret, sometimes it's best to keep it to yourself. Not to tell Mum and Dad."

Jack was subtly shocked at her words. Why keep something from Mum and Dad? Wasn't that lying? But Mandy answered for him.

"Sometimes, grown-ups don't understand their kid's secret. And I'll tell you one now."

He sat up in bed, all wide-eyed and snotty-nosed. He wondered why Mandy was crying.

"I'm leaving home. At the weekend. Going to live in Tewton. But Jack, please, don't tell Mum and Dad until I'm gone."

255

Jack blinked as tears stung his eyes. Mandy hugged him and kissed his cheeks.

He didn't want his sister to go. But he listened to what she said, and he did not tell their parents the secret.

Three days later, Mandy left home.

In the morning Jack went to fetch the milk, but the milkman hadn't been there. His father appeared behind him in the doorway, scowling out at the sunlight and the dew steaming slowly from the ground, hands resting lightly on his son's shoulders.

Something had been playing on Jack's mind all night, ever since it happened. An image had seeded there, grown and expanded and, in the silence of his parents' bedroom where none of them had slept, it had blossomed into an all-too-plausible truth. Now, with morning providing an air of normality—though it remained quieter than usual, and stiller—he was certain of what he would find. He did not *want* to find it, that was for sure, yet he had to see.

He darted away from the back door and was already at the corner of the house before his dad called after him. The shout almost stopped him in his tracks because there was an unbridled panic there, a desperation . . . but then he was looking around the side of the cottage at something he had least expected.

There was no body, no blood, no disturbed flower bed where someone had thrashed around in pain. He crunched along the gravel path, his father with him now, standing guard above and behind.

"You *didn't* shoot anyone," Jack said, and the sense of relief was vast.

Then he saw the rosebush.

The petals had been stripped, and they lay scattered on the ground alongside other things. There were bits of clothing there, and grimy white shards of harder stuff, and clumps of something else. There was also a watch.

"Dad, whose watch is that?" Jack could not figure out what he was seeing. If that was bone, where was the blood? Why was there a watch lying in their garden, its face shattered, hands frozen at some cataclysmic hour? And those dried things, tattered and ragged around the edges, like shriveled steak . . .

"Gray!" his mother called from the back door. "Where are you? Gray! There's someone coming down the hill."

"Come on," Jack's dad said, grabbing his arm and pulling him to the back door.

Jack twisted around to stare up the hillside, trying to see who his mother was talking about, wondering whether it was the Judes from Berry Hill Farm. He liked Mr. Jude—he had a huge Mexican mustache and he did a great impression of a *bandito*.

"We should stay in the house," his mum said as they reached the back door. "There's nothing on the radio."

If there's nothing on the radio, what is there to be worried about? Jack wondered.

"Nothing at all?" his dad said quietly.

His mother shook her head, and suddenly she looked older and grayer than Jack had ever noticed. It shocked him, frightened him. Death was something he sometimes thought about on the darkest of nights, but his mother's death . . . its possibility was unbearable, and it made him feel black and unreal and sick inside.

"I thought there may be some news . . ."

And then Jack realized what his mum had really meant . . . no radio, no radio *at all* . . . and he saw three people clambering over a fence higher up the hill.

"Look!" he shouted. "Is that Mr. Jude?"

His father darted into the cottage and emerged seconds later with the shotgun—locked and held ready in both hands—and a pair of binoculars hanging around his neck. He handed his mother the shotgun and she held it as if it were a living snake. Then he lifted the binoculars to his eyes and froze, standing there for a full thirty seconds while Jack squinted and tried to see what his dad was seeing. He pretended he had a bionic eye, but it didn't do any good.

His dad lowered the glasses, and slowly and carefully took the gun from his wife.

"Oh no," she said. "Oh no, Gray, no, no, no . . ."

"They did warn us," he murmured.

"But why the Judes? Why not us as well?" his mum whispered.

Jack's father looked down at him, and suddenly Jack was very afraid. "What, Dad?"

"We'll be leaving now, son," he said. "Go down to the car with your mum, there's a good boy."

"Can I take my books?"

"No, we can't take anything. We have to go now because Mr. Jude's coming."

"But I like Mr. Jude!" A tear had spilled down his dad's cheek. That was terrible, that was a leak in the dam holding back chaos and true terror because while

his dad was here—firm and strong and unflinching—
there was always someone to protect him.

His father knelt in front of him. "Listen, Jackie. Mr.
Jude and his family have a . . . a disease. If we're still
here when they arrive, they may try to hurt us, or we
may catch the disease. I don't know which, if either.
So we have to go—"

"Why don't we just not let them in? We can give
them tablets and water through the window and . . ."
He trailed off, feeling cold and unreal.

"Because they're not the only ones who have the
disease. Lots of other people will have it too by now.
We may have to wait a long time for help."

Jack turned and glanced up the hill at the three people coming down. They didn't look ill. They looked
odd, it was true. They looked *different*. But not ill. They
were moving too quickly for that.

"Okay." Jack nodded wisely, and he wondered who
else had been infected. He guessed it may have had
something to do with what was on the telly yesterday,
the thing his mum and dad had been all quiet and
tense and pale about. An explosion, he remembered,
an accident in a place so far away he didn't even recognize the name. "Mandy said we should go to Tewton. She said it was safe there."

"We will." His father nodded, but Jack knew it was
not because Mandy had said so. His parents rarely listened to her anymore.

"That big bonfire's still burning," Jack said, looking
out across the valley for the first time. A plume of
smoke hung in the sky like a frozen tornado, spreading
out at the top and dispersing in high air currents. And

then he saw it was not a bonfire, not really. It was the white farm on the opposite hillside; the whole white farm, burning. He'd never met the people who lived there, but he had often seen the farmer in his fields, chugging silently across the landscape in his tractor.

Jack knew where the word *bonfire* came from, and he could not help wondering whether today this was literally that.

His dad said nothing but looked down at Jack, seeing that he knew what it really was, already reaching out to pick up his son and carry him to their car.

"Dad, I'm scared!"

"I've got you, Jackie. Come on, Janey. Grab the keys. The shotgun cartridges are on the worktop."

"Dad, what's happening?"

"It's okay."

"Dad . . ."

As they reached the car, they could hear the Jude family swishing their feet through the sheen of bluebells covering the hillside. There were no voices, no talking or laughing. No inane *bandito* impressions this morning from Mr. Jude.

His parents locked the car doors from the inside and faced forward.

Jack took a final look back at their cottage. The car left the gravel driveway, and just before the hedge cut off the house from view, he saw Mr. Jude walk around the corner. From this distance, it looked like he was in black and white.

Jack kept staring from the back window so he did not have to look at his parents. Their silence scared him, and his mum's hair was all messed up.

Trees passed overhead, hedges flashed by on both sides, and seeing where they had been instead of where they were going presented so much more for his consideration.

Like the fox, standing next to a tree where the woods edged down to the road. Its coat was muddied; its eyes stared straight ahead. It did not turn to watch them pass. Jack thought it may have been *his* fox—the creature he had listened to each night for what seemed like ages—and as he mourned its voice he heard its cry, faint and weak, like a baby being dragged from its mother's breast and slaughtered.

They had left the back door open. His mum had dashed inside to grab the shotgun cartridges, his dad already had the car keys in his pocket, they'd left the back door open and he was sure—he was *certain*—that his mum had put some toast under the grille before they ran away. Maybe Mr. Jude was eating it now, Jack thought, but at the same time he realized that this was most unlikely. Mr. Jude was sick, and from what Jack had seen of him as he peered around the corner of their cottage, toast was the last thing on his mind.

Living, perhaps, was the first thing. Surviving. Pulling through.

Jack wondered whether the rest of Mr. Jude's family looked as bad.

The sense of invasion, of having his own space trespassed upon, was immense. They had left the back door open, and anyone or anything could wander into their house and root through their belongings. Not only the books and cupboards and food and fridge and dirty washing, but the private stuff. Jack had a lot of private stuff in his room, like letters from Mandy that he kept under a loose corner of carpet, his diary shoved into the tear in his mattress along with the page of a magazine he had found in the woods, a weathered flash of pink displaying what a woman *really* had between her legs.

But that sense of loss was tempered by a thought Jack was suddenly proud of, an idea that burst through the fears and the doubts and the awful possibilities this strange morning presented: that he actually had his whole life with him now. They may have left their home open to whatever chose to abuse it, but home was really with his family, wherever they may be. He was with them now.

All except Mandy.

He named his fears:

Loss, his parents disappearing into memory. Loneliness, the threat of being unloved and unloving. Death . . . that great black death . . . stealing away the ones he loved.

Stealing *him* away.

For once, the naming did not comfort him as much as usual. If anything it made him muse upon things more, and Mandy was on his mind and why she had run away, and what had happened to start all the bad stuff between the people he loved the most.

Jack had come home from school early that day, driven by the head teacher because he was feeling sick. He was only eight years old. The teacher really should have seen him into the house, but instead she dropped him at the gate and drove on.

As he entered the front door he was not purposely quiet, but he made sure he did not make any unnecessary noise, either. He liked to frighten Mandy—jump out on her or creep up from behind and smack her bum—because he loved the startled look on her face when he did so. And to be truthful, he loved the playful fight they would always have afterward even more.

He slipped off his shoes in the hallway, glanced in the fridge to see if there were any goodies, ate half a jam tart . . . and then he heard the sound from the living room.

His father had only ever smacked him three times, the last time more than a year before. What Jack remembered more than the pain was the loud noise as his dad's hand connected with him. It was a sound that signified a brief failure in their relationship; it meant an early trip to bed, no supper and a dreadful look on his mother's face that he hated even more, a sort of dried-up mix of shame and guilt.

Jack despised that sound. He heard it now, not only once, not even three times. Again, and again, and again—smacking. And even worse than that, the little cries that came between each smack. And it was Mandy, he knew that it was Mandy being hit over and over.

Their mum and dad were at work. So who was hitting Mandy?

Jack rushed to the living room door and flung it open.

His sister was kneeling on the floor in front of the settee. She had no clothes on and her face was pressed into the cushions, and the man from the bakery was kneeling behind her, grasping her bum, and he looked like he was hurting too. Jack saw the man's willy—at least he thought that's what it was, except this was as big as one of the French bread sticks he sold—sliding in and out of his sister, and it was all wet and shiny like she was bleeding, but it wasn't red.

"Mandy?" Jack said, and in that word was everything: *Mandy what are you doing? Is he hurting you? What should I do?* "Mandy?"

Mandy turned and stared at him red-faced, and then her mouth fell open and she shouted: "What the fuck are you doing here?"

Jack turned and ran along the hallway, forgetting his shoes, feet slapping on quarry tiles. He sprinted across the lawn, stumbling a couple of times. And then he heard Mandy call after him. He did not turn around. He did not want to see her standing at the door with the baker bouncing at her from behind. And he didn't want her to swear at him again, when he had only come home because he felt sick.

All he wished for was to un-see what he had seen.

Jack spent that night lost in the woods. He could never remember any of it, and when he was found and taken home the next day he started to whoop, coughing up clots of mucus and struggling to breathe. He was ill for two weeks, and Mandy sat with him for a couple of hours every evening to read him the fantastic tales of Narnia, or sometimes just to talk. She would always kiss him goodnight and tell him she was sorry, and Jack would tell her it was okay, he sometimes said *fuck* too, but only when he was on his own.

It seemed that as Jack got better everything else in their family got worse.

It was a little over two miles to the nearest village, Tall Stennington. Jack once asked his father why they lived where they did, why didn't they live in a village or a town where there were other people, and shops, and gas in pipes under the ground instead of oil in a big green tank. His dad's reply had confused him at the time, and it still did to an extent.

You've got to go a long way nowadays before you can't hear anything of Man.

Jack thought of that now as they twisted and turned through lanes that still had grass clumps along their spines. There was no radio, his mum had said, and he wondered exactly what they would hear outside were they to stop the car now. He would talk if they did, sing, shout, just to make sure there was a sound other than the silence of last night.

The deathly silence.

"Whose watch was that in the garden, Dad?"

"I expect it belonged to one of the robbers."

Jack thought about this for a while, staring from his window at the hedges rolling by. He glanced up at the trees forming a green tunnel over the road, and he knew they were only minutes from the village. "So, what was the other stuff lying around it? The dried stuff, like meat you've left in the fridge too long?"

His dad was driving so he had an excuse, but his mum didn't turn around either. It was she who spoke, however.

"There's been some stuff on the news—"

"Janey!" his dad cut in. "Don't be so bloody stupid!"

"Gray, if it's really happening he has to know . . . he will know. We'll see them, lots of them, and—"

"All the trees are pale," Jack said, the watch and dried meat suddenly forgotten. He was looking from the back window at the avenue of trees they had just passed, and he had figured out what had been nagging him about the hedges and the fields since they'd left the cottage: their color; or rather, their lack of it. The springtime flush of growth had been flowering across the valley for the last several weeks, great explosions of rich greens, electric blues and splashes of colors which, as his dad was fond of saying, would put a Monet to shame. Jack didn't know what a Monet was, but he was sure there was no chance in a billion it could ever match the slow-burning fireworks display nature put on at the beginning of every year. Spring was his favorite season, followed by autumn. They were both times of change, beautiful in their own way, and Jack loved to watch stuff happen.

Now, something *had* happened. It was as though autumn had crept up without anyone or anything noticing, casting its pastel influence secretly across the landscape.

"See?" he said. "Mum? You see?"

His mum turned in her seat and stared past Jack. She was trying to hide the fact she had been crying; she looked embarrassed and uncertain.

"Maybe they're dusty," she said.

He knew she was lying; she didn't really think that at all. "So what was on the news?" he asked.

"We're at the village." His dad slowed the car at the

hump-back bridge, which marked the outskirts of Tall Stennington.

Jack leaned on the backs of his parents' seats and strained forward to see through the windscreen. The place looked as it always had: The church dominated with a recently sand-blasted tower; stone cottages stood huddled beneath centuries-old trees; a few birds flitted here and there. A fat old Alsation trundled along the street and raised its leg in front of the Dog and Whistle, but it seemed unable to piss.

The grocer's was closed. It opened at six every morning, without fail, even Sundays. In fact, Jack could hardly recall ever seeing it closed, as if old Mrs. Haswell had nothing else to do but stock shelves, serve locals and natter away about the terrible cost of running a village business.

"The shop's shut," he said.

His dad nodded. "And there's no one about."

"Yes there is," his mum burst out. "Look, over there, isn't that Gerald?"

"Gerald the Geriatric!" Jack giggled because that's what they called him at school. He'd usually be told off for that, he knew, on any normal day. After the first couple of seconds he no longer found it all that funny himself. There was something wrong with Gerald the Geriatric.

He leaned against a wall, dragging his left shoulder along the stonework with jerky, infrequent movements of his legs. He was too far away to see his expression in full, but his jowls and the saggy bags beneath his eyes seemed that much larger and darker this morning. He also seemed to have mislaid his trademark walking stick. There were legends that he had once beaten a rat to death with that stick in the kitchen of the Dog and Whistle, and the fact that he had not frequented that pub for a decade seemed to hint at its truth. Jack used to imagine him striking out at the darting rodent with the knotted length of oak, spittle flying from his mouth, false teeth chattering with each impact. Now, the image seemed grotesque rather than comical.

His mother reached for the door handle.

"Wait, Mum!" Jack said.

"But he's hurt!"

"Jack's right. Wait." His dad rested his hand on the stock of the shotgun wedged beneath their seats.

Gerald paused and stood shakily away from the wall, turning his head to stare at them. He raised his hands, his mouth falling open into a toothless grin or grimace. Jack could not even begin to tell which.

"He's in pain!" Jack's mum said, and this time she actually clicked the handle and pushed her shoulder to the door, letting in cool morning air.

"Janey, remember what they said—"

"What's that?" Jack said quietly. It was the sound a big spider's legs made on his posters in the middle of the night. The fear was the same, too—unseen things.

His mum had heard it as well, and she *snicked* the door shut.

There was something under the car. Jack felt the subtle tickle of soft impacts beneath him, insistent scrapings and pickings, reminiscent of the window fumblers of last night.

"Maybe it's a dog," his mum said.

His dad slammed the car into reverse and burnt rubber. The skid was tremendous, the stench and reverberation overpowering. As soon as the tires caught Jack knew that they were out of control. The car leapt back, throwing Jack forward so that he banged his head on his mother's headrest. As he looked up he saw what had been beneath the car . . . Mrs. Haswell, still flipping and rolling where the chassis had scraped her along the road, her hair wild, her skirts torn to reveal pasty, pitted thighs . . .

His father swore as the brakes failed and the car dipped sickeningly into the ditch. Jack fell back, cracking his head on the rear window and tasting the sudden salty tang of blood as he bit his tongue. His mum screeched, his dad shouted and cursed again, the engine rose and sang and screamed until, finally, it cut out.

The sudden silence was huge. The wrecked engine ticked and dripped, Jack groaned, and through the tilted windscreen he could see Mrs. Haswell hauling herself to her feet.

Steadying her tattered limbs.

Setting out for their car with slow, broken steps.

"Okay, Jackie?" his mum said. She twisted in her seat and reached back, the look in her eyes betraying her thoughts: *My son, my son!*

Jack opened his mouth to speak, but only blood came out. He shuddered a huge breath and realized he'd been winded, things had receded, and only the blood on his chin felt and smelled real.

"What's wrong with her?" his dad said, holding the steering wheel and staring through the windscreen.

"That's Mrs. Haswell. Under our car. Did I run her over? I didn't hit her, did you see me hit her?"

"Gray, Jackie's bleeding."

Jack tried to talk again, to say he was all right, but everything went fluid. He felt queasy and sleepy, as if he'd woken up suddenly in the middle of the night.

"Gray!"

"Jack? You okay, son? Come on, out of the car. Janey, grab the binoculars. And the shells. Wait on your side. I'll get Jack out." He paused and looked along the road again. Mrs. Haswell was sauntering between the fresh skidmarks, and now Gerald the Geriatric was moving their way as well. "Let's hurry up."

Jack took deep, heavy breaths, feeling blood bubble in his throat. The door beside him opened and his dad lifted him out, and as the sun touched his face he began to feel better. His mum wiped at his bloody chin with the sleeve of her jumper.

There was a sound now, a long, slow scraping, and Jack realized it was Mrs. Haswell dragging her feet. She'd never done that before. She was eighty, but she'd always been active and forceful, like a wind-up toy that never ran out. She hurried through the village at lunchtime, darted around her shop as if she had wheels for feet . . . she had never, in all the times Jack had seen her or spoken to her, been slow.

Her arms were draped by her sides, not exactly swinging as she walked, but moving as if they were really no part of her at all. Her mouth hung open, but she did not drool.

"What's wrong with her, Dad?"

"She's got the disease," his dad said quickly, dismissively, and Jack felt a pang of annoyance.

"Dad," he said, "I think I'm old enough for you to tell me the truth." It was a childish thing to say, Jack understood that straightaway at some deeper level; petulant and prideful, unmindful of the panic his parents so obviously felt. But Jack was nearly a teenager—he felt he deserved some trust. "Anyway," he said, "she looks like she's dead." He'd seen lots of films where people died, but hardly any of them looked like the old woman. She seemed lessened somehow, shrunken into herself, drained. She had lost what little color she once possessed. In his mind's eye, this was how a true, real-life dead person should look.

His dad aimed the shotgun at Mrs. Haswell.

Jack gasped. For the second time in as many minutes, he found himself unable to talk.

"Gray," his mother said cautiously, quietly, hands raised in a warding-off gesture, "we should go across the fields."

Jack saw his dad's face then—tears stinging the corners of his eyes; lips pressed together tight and bloodless, the way they'd been on the day Mandy left home for the last time—and he realized what a dire situation they were in.

His dad had no idea what to do.

"Across the fields to the motorway," his mum continued. "If there's any help, we may find it there. And I'm sure they couldn't drive." She nodded at Mrs. Haswell as she spoke. "Could they? You don't think they could, do you?"

His dad was breathing heavily, just as Jack did

whenever he was trying not to cry. He grabbed Jack's hand.

Jack felt the cool sweat of his father's palms . . . like touching a hunk of raw meat before it was cooked.

They walked quickly back the way they had come, then hopped over a stile into the field.

Jack glanced back at their car, canted at a crazy angle in the ditch, and saw that the two old people had stopped in their tracks. They stood as still as statues, and just as lifeless. This was more disturbing than ever—at least before, they had seemed to possess some purpose.

She was under our car, Jack thought. *What purpose in that?*

And then his own words sprang back at him: *She looks like she's dead.*

"You know what an open mind is, Jack?" Mandy said. She had crept into his room in the middle of the night after hearing him whooping and crying. Sometimes she would sit on the edge of the bed until daybreak, just talking. Much of what she said confused him—she read all the time, and occasionally she even confused their mum and dad—but he remembered it all . . . and later, some of it began to make sense.

Jack had a grotesque vision of someone with a trap-door in their skull, their brain pulsing and glowing underneath. He smiled uncertainly at this bloody train of thought.

"It's the ability to believe in the unbelievable," she continued, apparently unconcerned at his silence. "It's a free mind. Imagination. Growing up closes off so many

doors. The modern world doesn't allow for miracles, so we don't see them. It's a very precious gift, an open mind, but it's not passive. You've got to nurture it like a bed of roses; otherwise it will wither and die. Make sure you don't close off your mind to things you find strange, Jack. Sometimes they may be the only truth."

They sat silently for a while, Jack croaking as he breathed past the phlegm in his throat, Mandy twirling strands of her long black hair between her fingers.

"It's something you have," she said suddenly, "and you always will. And that's another secret, to keep and tend."

"How do you know I have it?" he asked.

Mandy smiled at him and he saw a sadness behind her eyes. Maybe she still blamed herself for him being lost in the woods. Maybe she could already see how different their family was going to be.

"Hey," she said, "you're my brother." As if that was an answer.

The farther they moved away, the more Tall Stennington appeared normal. Halfway across the field they lost sight of the shuffling shapes in the road, the empty streets beyond, the pigeons sitting silently on the church tower. Jack found himself wishing for any sign of life. He almost called out, wanting to see windows thrust open and people he knew by name or sight lean out, wave to him, comment on what a lovely brisk spring morning it was. But his tongue hurt from the car wreck. His dad had crashed because a busy old lady had cut or torn the brake cables. And she had done that because . . . because . . .

There was nothing normal this morning. Not with Tall Stennington, not with Mr. Jude, not with the fox at the edge of the woods. Not even with his parents because they were tense and worried and hurrying across a newly planted field, and his mum still had on her slippers. His dad carried a shotgun. His mum had her arms crossed, perhaps against the cold but more likely, Jack thought, against something else entirely.

No, nothing was normal today.

They followed the furrows plowed into the field, stepping on green shoots and crushing them back into the earth from whence they came. Jack glanced behind at his footprints, his identity stamped into the landscape only to be brushed away by the next storm. When he was younger he wanted to be an astronaut, purely for the excitement of zero-G, piloting experimental spacecraft and dodging asteroids on the way out of the solar system. The idea still appealed to him, but his main reason now would be to walk on the moon and leave his footprints behind. He'd heard that they would be there forever, or at least near enough. When he was dead—perhaps when *everyone* was dead—some aliens might land on the moon, and see his footprints, and think, *Here was a guy willing to explore. Here was a guy with no closed doors in his head, with an open mind. Here was a guy who might have believed in us.*

Jack looked up at the ghost of the moon where it still hung in the clear morning sky. He wondered if his exact center line of sight were extended, would he be looking at Neil Armstrong's footprints right now?

He looked down at his feet and one of those doors in his mind flapped wide open.

Falling to his knees, he plucked at a green shoot. It felt dry and brittle between his fingers, not cool and damp as it should have. He rubbed at it and it came apart, shedding its faded outer skin and exposing powdery insides.

He picked another shoot and it was the same. The third bled a smear of greenish fluid across his fingertips, but the next was as dry as the first, and the next.

"Jack, what's up son? What are you doing?" His dad had stopped and turned, glancing nervously past Jack at the stile as if constantly expecting Mrs. Haswell and Gerald the Geriatric to come stumbling after them.

Jack shook his head, not *unable* to understand—he understood perfectly well, even for a twelve-year-old— but *unwilling*. The doors were open, but he was stubbornly grasping the frames, not wanting to enter the strange rooms presenting themselves to him now.

"This crop's dead," he said. "It looks fresh, Dad. Mum? Doesn't it all look so fresh?" His mum nodded, cupping her elbows in her hands and shivering. Jack held up a palm full of crushed shoot. "But look. It's all dead. It's still green, but it's not growing anymore."

He looked back at the village. Their footprints stood out in the young crop, three wavering lines of bent and snapped shoots. And the hedge containing the stile they had hopped over . . . its colors like those of a faded photograph, not lush and vibrant with the new growth of spring . . . He'd once read a book called *The Death of Grass*. Now, he might be living it.

To his left the hillsides, speckled with sheep so still

they looked like pustules on the face of the land.

To his right the edge of a stretch of woodland, at the other end of which stood their house, doors open, toast burnt in the grille, perhaps still burning.

"Everything's dying."

His dad sighed. "Not everything," he said.

Jack began to shake, his stomach twisted into a knot and he was sure he was going to puke. Another terrible admission from his father, another fearful idea implanted when really, he should be saying, *There, there, Jackie boy, nothing's changed, it's all in your imagination.*

What could he name? How could he lay all this out to understanding, to comprehension, to acceptance, all as he had been told? He tried, even though he thought it was useless: *The villagers, like walking dead, perhaps they are. The plants, dry and brittle even though it's springtime. Mum and Dad, scared to death* . . . He thought at first there was nothing there that would work, but then he named another part of this terrible day and a sliver of hope kept the light shining: *Mandy, in the town, saying it's safe.*

"Not everything, Jack," his dad said again, perhaps trying to jolt his son back to reality.

"Let's go," his mum said. "Come on, Jack, we'll tell you while we're walking . . . it's only two or three fields away . . . and there'll be help there." She smiled, but it could not reach her eyes.

The motorway was not three fields away; it was six. His parents told Jack all they knew by the time they'd reached the end of the second field. He believed what they said because he could smell death in the third field, and he mentioned it, but his mum and dad lied to themselves by not even answering. Jack was sure as hell he knew what death smelled like; he'd found a dead badger in the woods a year ago, after all, and turned it over with a stick, and run home puking. This was similar, only richer, stronger, as if coming from a lot more bodies. Some of them smelled cooked.

They saw the stationary cars on the motorway from two fields away. Wisps of smoke still rose here and there. Several vehicles were twisted on their backs like dead beetles.

From the edge of the field abutting the motorway they saw the shapes sitting around the ruined cars— the gray people in their colorful clothes—and although they could not tell for sure what they were eating, it was mostly red.

Jack's dad raised his binoculars. Then he turned, grabbed Jack's and his mother's hands and ran back they way they had come.

"Were they eating the people from the cars?" Jack asked, disgusted but fascinated.

His father—white-faced, frowning, shaking his head slightly as if trying to dislodge a memory—did not answer.

They walked quickly across another field, their path taking them away from the woods and between Tall Stennington and the motorway. Neither was in view any longer—the landscape here dipped and rose, and all they could see around them was countryside. Nothing to give any indication of humankind's presence;

no chimney smoke or aircraft trails; no skyscrapers or whitewashed farm buildings.

No traffic noise. None at all.

Jack realized that he only noticed noise when it was no longer there.

"Dad, tell me!" Jack said. "The dead people—were they eating the people from the cars?"

"No," his father said.

Jack saw straight through the lie.

He had taken it all in, everything his parents had told him, every snippet of information gleaned from the panicked newscasts yesterday, the confused reports from overseas. He had listened and taken it all in, but he did not really understand. He had already seen it for himself—Mr. Jude and the people in the village did not have a disease at all, and the young crop really was dead—but he could not believe. It was too terrifying, too unreal. Too crazy.

He whispered as they walked, naming the parts that scared him the most: *Dead people, dead things, still moving and walking. Dumb and aimless, but dangerous just the same.*

Those fingers last night had not sounded aimless, those probings and proddings at their locked-up, safe cottage. They had sounded anything *but* aimless.

He carried on naming. *Those of you who are immune, stay at home.* The broadcasts his parents had listened to had told of certain blood groups succumbing slower than others, and some being completely immune. In a way, these positive elements to the broadcasts—the mentions of immunity—scared Jack more. They made him feel increasingly isolated, one

of the few survivors, and what was left? What was
there that they could use now, where would they go
when dead people could cut your brake cables (and
that sure as shit wasn't aimless, either), when they
caused crashes on the motorway so they could . . .
they could . . . ?

Jack stumbled, dug his toes into a furrow and hit
the dirt. His face pressed into the ground and he felt
dry dead things scurrying across his cheeks. He
wanted to cry but he could not, neither could he shout
nor scream, and then he realized that what he wanted
most was comfort. His mother's arms around him, his
father sitting on the side of his bed stroking his brow
as he did when Jack had the occasional nightmare, a
cup of tea before bed, half an hour reading before he
turned out his light and lay back to listen to the night.

Hands did touch him, voices did try to soothe, but
all Jack could hear was the silence. All he could smell
was the undercurrent of death in the motionless spring
air.

Before the world receded into a strange flat brightness, Jack saw in sharp detail a line of ants marching
along a furrow. They were moving strangely—too
slowly, much slower than he'd ever seen one moving
before, as if they were in water—and he passed out
wondering how aimless these red ants really were.

He was not unconscious for long. He opened his eyes
to sunlight and sky and fluffy clouds, and he suddenly
knew that his parents had left him. They'd walked on,
leaving him behind like an injured commando on a
raid into enemy territory, afraid that he would slow

them down and give the dead things a chance—

And then his mother's face appeared above his and her tears dropped onto his cheeks. "Jackie," she said, smiling, and Jack could hear the love in her voice. He did not know how—it did not sound any different than usual—but out here, lost in a dying landscape, he knew that she loved him totally. She would never leave him behind. She would rather die.

"I want to go home," Jack said, his own tears mixing with his mother's on his face. He thought of the cottage and all the good times he had spent there. It would be cold inside by now, maybe there were birds . . . dead birds, arrogantly roosting on plate racks and picture frames. "Mum, I want to go home. I want none of this to happen." He held up his arms and she grabbed him, hugging him so tightly that his face was pressed into her hair, his breath squeezed out. He could smell her, a warm musk of sweat and stale perfume, and he took solace in the familiar.

"We can't stay here too long," his father said, but he sat down in the dirt next to his wife and son. "We've got to get on to Tewton."

"To find Mandy?"

"To find safety," his dad said. He saw Jack's crest-fallen expression and averted his eyes. "And to find Mandy."

"She never hurt me, you know," Jack muttered.

"She scared you, made you run away!"

"I ran away myself! Mandy didn't make me. She only ever hurt herself!" Once more, he tried to recall his time in the woods, but the effort conjured only sensations of cold, damp and dark. Ironically, he could remember what happened afterward with ease—the coughing, the fevers, the nightmares, Mandy by his bed, his shouting parents, Mandy running down their driveway, leaving her home behind—but still a day and a night were missing from his life.

It was a pointless argument, a dead topic, an aimless one. So nothing more was said.

They were silent for a while, catching their breath and all thinking their own thoughts. His mother continued to rock him in her lap, but Jack knew she was elsewhere, thinking other things. His dad had broken open the shotgun and was making sure the two cartridges in there were new.

"How do you kill a dead thing, Dad?" Jack asked. A perfectly simple question, he thought. Logical. Reasonable.

His dad looked across the fields. "Tewton should be a few miles that way," he said. He looked at his watch, then up at the sun where it hung low over the hills. "We could make it by tonight if we really push it."

Jack's mum began to cry. She pulled a great clod of mud from one of her slippers and threw it at the ground. "We can't go that far alone," she said. "Not on foot. Gray, we don't know what's happened, not really. They'll come and help us, cure everyone, send us home."

" 'They'?"

"You know what I mean."

"There was a film called *Them* once," Jack said. "About giant ants and nuclear bombs. It was nothing like this, though." Even as he spoke it, he thought maybe he was mistaken. He thought maybe the film was *very much* like this, a monstrous horror of human-kind's abuse of nature, and the harvest of grief it reaped.

"It's all so sudden," his dad said then. Jack actually saw his shoulders droop, his head dip down, as if he were being shrunken and reduced by what had happened. "I don't think there's much help around, not out here. Not yet."

"It'll be all right in Tewton," Jack said quietly. "Mandy said it was safe there. She phoned us because she was worried, so we've got to go. I don't want to stay out in the dark. Not after last night, Mum. Remember the noises?"

His mother nodded and tightened her lips.

"I don't want to know what made those noises." Jack felt close to tears once more, but he could not let them come, he would not.

A breeze came up and rustled through the dead young crop.

Jack jerked upright, eyes wide, mouth hanging open.

There was something around the corner of the L-shaped field, out of sight behind a clump of trees. He could not hear it, or smell it exactly, but he knew it was dead, and he knew it was moving this way.

"Mum," he said. "Dad. There's something coming."

They looked around and listened hard, his dad tightening his grip on the shotgun. "I can't—"

"There!" Jack said, pointing across the field a second before something walked into view.

His mother gasped. "Oh, no."

His dad stood and looked behind them, judging how far it was to the hedge.

Eight people emerged from the hidden leg of the field, one after another. There were men and women and one child. All of them moved strangely, as if they only just learned how to walk, and most of them wore night clothes. The exceptions were a policeman—his uniform torn and muddied—and someone dressed in a thick sweater, ripped jeans and a bobble hat. He had something dangling from his left hand; it could have been a leash, but there was no dog.

One of the women had fresh blood splattered across the front of her nightgown.

The child was chewing something bloody. Flies buzzed around his head, but none seemed to be landing.

Perhaps, Jack thought, *the flies are dead as well.*

The people did not pause. They walked straight at Jack and his parents, arms swinging by their sides from simple motion, not habit.

"I doubt they can run that fast," Jack's dad said.

"I'm scared," his mother whispered.

"But can they get through the hedge, Dad? Once we're through, will they follow us?"

Jack looked from the people to the hedge, and back again. He knew what was wrong with them—they were dead and they craved live food, his parents had learned all that from the news yesterday—but still he did not want to *believe*.

Their nostrils did not flare, their mouths hung open but did not drool, their feet plodded insistently . . . but not aimlessly. These dead things had a purpose, it seemed, and that purpose would be in their eyes, were they moist enough to throw back reflections.

"They're looking at us," Jack said quietly.

They walked slowly, coming on like wind-up toys with broken innards; no life in their movements at all.

Seconds later, they charged.

Whatever preconceptions Jack had about the ability of dead things to move were slaughtered here and now. The dead folk did not run, they rampaged, churning up the earth with heavy footfalls, shattering the strange peace with the suddenness of their movement. Yet their faces barely changed, other than the slack movement of their jaws snapping shut each time their feet struck mud. They did not shout or pant because, Jack guessed, they had no breath.

His dad fired the shotgun and then they all ran toward the hedge. Jack did not see what effect the shot had; he did not want to. He could sense the distance rapidly closing between them. The hedge seemed a hundred steps away, a thousand miles, and then he saw his father slowly dropping behind.

"Dad, come on!"

"Run, Jackie!"

"Dad!" He was fumbling with the shotgun, Jack saw, plucking out the spent cartridges and trying to load fresh ones. "Dad, don't bother, just run!"

"Gray, Gray," he heard his mother panting under her breath, but she did not turn around. She reached the hedge first and launched herself at what she thought was an easy gap to squeeze through. She squealed, and then screamed, when she became impaled on barbed wire and sharp sticks.

Jack was seconds from the hedge but his dad was

now out of sight, behind him and to the left. Jack was watching his feet so he did not trip, but in his mind's eye he saw something else: his father caught, then trampled, then gnawed into, eaten alive while he lay there broken-backed and defenseless . . .

He reached the hedge but did not slow down. Instead he jumped, scrabbling with his hands and feet even before he struck the tangled growth, hauling himself up and through the sharp thorns, the biting branches, the crisp spring foliage. Bloody tears sprang from cuts on his hands and arms.

"Mum!" he shouted as he tumbled over the other side. The breath was knocked from him as he landed, and he crawled back to the hedge in a kind of silent, airless void.

As he found his breath, he heard the blast of the shotgun once more. Something hit the ground.

His mum was struggling in the heart of the hedge and Jack went to her aid. She was already cut and bleeding, the splashes of blood vivid against withered leaves and rotting buds. "Stop struggling!" he shouted.

The shotgun again.

"Dad!"

He could see glimpses of frantic movement through the hedge—

And then he knew it was going to be all right. Not forever—in the long term everything was dark and lonely and different—but for now they would all pull through. He saw his bloodied parents hugging each other, felt the coolness of blood on his neck, smelled the scent of death receding as they left the mindless dead behind to feed on other things. He also saw a place where everything would be fine, but he had no idea how to get there.

"Jack, help me!" his mother shouted, and everything rushed back. He reached out and grabbed her arms, and although she screamed, still he pulled.

The hedge moved and shuddered as bodies crashed into it on the other side. He could not see his dad, but he did not worry; there was nothing to worry about

(*yet*, nothing to worry about *yet*)

and then he came scrambling over, throwing the shotgun to the ground and following close behind.

His mother came free with a final harsh scream. Jack saw the wounds on her arms and shoulders where the barbed wire had slashed in and torn out, and he began to cry.

"Oh, Janey," his dad said, hugging his wife and letting his tears dilute her blood. Jack closed his eyes because his mum was bleeding . . . she was hurt and she was bleeding . . . But then she was hugging him and her blood cooled on his skin.

"Come on, I don't want to stay here a minute longer," his father said. "And maybe they'll find a way through. Maybe."

They hurried along the perimeter of the new field, keeping a wary look out in case this place, too, had occupants ready to chase them into the ground.

Jack looked back only once. Shapes were silhouetted on and in the hedge like grotesque fruits, their arms twitching uselessly, clothes and skin stretched and torn on barbed wire and dead wood.

He did not look again, but he heard their struggles for a long while. By the time he and his family reached the gate that led out into a little country lane, their stench had been carried away on the breeze.

The lane looked unused, but at least it was a sign of humanity.

Jack was so glad to see it.

They turned east. Jack wondered at his conviction that there was something dangerous approaching, moments before the crowd had rounded the corner in the field. He had smelled them, of course, that was it. Or perhaps he had heard them. He had a good sense of hearing, his mother always said so.

Or perhaps he had simply known that they were there.

His mother and father were walking close together behind him, almost rubbing shoulders. Almost, but not quite, because his mum's arm was a mess. There was blood dripping from her fingertips as they walked, and Jack had seen her shoulder where a flap of skin hung down across her armpit, and he'd seen the *meat* of her there where the barbed wire had torn her open.

It didn't hurt, she said. It was numb, but it didn't hurt. Jack knew from the way she talked that the numbness would not last. Once the shock had worn off and the adrenaline drained from her system, the slow fire would ignite and the pain would come in surges. For his mother, the future was a terrifying place promising nothing but worse to come.

Total silence surrounded them. The landscape had taken on an eerie appearance, one normally reserved for the strangest of autumn evenings, when the sun was sinking behind wispy clouds and the moon had already revealed itself. The hills in the distance were smothered in mist, only occasional smudges of green showing through like old bruises. Nearer by, clumps of trees sprouted on ancient hillocks. The trees were all old, Jack knew, otherwise the farmers would have cut them down; but today they looked positively ancient. Today they looked fossilized, petrified like the wood his friend Jamie had brought back from his holiday in the Dominican Republic the year before, wood so old it was like stone.

What would those trees feel like now? Jack wondered. Would their trunks be cold and dry as rock, or was there still that electric dampness of something alive? Were their leaves as green and fresh and vibrant as they should be in the spring . . . or were they as dead inside as the young harvest across the fields?

If I cut them, Jack thought, *will they bleed?*

"Hang on," his mum said, and he knew that the pain had begun. He turned back and saw her sink slowly to her knees in the lane, his dad standing over her, one hand reaching out but not touching her shoulder because he did not know what to do. It was always Jack's mum who did the comforting, the mollycoddling when Dad had a cold, the reassuring when Jack woke from nightmares and became frustrated when he just could not explain exactly what they were about. And now that she needed comforting, his dad was standing there like he was balancing a teacup on the back of his hand, unable to help his wife where she knelt bleeding and crying into the muck.

"Mum," Jack said, "my teacher said that pain is transitory."

"Big words, Jackie," she said, trying to smile for him.

"It's what he said, though. He was telling us because Jamie was going to the dentist for a filling, and he was scared of the needle. Mr. Travis said pain is transitory, you feel it when it happens but afterward you can't remember exactly what it was like. You can't recreate pain in your memories because your body won't let you. Otherwise it'll only hurt again."

His dad handed her a handkerchief and she lifted her sleeve slowly, revealing some of the smaller cuts and dabbing at them as if that would take her attention from the gaping wound in her shoulder. "The point being?" she said, sharply but not unkindly. Jack could see that she was grateful for the distraction.

"Well, if you're hurting just cast your mind into the future. When you're all better, you won't even remember what the hurting was like. And pain doesn't actually *hurt* you, anyway. It's only in your head. Your cuts will heal, Mum. In a few days it won't matter."

"In a few days . . ." she said, smiling and sighing and opening her mouth as if to finish the sentence. But she left it at that.

"It's almost midday," his dad said.

"I should be in school."

"School's off, kiddo!" Tears were cascading past his mum's smiling mouth.

"We should get moving, if we can. Janey, you think you can move, honey? If we're going to get to Tewton—"

"Where are we now?" Jack's mum asked suddenly.

His dad frowned but did not answer.

"Gray? Don't tell me that. Don't say we're lost."

"Well," he said, "Tall Stennington is maybe three miles back thataway." He turned and pointed the way they had come, though Jack thought he was probably off by about a sixth of a circle anyway. "So we must be nearing the river by now. You think, Jackie?"

You think, Jackie? His dad, asking him for advice in something so important. He tried to see himself from his father's eyes. Short, skinny, into books instead of his dad's beloved football, intelligent in his own right but academically average . . . a kid. Just a kid. However much Jack thought about things, used big words, had a hard-on when he watched bikini-clad women on holiday programs . . . he was just a kid to his dad.

"No," Jack said. "I think you're a bit off there, Dad. I reckon we're closer to Peter's Acre than anything, so we really need to head more that way, if we can." He pointed off across the fields to where the landscape rose in the distance, lifting toward a heavily wooded hillside. "Tewton is over that hill, through the woods. If you drive you go that way, yes," he said, indicating the direction his father had suggested. "But if I were a crow, I'd go there."

"So by the time we get that far," his mum said, "what I'm feeling now I'd have forgotten."

Jack nodded, but he was frowning.

"Ok, Jackie. Let's hit it." And up she stood, careful not to look down at the strip of her husband's T-shirt wrapped around her shoulder, already stained a deep, wet red.

They left the lane and moved off across the fields toward the tree-covered hillside in the distance. Between them and the woods lay several fields, a veiny network of hedges, hints of other lanes snaking from here to there and a farmstead. It looked quiet and deserted; no smoke rose from its chimneys; its yard seemed, from this distance, empty and still. Yet for the first time, Jack was glad that his dad was carrying the gun.

Something had changed, Jack thought, since before their flight from the dead people and his mother being tangled and wounded in the hedge. It was her attitude to things—the nervousness had been swept aside by the pain, so that now she seemed to accept things more as they came than as she expected them to be. But this change in his mother had also moved down the line to his father and himself, altering the subtle hierarchy of the family, shifting emphases around so that none of them were quite the people they had been that morning.

Jack suddenly wanted to see Mandy. In the four years since her leaving home she had become something of a stranger. They still saw her on occasion— though it was always she who came to visit them— but she changed so much every time that Jack would see a different person walking in the door. She and Jack were still very close and there was an easy atmosphere between them that his parents seemed to resent, but she was not the Mandy he remembered.

Sometimes Jack would imagine that his sister was still living at home. He would go into her bedroom, and although it had been cleared out by his parents and left sterile and bland—forever awaiting a visitor to abuse its neatness—he could sense her and hear her and smell her. Only his memories placed her there, of course, but he would sit and chat with her for hours.

Sometimes, when he next spoke to her on the phone, they would carry on their conversation.

"When can we go to see Mandy?" he asked, realizing as he spoke that he sounded like a whiner. They were going, that was that, and they certainly could not move any faster.

"We'll be there by tonight, Jackie," his mother said comfortingly.

"You do love her, don't you?" he asked.

"Of course we do! She's our daughter—your sister—so of course we love her!"

"So why don't we go to see her anymore?"

His mother was silent for a while, his father offering no help. There was only the crunch of their feet crushing new grass into crisp green fragments in the dirt. It sounded to Jack as though they were walking on thin ice.

"Sometimes people fall out," his mother said. "There was that time she made you run away—"

"She didn't make me. I told you, I did it myself!"

His mother winced in pain as she turned to him and Jack felt ashamed, ashamed that he was putting her through this soon after she had been dragged through a wire fence and torn to shreds. But then, he thought, maybe there was no better time. Her defenses were down, the pain was filtering her thoughts and letting only essential ones through, holding back the ballast and, maybe, discarding it altogether.

"Mandy scared you," she said. "She was doing something she shouldn't have been doing and she scared you and you ran away. We didn't find you until the next day, and you don't . . ." She looked up at the sky, but Jack could still see the tears. "You don't know what that night did to your Dad and me."

"But you still love her?"

His mother nodded. "Of course we do."

Jack thought about this for a while, wondering whether easy talk and being together were really the most important things there were. "That's okay then," he said finally. "I'm hungry."

Mum dying because she's hurt, he thought, naming his fears automatically. *Things changing, it's all still changing. Dead people. I'm afraid of the dead people.*

"We'll eat when we get to Tewton," his dad said from up ahead.

"And I'm thirsty." *No food, no drink . . . no people at all. Death; we could die out here.*

"When we get to Tewton, Jackie," his dad said, more forcefully than before. He turned around and Jack could see how much he had changed, even over the last hour. The extraordinary had been presented to him, thrust in his face in the form of a gang of dead people, denying disbelief. Unimaginable, impossible, true.

"I expect those people just wanted help, Dad." He knew it was crazy even as he said it—he *knew* they'd wanted more than that; he had seen the fresh blood— but maybe the idea would drain some of the strain from his dad's face. And maybe a lie could hide the truth, and help hold back his mother's pain, and bring Mandy back to them where she belonged, and perhaps they were only on a quiet walk in the country. . . .

"Come on, son," his father said, and Jack did not

know whether he meant *move along,* or *give me a break.* Whatever, he hated the air of defeat in his voice.

My dad, failing, he thought. *Pulling away from things already, falling down into himself. What about Mum? What about me?*

Who's going to protect us?

They had crossed one field and were nearing the edge of another when Jack suddenly recognized their surroundings. To the left stood an old barn, doors rotted away and ivy making its home between the stones. The ivy was dead now, but still it clotted the building's openings, as if holding something precious inside. To the right, at the far corner of the field, an old metal plow rusted down into the ground. He remembered playing war here, diving behind the plow while Jamie threw mud grenades his way, *ack—ack—ack*ing a stream of machine-gun fire across the field, crawling through the rape crop and plowing their own paths toward and away from each other. Good times, and lost times, never to be revisited; he felt that now more than ever. Lost times.

"I know this place!" he said. "There's a pond over there behind that hedge, with an island in the middle and everything!" He ran to the edge of the field, aiming for the gate where it stood half open.

"Jack, wait!" his dad shouted, but Jack was away, cool breeze ruffling his hair and lifting some of the nervous sweat from his skin. The crinkle of shoots beneath his feet suddenly seemed louder and Jack wanted nothing more than to get out onto the road, leave these dead things behind, find a car or thumb a lift into Tewton where there would be help, where there had to be help, because if there wasn't then where the hell *would* there be help?

Nowhere. There's no help anywhere. The thought chilled him, but he knew it was true, just as he had known that there were dead people around the corner of the field—

—just as he knew that there was something very, very wrong here as well. He could smell it already, a rich, warm tang to the air instead of the musty smell of death they had been living with all morning. A *fresh* smell. But he kept on running because he could not do anything else, even though he knew he should stay in the field, knew he *had* to stay in the field for his own good. He had played here with Jamie. They had shared good times here so it must be a good place.

Jack darted through the gate and out onto the pitted road.

The colors struck him first. Bright colors in a landscape so dull with death.

The car was a blazing yellow, a metal banana his mum would have called it, never lose that in a car park she would say. Inside the car sat a woman in a red dress, and inside the woman moved something else, a squirrel, its tail limp and heavy with her blood. The dress was not all red, he could see a white sleeve and a torn white flap hanging from the open door, touching the road.

Her face had been ripped off, her eyes torn out, her throat chewed away.

There was something else on the road next to the car, a mass of meat torn apart and spread across the tarmac. Jack saw the flash of bone and an eyeless head and a leg, still attached to the bulky torso by strands of stuff, but they did not truly register. What he did see and understand were the dozen small rodents chewing at the remnants of whatever it had been. Their tails were long and hairless, their bodies black and slick with the blood they wallowed in. They chewed slowly, but not thoughtfully because there could not have been a single thought in their little dead minds.

"Dad," Jack gasped, trying to shout but unable to find a breath.

More things lay farther toward the pond, and for a terrible moment Jack thought it was another body that had been taken apart (because that's what he saw, he knew that now, his mind had permitted understanding on the strict proviso that he—)

He turned and puked and fell to his knees in his own vomit, looking up to see his father standing at the gate and staring past him at the car.

Jack looked again, and he realized that although the thing farther along the road had once been a person— he could see its head, like a shop dummy's that had been stepped on and covered in shit and set on fire so the eyes melted and rolled out to leave black pits— there was no blood at all, no wetness there. Nothing chewed on these sad remains.

Dead already when the car ran them over. Standing there in the road, dead already, letting themselves be hit so that the driver—he had been tall, good looking, the girl in his passenger seat small and mouselike and scared into a gibbering, snotty wreck—would get out and go to see what he had done. Opening himself up to attack from the side, things darting from the ditches and downing him and falling on him quickly . . . and quietly. No sound apart from the girl's screams as she saw what was happening, and then her scream had changed in tone.

When they'd had their fill, they dragged themselves away to leave the remains to smaller dead things.

"Oh God, Dad!" Jack said, because he did not want to know anymore. Why the hell should he? How the hell did he know what he knew already?

His dad reached down and scooped him up into his arms, pressing his son's face into his shoulder so he did not have to look anymore. Jack raised his eyes and saw his mother walk slowly from the field, and she was trying not to look as well. She stared straight at Jack's face, her gaze unwavering, her lips tensed with the effort of not succumbing to human curiosity and subjecting herself to a sight that would live with her forever.

But of course she looked, and her liquid scream hurt Jack as much as anything ever had. He loved his mum because she loved him; he knew how much she loved him. His parents had bought him a microscope for Christmas and she'd pricked her finger with a needle so that he could look at her blood, that's how much she loved him. He hated to hear her scared, hated to see her in pain. Her fear and agony were all his own.

His father turned and ushered his mum down the road, away from the open banana car with its bright red mess, away from the bloody dead things eating up what was left. Jack, facing back over his dad's shoulder, watched the scene until it disappeared around a bend in the road. He listened to his father's labored breathing and his mother's panicked gasps. He looked at the pale green hedges, where even now hints of rot were showing through. And he wanted to go home.

"Are you scared, Jack?" Mandy had asked.

"No," he said truthfully.

"Not of me," she smiled. "Not of Mum and Dad and what's happening, that'll sort itself out. I mean ever. Are you ever scared of things? The dark, spiders, death, war, clowns? Ever, ever, ever?"

Jack went to shake his head, but then he thought of things that did frighten him a little. Not outright petrified, just disturbed, that's how he sometimes felt. Maybe that's what Mandy meant.

"Well," he said, "there's this thing on TV. It's Planet of the Apes, *the TV show, not the film. There's a bit at the beginning with the gorilla army man, Urko. His face is on the screen and sometimes it looks so big that it's bigger* than *the screen. It's really in the room, you know? Well . . . I hide behind my hands."*

"But do you peek?"

"No!"

"I've seen that program," Mandy said, even though Jack was pretty sure she had not. "I've seen it, and you know what? There's nothing at all to be scared of. I'll tell you why: The bit that scares you is made up of a whole bunch of bits that won't. A man in a suit; a camera trick, an actor, a nasty voice. And that man in the suit goes home at night, has a cup of tea, picks his nose and goes to the toilet. Now that's not very scary, is it?"

Even though he felt ill Jack giggled and shook his

head. "No!" He wondered whether the next time he watched that opening sequence, he'd be as scared as before. He figured maybe he would, but in a subtly different way. A grown-up way.

"Fear's made up of a load of things," she said, "and if you know those things . . . if you can name them . . . you're most of the way to accepting your fear."

"But what if you don't know what it is? What if you can't say what's scaring you?"

His sister looked up at the ceiling and tried to smile, but she could not. "I've tried it, over the last few days," she whispered. "I've named you, and Mum, and Dad, and the woods, and what happened, and you . . . out there in the woods, alone . . . and loneliness itself. But it doesn't work." She looked down at Jack again, looked straight into his eyes. "If that happens then it should be scaring you. Real fear is like intense pain. It's there to warn you something's truly wrong."

I hope I always know, *Jack thought.* I hope I always know what I'm afraid of.

Mandy began singing softly. Jack slept.

"Oh no! Dad, it's on fire!"

They had left the scene of devastation and headed toward the farm they'd spotted earlier, intending to find something to eat. It went unspoken that they did not expect to discover anyone alive at the farm. Jack only hoped they would not find anyone dead, either.

They paused in the lane, which was so infrequently used that grass and dock leaves grew in profusion along its central hump. Insipid green grass and yellowed dock now, though here and there tufts of rebellious life still poked through. The puddled wheel ruts held the occasional dead thing swimming feebly.

Jack's dad raised his binoculars, took a long look at the farm and lowered them again. "It's not burning. Something is, but it's not the farm. A bonfire, I think. I think the farmer's there, and he's started a bonfire in his yard."

"I wonder what he could be burning," Jack's mother said. She was pale and tired, her left arm tucked between the buttons of her shirt to try to ease the blood loss. Jack wanted to cry every time he looked at her, but he could see tears in her eyes as well, and he did not want to give her cause to shed any more.

"We'll go and find out."

"Dad, it might be dangerous. There might be . . . those people there. Those things." *Dead things,* Jack thought, but the idea of dead things walking still seemed too ridiculous to voice.

"We need food, Jack," his dad said, glancing at his mother as he said it. "And a drink. And some bandages for your mum, if we can find some. We need help."

"I'm scared. Why can't we just go on to Tewton?"

"And when we get there, and there are people moving around in the streets, will you want to hold back then? In case they're the dead things we've seen?"

Jack did not answer, but he shook his head because he knew his dad was right.

"I'll go on ahead slightly," his dad said. "I've got the gun. That'll stop anything that comes at us. Jack, you help your mum."

Didn't stop the other people, Jack thought. *And you*

couldn't shoot at Mrs. Haswell, could you, Dad? Couldn't shoot at someone you knew.

"Don't go too fast," his mum said quietly. "Gray, I can't walk too fast. I feel faint, but if I walk slowly I can keep my head clear."

He nodded, then started off, holding the shotgun across his stomach now instead of dipped over his elbow. Jack and his mother held back for a while and watched him go, Jack thinking how small and scared he looked against the frightening landscape.

"You all right, Mum?"

She nodded but did not turn her head. "Come on, let's follow your dad. In ten minutes we'll be having a nice warm cup of tea and some bread in the farmer's kitchen."

"But what's he burning? Why the bonfire?"

His mother did not answer, or could not. Perhaps she was using all her energy to walk. Jack did the only thing he could and stayed along beside her.

The lane crossed a B-road and then curved around to the farmyard, bounded on both sides by high hedges. There was no sign of any traffic, no hint that anyone had come this way recently. Jack looked to his left where the road rose slowly up out of the valley. In the distance he saw something walk from one side to the other, slowly, as if unafraid of being run down. It may have been a deer, but Jack could not be sure.

"Look," his mum said quietly. "Oh Jackie, look."

There was an area of tended plants at the entrance to the farm lane, rose bushes pointing skeletal thorns skyward and clematis smothered in pink buds turning brown. But it was not this his mother was pointing at with a finger covered in blood; it was the birds. There were maybe thirty of them, sparrows from what Jack could make out, though they could just as easily have been siskins that had lost their color. They flapped uselessly at the air, heads jerking with the effort, eyes like small black stones. They did not make a sound, and that is perhaps why his father had not seen them as he walked by. Or maybe he had seen them and chosen to ignore the sight. Their wings were obviously weak, their muscles wasting. They did not give in. Even as Jack and his mother passed by they continued to flap uselessly at air that no longer wished to support them.

Jack kept his eyes on them in case they followed.

They could smell the bonfire now, and tendrils of smoke wafted across the lane and into the fields on either side. "That's not a bonfire," Jack said. "I can't smell any wood." His mother began to sob as she walked. Jack did not know whether it was from her pain, or something else entirely.

A gunshot coughed at the silence. Jack's father crouched down low, twenty paces ahead of them. He brought his gun up but there was no smoke coming from the barrel. "Wait—!" he shouted, and another shot rang out. Jack actually saw the hedge next to his dad flicker as pellets tore through.

"Get away!" a voice said from a distance. "Get out of here! Get away!"

His dad backed down the lane, still in a crouch, signaling for Jack and his mum to back up as well. "Wait, we're all right, we're normal. We just want some help."

There was silence for a few seconds, then another two aimless shots in quick succession. "I'll kill you!" the voice shouted again, and Jack could tell its owner was crying. "You killed my Janice, you made me kill her again, and I'll kill you!"

Jack's dad turned and ran to them, keeping his head tucked down as if his shoulders would protect it against a shotgun blast. "Back to the road," he said.

"But we could reason with him."

"Janey, back to the road. The guy's burning his own cattle and some of them are still moving. Back to the road."

"Some of them are still moving," Jack repeated, fascination and disgust—two emotions which, as a young boy, he was used to experiencing in tandem—blurring his words.

"Left here," his father said as they reached the B-road. "We'll skirt around the farm and head up toward the woods. Tewton is on the other side of the forest."

"There's a big hill first, isn't there?" his mum said. "A steep hill?"

"It's not that steep."

"However steep it is . . ." But his mum trailed off, and when Jack looked at her he saw tears on her cheeks. A second glance revealed the moisture to be sweat, not tears. It was not hot, hardly even warm. He wished she was crying instead of sweating.

His father hurried them along the road until the farm was out of sight. The smell of the fire faded into the background scent of the countryside, passing over from lush and alive, to wan and dead. Jack could still not come to terms with what he was seeing. It was as if his eyes were slowly losing their ability to discern colors and vitality in things, the whole of his vision turning into one of those sepia-tinted photographs he'd seen in his grandmother's house, where people never smiled and the edges were eaten away by time and too many thumbs and fingers. Except the bright red of his mother's blood was still there, even though the hedges were pastel instead of vibrant. His dad's face was pale, yes, but the burning spots on his cheeks—they flared when he was angry or upset, or both—were as bright as ever. Some colors, it seemed, could not be subsumed so easily.

"We won't all fade away, will we, Dad? You won't let me and Mum and Mandy fade away, will you?"

His dad frowned, then ruffled his hair and squeezed the back of his neck. "Don't worry, son. We'll get to Tewton and everything will be all right. They'll be doing something to help, they're bound to. They have to."

"Who are 'they,' Dad?" Jack said, echoing his mum's question from that morning.

His dad shook his head. "Well, the government. The services, you know, the police and fire brigade."

Maybe they've faded away too, Jack thought. He did not say anything. It seemed he was keeping a lot of his thoughts to himself lately, making secrets. Instead, he tried naming some of his fears—they seemed more expansive and numerous every time he thought about them—but there was far too much he did not know. Fear is like pain, Mandy had told him. Maybe that's why his mum was hurting so much now. Maybe that's why *he* felt so much like crying. Underneath all the running around and the weirdness of today, perhaps he was truly in pain.

They followed the twisting road for ten minutes before hearing the sound of approaching vehicles.

"Stand back," Jack's dad said, stretching out and ushering Jack and his mum up against the hedge. Jack hated the feel of the dead leaves and buds against the back of his neck. They felt like long fingernails, and if he felt them move . . . if he felt them twitch and begin to scratch . . .

The hedges were high and overgrown here, though stark and sharp in death, and they did not see the cars until they were almost upon them. They were both battered almost beyond recognition, paint scoured off to reveal rusting metal beneath. *It's as if even the cars are dying,* Jack thought, and though it was a foolish notion it chilled him and made him hug his dad.

His dad brought up the gun. Jack could feel him shaking. He could feel the fear there, the tension in his legs, the effort it was taking for him to breathe.

"Dad?" he said, and he was going to ask what was wrong. He was going to ask why was he pointing a gun at people who could help them, maybe give them a lift to Tewton.

"Oh dear God," his mum said, and Jack heard the crackle as she leaned back against the hedge.

There were bodies tied across the bonnets of each car. He'd seen pictures of hunters in America, returning to town with deer strapped across the front of their cars, parading through the streets with kills they had made. This was not the same because these bodies were not kills. They were dead, yes, but not kills, because their heads rolled on their necks, their hands twisted at the wrist, their legs shook and their heels banged on the hot metal beneath them.

Jack's father kept his gun raised. The cars slowed and Jack saw the faces inside, young for the most part, eyes wide and mouths open in sneers of rage or fear or mockery, whatever it was Jack could not tell. Living faces, but mad as well.

"Wanna lift?" one of the youths shouted through the Ital's smashed windscreen.

"I think we'll walk," Jack's dad said.

"It's not safe." The cars drifted to a standstill. "These fuckers are everywhere. Saw them eating a fucking bunch of people on the motorway. Ran them over." He leaned through the windscreen and patted the dead woman's head. She stirred, her eyes blank and black, skin ripped in so many places it looked to Jack like she was shedding. "So, you wanna lift?"

"Where are you going?" Jack asked.

The boy shrugged. He had a bleeding cut on his face; Jack was glad. The dead didn't bleed. "Dunno. Somewhere where they can figure out what these fuckers are about."

"Who are 'they'?" Jack's dad asked.

The youth shrugged again, his bravado diluted by doubt. His eyes glittered and Jack thought he was going to cry, and suddenly he wished the youth would curse again, shout and be big and brave and defiant.

"We'll walk. We're going to Tewton."

"Yes, Mandy rang and said it's safe there!" Jack said excitedly.

"Best of luck to you then, little man," the driver said.

Then he accelerated away. The second car followed, frightened faces staring out. The cars—the dead and the living—soon passed out of sight along the road.

"Into the fields again," Jack's dad said. "Up the hill to the woods. It's safer there."

Safer among dead things than among the living, Jack thought. Again, he kept his thought to himself. Again, they started across the fields.

They saw several cows standing very still in the distance, not chewing, not snorting, not flicking their tails. Their udders hung slack and empty, teats already black. They seemed to be looking in their direction. None of them moved. They looked like photos Jack had seen of the concrete cows in Milton Keynes, though those looked more lifelike.

It took an hour to reach the edge of the woods. Flies buzzed them but did not bite, the skies were empty of birds, things crawled along at the edges of fields, where dead crops met dead hedges.

The thought of entering the woods terrified Jack, though he could not say why. Perhaps it was a subconscious memory of the time he had been lost in the woods. That time had been followed by a mountain of heartache. Maybe he was anticipating the same now.

Instead, as they passed under the first stretch of dipping trees, they found a house, and a garden and more bright colors than Jack had names for.

"Look at that! Janey, look at that! Jack, see, I told you, it's not all bad!"

The cottage was small, its roof slumped in the middle and its woodwork painted a bright, cheery yellow. The garden was a blazing attack of color, and for a while Jack thought he was seeing something from a fairy tale. Roses were only this red in stories, beans this green, grass so pure, ivy so darkly gorgeous across two sides of the house. Only in fairy tales did potted plants stand in windowsill ranks so perfectly, their petals kissing each other but never stealing or leeching color from their neighbor. Greens and reds and blues and violets and yellows, all stood out against the backdrop of the house and the limp, dying woods behind it. In the woods there were still colors, true, vague echoes of past glories clinging to branches or leaves or fronds. But this garden, Jack thought, must be where all the color in the world had fled, a Noah's Ark for every known shade and tint and perhaps a few still to be discovered. There was magic in this place.

"Oh, wow," his mum said. She was smiling, and Jack was glad. But his father, who had walked to the garden gate and pulled an overhanging rose stem to his nose, was no longer smiling. His expression was as far away from a smile as could be.

"It's not real," his dad said.

"What?"

"This rose isn't real. It's . . . synthetic. It's silk, or something."

"But the grass, Dad . . ."

Jack ran to the gate as his father pushed through it, and they hit the lawns together.

"Astroturf. Like they use on football pitches, sometimes. Looks pretty real, doesn't it, son?"

"The beans. The fruit trees, over there next to the cottage."

"Beans and fruit? In spring?"

Jack's mum was through the gate now, using her one good hand to caress the plants, squeeze them and watch them spring back into shape, bend them and hear the tiny *snap* as a plastic stem broke. Against the fake colors of the fake plants, she looked very pale indeed.

Jack ran to the fruit bushes and tried to pluck one of the red berries hanging there in abundance. It was difficult parting it from its stem, but it eventually popped free and he threw it straight into his mouth. He was not really expecting a burst of fruity flesh, and he was not proved wrong. It tasted like the inside of a yogurt carton: plastic and false.

"It's not fair!" Jack ran to the front door of the cottage and hammered on the old wood, ignoring his father's hissed words of caution from behind him. His mum was poorly, they needed some food and drink, there were dead things—*dead* things, for fucking hell's sake—walking around and chasing them and eating people. Saw them eating a fucking bunch of people on the motorway, the man in the car had said.

All that, and now this, and none of it was fair.

The door drifted open. There were good smells from within, but old smells as well: the echoes of fresh bread; the memory of pastries; a vague idea that chicken had been roasted here recently, though surely not today and probably not yesterday.

"There's no one here!" Jack called over his shoulder.

"They might be upstairs."

Jack shook his head. No, he knew this place was empty. He'd known the people in the field were coming and he'd seen what the dead folk in the banana car were like before . . . before he saw them for real. And he knew that this cottage was empty.

He went inside.

His parents dashed in after him, even his poor mum. He felt bad about making her rush, but once they were inside and his dad had looked around, they knew they had the place to themselves.

"It's just not fair," Jack said once again, elbows resting on a windowsill in the kitchen, chin cradled in cupped hands. "All those colors . . ."

There was a little bird in the garden, another survivor drawn by the colors. It was darting here and there, working at the fruit, pecking at invisible insects, fluttering from branch to plastic branch in a state of increasing agitation.

"Why would someone do this?" his mum asked. She was sitting at the pitted wooden table with a glass of orange juice and a slice of cake. Real juice, real cake. "Why construct a garden so false?"

"I feel bad about just eating their stuff," his dad said. "I mean, who knows who lives here? Maybe it's a little old lady and she has her garden like this because she's too frail to tend it herself. We'll leave some money when we go." He tapped his pockets, sighed. "You got any cash, Janey?"

She shook her head. "I didn't think to bring any when we left this morning. It was all so . . . rushed."

"Maybe everything's turning plastic and this is just

where it begins," Jack mused. Neither of his parents
replied. "I read a book once where everything turned
to glass."

"I'll try the TV," his dad said after a long pause.

Jack followed him through the stuffy hallway and
into the living room, a small room adorned with faded
tapestries, brass ornaments and family portraits of
what seemed like a hundred children. Faces smiled
from the walls, hair shone in forgotten summer sunshine, and Jack wondered where all these people were
now. If they were still children, were they in school? If
they were grown up, were they doing what he and his
parents were doing, stumbling their way through
something so strange and *unexpected* that it forbore
comprehension?

Or perhaps they were all dead. Sitting at home. Staring at their own photographs on their own walls, seeing how things used to be.

"There it is," his dad said. "Christ, what a relic." He
never swore in front of Jack, not even damn or Christ
or shit. He did not seem to notice his own standards
slipping.

The television was an old wooden cabinet type, buttons and dials running down one side of the screen,
no remote control, years of mugs and plates having
left their ghostly impressions on the veneered top. His
dad plugged it in and switched it on, and they heard
an electrical buzz as it wound itself up. As the picture
coalesced from the soupy screen Jack's dad glanced
at his watch. "Almost six o'clock. News should be on
anytime now."

"I expect they'll have a news flash, anyway," Jack said confidently.

His dad did something then that both warmed his heart and disconcerted him. He laughed gently and gave him a hug, and Jack felt tears cool and shameless on his cheek. "Of course they will, son," he said, "I'm sure they will."

"Anything?" called his mum.

"Nearly," Jack shouted back.

There was no sound. The screen was stark and bland, and the bottom half stated: "This is a Government Announcement." The top half of the screen contained scrolling words: "Stay calm . . . Remain indoors . . . Help is at hand . . . Please await further news."

And that was it.

"What's on the other side, Dad?"

Buttons clicked in, the picture fizzled and changed. BBC1, BBC2, ITV, Channel 4, Channel 5, there were no others. But if there were, they probably would have contained the same image. The government notice, the scrolling words that should have brought comfort but which, in actual fact, terrified Jack. "I wonder how long it's been like that," he said, unable to prevent a shiver in his voice. "Dad, what if it isn't changing."

"It says 'Please await further news.' They wouldn't say that unless they were going to put something else up soon. Information on where to go or something."

"Yeah, but that's like a sign on a shop door saying 'Be back soon.' It could have been there for months."

His dad looked down at him, frowning, chewing his lower lip. "There's bound to be something on the radio.

312

dio. Come on, I think I saw one in the kitchen."

His mum glanced up as they entered and Jack told her what they had seen. The radio was on a shelf above the cooker. It looked like the sort of antique people spent lots of money to own nowadays, but it was battered and yellowed, and its back cover was taped on. It crackled into instant life. A somber brass band sprang from the speakers.

"Try 1215 medium wave," Jack said. "Virgin."

His dad tuned; the same brass band.

In six more places across the wavelengths, the same brass band.

"I'll leave it on. Maybe there'll be some news after this bit of music. I'll leave it on."

They tried the telephone as well, but every number was engaged. 999, the operator, the local police station, family and friends, random numbers. It was as if everyone in the world was trying to talk to someone else.

Twenty minutes later Jack's dad turned the radio off. They went to check the television and he switched that off as well. His mum laid down on the settee and Jack washed the cuts on her arms and the horrible wound on her shoulder, crying and gagging at the same time. He was brave, he kept it down. His mum was braver.

Later, after they had eaten some more food from the fridge and shared a huge pot of tea, his dad suggested they go to bed. No point trying to travel at night, he said, they'd only get lost. Besides, better to rest now and do the final part of the trip tomorrow than to travel all night, exhausted.

And there were those things out there as well, Jack

thought, though his dad did not mention them. Dead things. *These fuckers are everywhere.* Dead cows, dead birds, dead insects, dead grass, dead crops, dead trees, dead hedges . . . dead people. Dead things everywhere with one thing in mind—to keep moving. To find life.

How long before they rot away?

Or maybe the bugs that make things rot are dead as well.

There were two bedrooms. Jack said he was happy sleeping alone in one, so long as both doors were kept open. He heard his mother groan as she lowered herself onto their bed, his father bustling in the bathroom, the toilet flushing . . . and it was all so normal.

Then he saw a spider in the corner of his room and there was no way of telling whether it was alive or dead—even when it moved—and he realized that "normal" was going to have to change its coat.

Night fell unnaturally quickly, but when he glanced at his watch in the moonlight he saw that several hours had passed. Maybe he had been drifting in and out of sleep, daydreaming, though he could not recall what these fancies were about. He could hear his father's light snoring, his mother's breathing pained and uncomfortable. *What if something tries to get in now?* he thought. *What if I hear fingers picking at window latches and tapping at the glass, nails scratching wood to dig out the frames?* He looked up at the misshapen ceiling and thought he saw tiny dark things scurrying in and out of cracks, but it may have been fluid shapes on the surfaces of his eyes.

Then he heard the noises beginning outside. They

may have been the sounds of dead things crawling through undergrowth, but so long as he did not hear them shoving between plastic stems and false flowers, everything would be fine. The dark seemed to allow sounds to travel farther, ring clearer, as if light could dampen noise. Perhaps it could; perhaps it would lessen the sound of dead things walking.

The night was full of furtive movements, clawed feet on hard ground, sagging bellies dragging through stiff grasses. There were no grunts or cries or shouts, no hooting owls or barking foxes screaming like tortured babies, because dead things couldn't talk. Dead things, Jack discovered that night, could only wander from one pointless place to another, taking other dead things with them and perhaps leaving parts of themselves behind. Whether he closed his eyes or kept them open he saw the same image, his own idea of what the scene was like out there tonight: no rhyme; no reason; no competition to survive; no feeding (unless there were a few unlucky living things still abroad); no point, no use, no ultimate aim . . .

. . . aimless.

He opened and closed his eyes, opened and closed them, stood and walked quietly to the window. The moon was almost full and it cast its silvery glare across a sickly landscape. He thought there was movement here and there, but when he looked he saw nothing. It was his poor night vision, he knew that, but it was also possible that the things didn't want to be seen moving. There was something secretive in that. Something intentional.

He went back to bed. When he was much younger

it had always felt safe, and the feeling persisted now in some small measure. He pulled the stale blankets up over his nose.

His parents slept on. Jack remained awake. Perhaps he was seeking another secret in the night, and that thought conjured Mandy again. All those nights she had sat next to his bed talking to him, telling him adult things she'd never spoken of before, things about fear and imagination and how growing up closes doors in your mind. He had thought she'd been talking about herself, but she'd really been talking about him as well. She'd been talking about both of them because they were so alike, even if she was twice his age. And because they loved each other just as a brother and sister always should, and whatever had happened in the past could never, ever change that.

Because of Mandy he could name his fears, dissect and identify them, come to know them if not actually come to terms with them. He would never have figured that out for himself, he was sure.

What she said had always seemed so right.

He closed his eyes to rest, and the dead had their hands on him.

They were grabbing at his arms, moving to his legs, pinching and piercing with rotten nails. One of them slapped his face and it was Mandy, she was standing at the bedside smiling down at him, her eyes shriveled prunes in her gray face, and you should always name your fears.

Jack opened his mouth to scream but realized he was not breathing. *It's safe here,* he heard Mandy say. She was still smiling, welcoming, but there was a sadness behind that smile—even behind the slab of meat she had become—that Jack did not understand.

He had not seen Mandy for several months. She should be pleased to see him.

Then he noticed that the hands on his arms and legs were her own and her nails were digging in, promising never, ever to let him go, they were together now, it was safe here, safe . . .

"Jack!"

Still shaking, still slapped.

"Jack! For fuck's sake!"

Jack opened his eyes and Mandy disappeared. His dad was there instead, and for a split second Jack was confused. Mandy and his dad looked so alike.

"Jackie, come with me," his dad said quietly. "Come on, we're leaving now."

"Is it morning?"

"Yes. Morning."

"Where's Mum?"

"Come on, son, we're going to go now. We're going to find Mandy."

Her name chilled him briefly, but then Jack remembered that even though she had been dead in his dream, still she'd been smiling. She had never hurt him; she *would* never hurt him. She would never hurt any of them.

"I need a pee."

"You can do that outside."

"What about food, Dad? We can't walk all that way without eating."

His dad turned his back and his voice sounded strange, as if forced through lips sewn shut. "I'll get some food together when we're downstairs, now come on."

"Mum!" Jack shouted.

"Jackie—"

"Mum! Is she awake yet, Dad?"

His father turned back to him, his eyes wide and wet and overflowing with grief and shock. Jack should have been shocked as well, but he was not, not really that shocked at all.

"Mum . . ." he whispered.

He darted past his father's outstretched hands and into the bedroom his parents had shared.

"Mum!" he said, relief sagging him against the wall. She was sitting up in bed, hands in her lap, staring at the doorway because she knew Jack would come running in as soon as he woke up. "I thought . . . Dad made me think . . ." *that you were dead.*

Nobody moved for what seemed like hours.

"She was cold when I woke up." His dad sobbed behind him. "Cold. So cold. And sitting like that. She hasn't moved, Jackie. Not even when I touched her. I felt for her pulse and she just looked at me . . . I felt for her heart, but she just stared . . . she just keeps staring. . . ."

"Mum," Jack gasped. Her expression did not change because there was no expression. Her face was like a child's painting: two eyes, a nose, a mouth, no life there at all, no heart, no love or personality or soul. "Oh Mum . . ."

She was looking at him. Her eyes were dry, so he could not see himself reflected there. Her breasts sagged in death, her open shoulder was a pale bloodless mass, like over-cooked meat. Her hands were crossed, and the finger she had pricked so that he could study her swarming blood under his microscope was pasty gray.

"We'll take her," Jack said. "When we get to Tewton they'll have a cure. We'll take her and—"

"Jack!" His father grabbed him under the arms and hauled him back toward the stairs. Jack began to kick and shout, trying to give life to his mother by pleading with her to help him, promising they would save her. "Jack we're leaving now, because Mum's dead. And Mandy is all we have left, Jackie. Listen to me!"

Jack continued to scream and his father dragged him downstairs, through the hallway and into the kitchen. He shouted and struggled, even though he knew his dad was right. They had to go on, they couldn't take his dead mum with them, they had to go on. They'd seen dead people yesterday, and the results of dead people eating living people. He knew his dad was right but he was only a terrified boy, verging on his teens, full of fight and power and rage. The doors in his mind were as wide as they'd ever been, but grief makes so many unconscious choices that control becomes an unknown quantity.

Jack sat at the kitchen table and cried as his father filled a bag with food and bread. He wanted comfort, he wanted a cuddle, but he watched his dad work and saw the tears on his face too. He looked a hundred years old.

At last Jack looked up at the ceiling—he thought he'd heard movement from up there, bedsprings flexing and settling—and he told his dad he was sorry.

"Jack, you and Mandy . . . I have to help you. We've got to get to Mandy, you see that? All the silly stuff, all that shit that happened . . . if only we knew how petty it all was. Oh God, if only I could un-say so much, son. Now, with all this . . . Mandy and Mum can never make up now." Bitter tears were pouring from his eyes, no matter how much he tried to keep them in. "But Mandy and I can. Come on, it's time to go."

"Is there any news, Dad?" Jack wanted him to say yes, to hear they'd found a cure.

His dad shrugged. "TV's the same this morning. Just like that 'Be back soon' sign."

"You checked it already?"

"And the phone and the radio. All the same. When I found your mum, I thought . . . I wanted help."

They opened the front door together. Jack went first and as he turned to watch the door close, he was sure he saw his mother's feet appear at the top of the stairs. Ready to follow them out.

It was only as they came to the edge of the grotesquely cheerful garden that Jack saw just how much things had changed overnight.

Looking down the hillside he could recognize little. Yesterday had come along to kill everything, and last night had leeched any remnants of color or life from those sad corpses. Everything was dull. Branches dipped at the ground as if trying to find their way back to seed, grasses lay flat against the earth, hedgerows snaked blandly across the land, their dividing purpose now moot. Jack's eye was drawn to the occasional hints of color in clumps of trees or hedges, where a lone survivor stood proudly against the background of its dead cousins. A survivor much like them.

Nothing was moving. The sky was devoid of birds, and for as far as they could see the landscape was utterly still.

"Through the woods. Back of the house. Come on, son, one hour and we'll be there." Jack thought it would be more like two hours, maybe three, but he was grateful for his dad's efforts on his behalf.

They skirted the garden. Jack tried desperately not to look at the cottage in case he saw a familiar face pressed against a window.

Ten minutes later they were deep in the woods, still heading generally upward toward the summit of the hill. The ground was coated with dead leaves—autumn in spring—and in places they were knee-deep. Jack had used to enjoy kicking through dried leaves piled along pavements in the autumn—his mother told him it was an indication of the rebirth soon to come—but today he did not enjoy it. His mum was not here to talk to him . . . and he was unsure of what sort of rebirth could ever come of this. He saw a squirrel at the base of one tree, grayer than gray, stiff in death but its limbs still twitching intermittently. It was like a wind-up toy whose key was on its final revolution. Some branches were lined with dead birds, and only a few of them were moving. There was an occasional rustle of leaves as something fell to the ground.

Grief was blurring Jack's vision, but even without tears the unreality of what was on view would have done the same. Where trees dipped down and tapped him on the shoulder, he thought they were skeletal fingers reaching from above. Where dead things lay twitching, he thought he could see some hidden hand moving them. There had to be something hidden, Jack thought, something causing and controlling all this. Otherwise what was the point? He believed strongly in reasons, cause and effect. Coincidence and randomness were just too terrifyingly cold to even consider. Without reason, his mum's death was pointless.

His dad kept reaching out to touch him on the head, or the shoulder, or the arm, perhaps to make sure he was still there, or maybe simply to ensure that he was real. Occasionally he would mumble incoherently, but mostly he was silent. The only other sound was the swish of dead leaves, and the intermittent impact of things hitting the ground for the final time.

Jack looked back once. After thinking of doing so, it took him several minutes to work up the courage. They had found an old track that led deep into the woods, always erring upward, and they were following that path now, the going easier than plowing across the forest floor. He knew that if he turned he would see his mother following them, a gray echo of the wonderful woman she had been yesterday, her blood dried black on her clothes, smile caused by stretched skin rather than love. She had pricked her finger for him that Christmas, and to the young boy he'd been then, that was the ultimate sign of love—the willingness to inflict pain upon herself for him. But now, now that she was gone, Jack knew that his mother's true love was something else entirely. It was the proud smile every time she saw him go out to explore and experience. It was the hint of sadness in that smile, because *every single time* she said goodbye, somewhere deep inside she knew it could be the last. And it was the hug and kiss at the end of the day, when once again he came home safe and sound.

So Jack turned around, knowing he would see this false shadow of all the wonderful things his mother had been.

There was nothing following them, no one, and Jack was pleased. But still fresh tears came.

They paused and tried to eat, but neither was hungry. Jack sat on a fallen tree and put his face in his hands.

"Be brave, Jack." His dad sat next to him and hugged him close. "Be brave. Your mum would want that, wouldn't she?"

"But what about you, Dad?" Jack asked helplessly. "Won't you be lonely?"

His dad lowered his head and Jack saw the diamond rain of tears. "Of course I will, son. But I've got you, and I've got Mandy. And your mum would want me to be brave as well, don't you think?"

Jack nodded and they sat that way for a while, alternately crying and smiling into the trees when unbidden memories came. Jack did not want to relive good memories, not now, because here they would be polluted by all the dead things around them. But they came anyway and he guessed they always would, and at the most unexpected and surprising times. They were sad but comforting. He could not bear to drive them away.

They started walking again. Here and there were signs of life, but they were few and far between: a bluebell still bright among its million dead cousins; a woodpecker burrowing into rotting wood; a squirrel, jumping from tree to tree as if following them, then disappearing altogether.

Jack began to wonder how long the survivors would survive. How long would it be before whatever had killed everything else killed them, like it had his mum? He was going to ask his dad, but decided against it. He must be thinking the same thing.

In Tewton it would be safe. Mandy had said so, Mandy was there, and now she and Dad could make up for good. At least then, there would still be something of a family about them.

They walked through the woods and nothing changed. Jack's dad held the shotgun in both hands but he had no cause to use it. Things were grayer today, blander, slower. It seemed also that things were deader. They found three dead people beneath a tree, not one of them showing any signs of movement. They looked as though they had been dead for weeks, but they still had blood on their chins. Their stomachs were bloated and torn open.

Just before midday they emerged suddenly from the woods and found themselves at the top of the hill, looking down into a wide, gentle valley. The colors here had gone as well; it looked like a fine film of ash had smothered everything in sight, from the nearest tree to the farthest hillside. In the distance, hunkered down behind a roll in the land as if hiding itself away, they could just make out the uppermost spires and roofs of Tewton. From this far away it was difficult to see whether there were any signs of life. Jack thought not, but he tried not to look too hard in case he was right.

"Let's take a rest here, Jackie," his dad said. "Let's sit and look." Jack's mum used that saying when they were on holiday, the atmosphere and excitement driving Jack and Mandy into a frenzy, his dad eager to find a pub, an eternity of footpaths and sight-seeing stretched out before them. *Let's just sit and look,* she had said, and they had heeded her words and simply enjoyed the views and surroundings for what they were. Here and now there was nothing he wanted to sit and look at. The place smelled bad, there were no sounds other than their own labored breathing, the landscape was a corpse laid out on a slab, perhaps awaiting identification, begging burial. There was nothing here he wanted to see.

But they sat and looked, and when Jack's heartbeat settled back to normal, he realized that he could no longer hear his father's breathing.

He held his breath. Stared down at the ground between his legs, saw the scattered dead beetles and ants, and the ladybirds without any flame in their wings. He had never experienced such stillness, such silence. He did not want to look up, did not want events to move on to whatever he would find next. *Dad dead,* he named. *Me on my own. Me, burying Dad.*

Slowly, he raised his head.

His father was asleep. His breathing was long and slow and shallow, a contented slumber or the first signs of his body running down, following his wife to that strange place which had recently become even stranger. He remained sitting upright and his hands still clasped the gun, but his chin was resting on his chest, his shoulders rising and falling, rising and falling, so slightly that Jack had to watch for a couple of minutes to make sure.

He could not bear to think of his father not waking up. He went to touch him on the shoulder, but wondered what the shock would do.

They had to get to Tewton. They were here—hell, he could even *see* it—but still they found no safety. If there was help to be had, it must be where Mandy had said it would be.

Jack stood, stepped from foot to foot, looked around as if expecting help to come galloping across the funereal landscape on a white charger. Then he gently lifted the binoculars from his dad's neck, negotiated the strap under his arms, and set off along the hillside. Ten minutes, he figured, if he walked for ten minutes he would be able to see what was happening down in Tewton. See the hundreds of people rushing hither and tither, helping the folks who had come in from the dead countryside, providing food and shelter and some scrap of normality among the insanity. There would be soldiers there, and doctors, and tents in the streets because there were too many survivors to house in the buildings. There would be food as well, tons of it ferried in by helicopter, blankets and medicines . . . maybe a vaccine . . . or a cure.

But there were no helicopters. And there were no sounds of life.

He saw more dead things on the way, but he had nothing to fear from them. Yesterday dead had been dangerous, an insane, impossible threat; now it was simply no more. Today, the living were unique.

Jack looked down on the edge of the town. A scattering of houses and garages and gardens spewed out into the landscape from between the low hills. There was a church there as well, and a row of shops with smashed windows, and several cars parked badly along the two streets he could see.

He lowered the binoculars and oriented himself from a distance, then looked again. A road wound into town from this side, trailing back along the floor of the valley before splitting in two, one of these arteries climbing toward the woods he and his father had just exited. Jack frowned, moved back to where the road passed between two rows of houses into the town, the blurred vision setting him swaying like a sunflower in the breeze.

He was shaking. The vibration knocked him out of focus. There was a cool hand twisting his insides and drawing him back the way he had come, not only to his father, but to his dead mother as well. It was as if she were calling him across the empty miles that now separated them, pleading that he not leave her alone in that strange color-splashed cottage, singing her love to tunes of guilt and with a chorus of childlike desperation so strong that it made him feel sick. However grown up Jack liked to think he was, all he wanted at that moment was his mother. And in a way he *was* older than his years, because he knew he would feel like that whatever his age.

Tears gave him a fluid outlook. He wiped his eyes

roughly with his sleeve and looked again, breathing in deeply and letting his breath out in a long, slow sigh.

There were people down there. A barricade of some sort had been thrown across the road just where houses gave way to countryside—there was a car, and some furniture, and what looked like fridges and cookers—and behind this obstruction heads bobbed, shapes moved. Jack gasped and smiled and began to shake again, this time with excitement.

Mandy must be down there somewhere, waiting for them to come in. When she saw it was just Jack and his dad she would know the truth, they would not need to tell her, but as a family they could surely pull through, help each other and hold each other and love each other as they always should have.

Jack began to run back to his dad. He would wake him and together they would go the final mile.

The binoculars banged against his hip and he fell, crunching dry grass, skidding down the slope and coming to rest against a hedge. A shower of dead things pattered down on his face, leaves and twigs and petrified insects. His mum would wipe them away. She would spit on her handkerchief and dab at the cuts on his face, scold him for running when he should walk, tell him to read a book instead of watching the television.

He stood and started off again, but then he heard a voice.

"Jack."

It came from afar, faint, androgynous with distance and panic. He could hear that well enough; he could hear the panic.

"Jack."

He looked uphill toward the forest, expecting to see the limp figure of his mother edge out from beneath the trees' shadows, coming at him from the woods.

"Jack!"

The voice was louder now and accompanied by something else—the rhythmic *slap slap slap* of running feet.

Jack looked down the hill and made out something behind a hedge denuded of leaves. Lifting the binoculars he saw his father running along the road, hands pumping at the air, feet kicking up dust.

"Dad!" he called, but his father obviously did not hear. He disappeared behind a line of brown evergreens.

Jack tracked the road through the binoculars, all the way to Tewton. His dad must have woken up, found him missing and assumed he'd already made his way to the town, eager to see Mandy, or just too grief-stricken to wait any longer. Now he was on his way into town on his own, and when he arrived he would find Jack absent. He would panic. He would think himself alone, alone but for Mandy. How would two losses in one day affect him?

His dad emerged farther down the hillside, little more than a smudge against the landscape now, still running and still calling.

Jack ran as well. He figured if he moved as the crow flies they would reach the barricade at the same time. Panic over. Then they would find Mandy.

He tripped again, cursed, hauled the binoculars from his shoulder and threw them away. As he stood and ran on down the hill, he wondered whether they would ever be found. He guessed not. He guessed they'd stay here forever, and one day they would be a fossil. There were lots of future fossils being made today.

He could no longer see his dad, but he could see the hedgerow hiding the road that led into Tewton. His feet were carrying him away, moving too fast, and at some point Jack lost control. He was no longer running, he was falling, plummeting down the hillside in a reckless dash that would doubtless result in a broken leg—at least—should he lose his footing again. He concentrated on the ground just ahead of him, tempted to look down the hillside at the road but knowing he should not. He should watch out for himself, for if he broke a limb now and there were no doctors in Tewton . . .

As the slope of the hill lessened so he brought his dash under control. His lungs were burning with exertion and he craved a drink. He did not stop running, though, because the hedge was close now, a tangled, bramble-infested maze of dead twigs and crumbling branches.

Tewton was close too. He could see rooftops to his right, but little else. He'd be at the barricade in a matter of minutes.

He hoped, how he hoped that Mandy was there to greet them. She and their father would have made up already, arms around each other, smiling sad smiles. *I've named my fears*, Jack would tell her, and though their father would not understand they would smile at each other and hug, and he would tell her how what she had told him had saved him from going mad.

He reached the hedge and ran along it until he found a gate. His knees were flaring with pain, his chest tight and fit to burst, but he could see the road. He climbed the gate—there was a dead badger on the other side; not roadkill, just dead, and thankfully unmoving—and jumped into the lane.

It headed around a bend, and he was sure he heard pounding footsteps for a few seconds. It may have been his heart; it was thumping at his chest, urging him on, encouraging him to safety. He listened to it and hurried along the lane, moving at a shuffle now, more than a run.

As he rounded the bend everything came into view.

The people first of all, a couple of them still dragging themselves from the drainage reens either side of the road, several more converging on his father. He stood several steps from the barricade, glancing frantically around, obviously searching for Jack but seeing only dead people circling him, staring at him.

"Dad!" Jack shouted, at least he tried to. It came out as a gasp, fear and dread and defeat all rolled into one exhalation. Tewton . . . hope . . . help, all given way to these dead things. For a fleeting instant he thought the barricade was a dividing line behind which hope may still exist, but then he saw that it wasn't really a barricade at all. It may have been once, maybe only hours ago, but now it was broken down and breached. Little more than another pile of rubbish that would never be cleared.

"Dad!" This time it *was* a shout. His dad spun around, and it almost broke Jack's heart to see the relief on his face. But then fear regained its hold and his dad began to shout.

"Jack, stay away, they're here, look! Stay away, Jack!"

"But, Dad—"

His father fired the shotgun and one of the dead people hit the road. It—Jack could not even discern its sex—squirmed and slithered, unable to regain its feet.

Mandy, he thought, *where's Mandy, what of Mandy? Mandy dead, Mandy gone, only me and Dad left—*

But the naming of his fears did him no good, because he was right to be afraid. He knew that when he heard the sounds behind him. He knew it when he turned and saw Mandy scrabbling out from the ditch, her long black hair clotted with dried leaves, her grace hobbled by death.

"Mandy," he whispered, and he thought she paused.

There was another gunshot behind him and the sound of metal hitting something soft. Then running feet coming his way. He hoped they were his father's. He remembered the dead people in the field yesterday, how fast they had moved, how quickly they had charged.

Mandy was gray and pale and thin. Her eyes showed none of his sister, her expression was not there, he could not *sense* her at all. Her silver rings rattled loose on long stick fingers. She was walking toward him.

"Mandy, Mandy, it's me, Jack—"

"Jack! Move!" His father's words were slurred because he was running, it *was* his footsteps Jack could hear. And then he heard a shout, a curse.

He risked a glance over his shoulder. His father had tripped and slid across the lane on his hands and knees, the shotgun clattering into the ditch, three of the dead folk closing on him from behind. "Dad, behind you!" Jack shouted.

His father looked up at Jack, his eyes widened, his mouth hung open, his hands bled. "Behind you!" he shouted back.

A weight struck Jack and he went sprawling. He half turned as he fell so that he landed on his side, and he looked up and back in time to see Mandy toppling over on top of him. The wind was knocked from him and for a few seconds his chest felt tight, useless, dead.

Perhaps this is what it's like, he thought. *To be like them.*

At last he drew a shuddering breath, and the stench of Mandy hit him at the same time. The worst thing . . . the worst thing of all . . . was that he could detect a subtle hint of Obsession beneath the dead animal smell of her. His mum and dad always bought Obsession for Mandy at the airport when they went on holiday, and Jack had had a big box of jelly-fruits.

He felt her hands clawing at him, fingers seeking his throat, bony knees jarring into his stomach, his crotch. He screamed and struggled but could not move, Mandy had always beaten him at wrestling, she was just so strong—

"Get off!" his dad shouted. Jack could not see what was happening—he had landed so that he looked along the lane away from Tewton—but he could hear. "Get the fuck off, get away!" A thump as something soft hit the ground, then other sounds less easily identifiable, like an apple being stepped on or a leg torn from a cooked chicken. Then the unmistakable metallic snap of the shotgun being broken, reloaded, closed.

Two shots in rapid succession.

"Oh God, oh God, oh . . . Jack, it's not Mandy, Jack, you know that don't you!"

Jack struggled onto his back and looked up at the thing atop him.

You can name your fears, Mandy had said, and Jack could not bear to look. This bastard thing resembling his beautiful sister was a travesty, a crime against everything natural and everything right.

Jack closed his eyes. "I still love you Mandy," he said, but he was not talking to the thing on top of him now.

There was another blast from the shotgun. A weight landed on his chest, something sprinkled down across his face. He kept his eyes closed. The weight twisted for a while, squirmed and scratched at Jack with nails and something else, exposed bones perhaps—

A hand closed around his upper arm and pulled.

Jack screamed, shouted until his throat hurt. Maybe he could scare it off. "It's alright, Jackie," a voice whispered into his ear. Mandy had never called him Jackie, so why now, why when—

Then he realized it was his father's voice. Jack opened his eyes as he stood and looked straight into his dad's face. They stared at each other because they both knew to stare elsewhere—to stare *down*—would invite images they could never, ever live with.

They held hands as they ran along the lane, away from Tewton. For a while there were sounds of possible pursuit behind them, but they came from a distance and Jack simply could not bring himself to look.

They ran for a very long time. For a while Jack felt like he was going mad, or perhaps it was clarity in a world gone mad itself. In his mind's eye he saw the dead people of Tewton waiting in their little town, waiting for the survivors to flee there from the countryside, slaughtering and eating them, taking feeble strength from cooling blood and giving themselves a few more hours before true death took them at last. The image gave him a strange sense of hope because he saw it could not go on forever. Hope in the death of the dead. A strange place to take comfort.

At last they could run no more. They found a petrol station and collapsed in the little shop, drinking warm cola because the electricity was off, eating chocolate and crisps. They rested until midafternoon. Then, because they did not know what else to do, they moved on once more.

Jack held his father's hand. They walked along a main road, but there was no traffic. At one junction they saw a person nailed high up on an old telegraph pole. Jack began to wonder why but then gave in because he knew he would never know.

The countryside began to flatten out. A few miles from where they were was the coast, an aim as good as any now, a place where help may have landed.

"You okay to keep going, son?"

Jack nodded. He squeezed his dad's hand as well. But he could not bring himself to speak. He had said nothing since they'd left the petrol station. He could not. He was too busy trying to remember what Mandy looked like, imprint her features on his mind so that he would never, ever forget.

There were shapes wandering the fields of dead crops. Jack and his dad increased their pace but the dead people were hardly moving, and they seemed to pose no threat. He kept glancing back as they fell behind. It looked like they were harvesting what they had sown.

As the sun hit the hillsides behind them they saw something startling in the distance. It looked like a flash of green, small but so out of place among this blandness that it stood out like an emerald in ash. They could not run because they were exhausted, but they increased their pace until they drew level with the field.

In the center of the field stood a scarecrow, very lifelike, straw hands hidden by gloves and face painted with a soppy sideways grin. Spread out around its stand was an uneven circle of green shoots. The green was surrounded by the rest of the dead crop, but it was alive, it had survived.

"Something in the soil, maybe?" Jack said.

"Farming chemicals?"

Jack shrugged. "Maybe we could go and see."

"Look," his dad said, pointing out towards the scarecrow.

Jack frowned, saw what his dad had seen, then saw the trail leading to it. It headed from the road, a path of crushed shoots aiming directly out toward the scarecrow. It did not quite reach it, however, and at the end of the trail something was slumped down in the mud,

FEARS UNNAMED

just at the boundary of living and dead crop. Jack thought he saw hair shifting in the breeze, the hem of a jacket lifting, dropping, lifting again, as if waving.

They decided not to investigate.

They passed several more bodies over the next couple of hours, all of them still, all of them lying in grotesque contortions in the road or the ditches. Their hands were clawed, as if they'd been trying to grasp something before coming to rest.

Father and son still held hands, and as the sun began to bleed across the hillsides they squeezed every now and then to reassure each other that they were all right. As all right as they could be, anyhow.

Jack closed his eyes every now and then to remember what Mandy and his mum had looked like. Each time he opened them again, a tear or two escaped.

He thought he knew what they would find when they reached the coast. He squeezed his father's hand once more, but he did not tell him. Best to wait until they arrived.

For now, it would remain his secret.